Graeme Williamson was born in Montreal, Canada, and lives in Glasgow. He has worked in factories, warehouses and offices – and has taught courses for adults in American and European literature. During the 1980s and 90s he wrote and performed with award-winning cult band The Pukka Orchestra, in Toronto. His short fiction and poetry has appeared in magazines on both sides of the Atlantic. *Strange Faith* is his first novel.

Strange Faith

www.11-9.co.uk

Strange Faith

Graeme Williamson

First published by

303a The Pentagon Centre
36 Washington Street
GLASGOW
G3 8AZ

Tel: 0141 204 1109
Fax: 0141 221 5363

E-mail: info@nwp.sol.co.uk
www.11-9.co.uk

THE SCOTTISH ARTS COUNCIL
National Lottery Fund

11:9 is funded by the Scottish Arts
Council National Lottery Fund

ISBN 1 903238 28 5

Typeset in Utopia
11:9 series designed by Mark Blackadder

Printed in Finland by WS Bookwell

For Iris

'To strangers they offer all the rites
of hospitality, but do not open their hearts. If
you ask them, they will tell you a story, but
it will not be such a story as they tell when alone.'

Elias Johnson
History of the Iroquois

Prologue

There was once a seafaring man, a Captain Jones by name, who was imprisoned by a tribe of cannibals; mutineers, it is said, from the Royal Navy.

These savages inhabited a remote region of the South Pacific, a place of the most unsavoury character, where they had been marooned many years before. Captain Jones had fallen among them at a time when food had become scarce and rationing was in force. The wretches had eaten the inhabitants of all the neighbouring villages, and despite the wealth of provender available in the surrounding jungle – mangoes, bananas, vine leaves, not to mention the ghastly durian fruit – they could only be satisfied by the consumption of their own kind. Captain Jones was confined in a small and unhygienic wattle cell to await his fate.

Among the Captain's qualities was an extreme fondness for animals, no species of which was too outlandish or repulsive to excite his compassion and curiosity. During the course of his travels he had discovered in himself a remarkable capacity to entice the fauna of every locality to approach him. In his presence even the most ferocious and volatile of creatures became a model of docility. Captain Jones achieved this effect by singing; not that he was particularly accomplished in that field, nor had he a vast repertoire from which to draw, but he did his best: Hearts Of Oak, *selections from Gilbert and Sullivan, the occasional Steven Foster song, supplemented by the poetry of Robert Service, all of which he delivered in a dark, stentorian baritone.*

It is a well known fact that animals enjoy a particular sensitivity to human music. The snake, for example, is easily bewitched by the bagpipe, and the wrath of the tiger may often be subdued by the playing of the harmonica. So it was that Captain Jones whiled away his leisure hours, for there were many, in this manner, and he had soon struck up a peculiar rapport with the various insects and animals which abounded in that melancholy place.

The head man of the tribe, a former medical officer, and graduate in medicine from the University of Edinburgh, boasted a knowledge of anatomy and physiology both uncanny and arcane.

He determined that due to the imposition of rationing, Captain Jones would be eaten piecemeal, over a number of weeks. He knew how this might be accomplished without killing the Captain until the very last moment, when all that would remain of him would be his head and vital organs, connected only by a few essential veins and nerves. Unpalatable as it might be to be consumed in toto by cannibals, there is often the consolation of a quick death by machete, or some other such implement. Nevertheless, this was not to be the lot of Captain Jones.

They began with his right arm. After drawing lots, two of the senior tribesmen climbed into the cage with him one evening and, without warning, began to gnaw at the flesh of his arm. Within moments they had consumed it all, from shoulder to fingertips, leaving only the bones, shining like white marble in the eerie jungle night.

It would be difficult to describe the grave impression this experience made on the Captain. Nevertheless, he was a man of mettle. He did not respond by crying out, cursing his ill-fortune, or pleading for mercy. Instead, he sang. In fact, he sang as he had never sung before, a great rhapsodic outpouring of sonorous vocalising, such as had never been heard previously in those parts. As the natives ate, and his discomfort increased, the more vigorous and tuneful his singing became; before long a strange hush descended over the jungle, so overwhelming was the impression his song made in that godforsaken place. And when the natives retired replete and contented to their squalid, litter-strewn hut, it was hours before the silence abated. Captain Jones lay down on the floor of his cell, rested his head on his good arm, and continued to sing softly to himself, while out of the dark the lizards and insects he had previously befriended came to lie beside him, or sit in clusters upon his exposed body, as if attempting, in their own primitive fashion, to solace and comfort him after this terrible ordeal.

The head man, who, as I have indicated, was a veritable paradigm of low cunning and cruelty, determined that Captain Jones would need time to recover from this first assault against his person. So it was, he was allowed to lie unmolested for several days to regain his strength. In fact, the women of the tribe, hideous creatures with long, painted fingernails and beehive hairdos, dressed in the ghastly fashions peculiar to naval wives, brought him items of vegetation to consume during this period of respite. But one sultry evening, as the sun set between the palm trees, two more men of the tribe climbed into his cage and began to dine on the Captain's left leg with the same scant regard for his comfort as that shown by those who had disposed of his arm.

Once again the extraordinary song erupted from his lips, and seemed to glide up into the sky like a huge, colourful bird, with a voice like a chorus of angels, and vast wings that cast a shade of euphonious profundity over the countryside. Soon the gruesome repast was completed and the men left him, exhausted, on the floor of his cage. From the silent jungle the reptilian and lepidopterous inhabitants crept out to join him, wrapping themselves around him to prevent the onset of shock.

It goes without saying that this horrible sequence of events was repeated a number of times, until there was nothing much left of Captain Jones but half of his torso and his head. However, the songs that now emanated from his diminished frame had assumed a grandeur to which few of us are likely to bear witness. The lizards and insects were joined by a veritable Noah's Ark of animals, wild cats with big spots and elegant tails encircled his cell, warming his flesh with their fur; tropical birds perched on the roof above his head and sang sweetly as he slept. Ironically, these prodigious occurrences only encouraged the anthropophagi in their filthy practices, believing as they did that the consumption of a man of such extraordinary qualities could only enhance their own paltry attributes.

As time passed a strange thing began to happen. From the moment two of their number entered the cage for another meal at Captain Jones's expense the remaining members of the tribe sang along with him, their voices rising together in a chorus of such harmonious magnificence that you would have believed it could be heard on the moon.

Within a month, however, they finished him off. There was no *rescue, no miraculous intervention, nor had Captain Jones anticipated there would be. But on the very last day, as the headman himself devoured Captain Jones's heart, the song of the village rose to a great crescendo and hovered briefly over the jungle like the very first raincloud at the beginning of time. Then, suddenly, it vanished; dissipating among the hills and streams and valleys, like morning mist in the first rays of the sun. As Captain Jones breathed his last, all the people of the village fell dead where they stood. A great legion of animals emerged from the forest to devour their remains, and never again was that place troubled by their barbarous presence.*

Melibee Robertson
June 1970

Part one

Part One

Chapter one

Martin stared blankly from the window overlooking Newcastle Terrace. Spring rain approached from the north, the first drops spitting against the glass. On the horizon a line of hill villages, scattered over mine-scarred fields, vanished in premature twilight. At the city's edge light drained out into the land. The city seemed eclipsed. Shadows flooded in. The immediate neighbourhood was taking on a sombre look; unlikely darkness shrouded tree-lined streets, a lake of slate roofs, the bowling green across the road. Below, someone was running after a taxi, but otherwise the street was empty.

The phone rang in the hall and Mrs Morrison shuffled by. He heard her speak, then a timid knock at the door. 'Martin?'

He pulled on his jeans and went into the hall as the landlady scuttled back into her sitting-room.

'We're meeting Carole in Wimpy's in half an hour,' Christine said. 'You coming?'

'I've never stolen anything before.'

'You don't have to now. That's Carole's speciality. Anyway, I thought you wanted some clothes.'

'I suppose, yes.'

'Besides, Ray's going on about London again and he's driving us mad.'

'Is he going?'

'Don't be soft.' Christine laughed. 'It's just his wee pipe-dream.'

He returned to his room, pulled some clothes from a pile by his bed and went to the window to dress. A cloud parted and sunlight brightened the room. Then the rain intensified.

It was impossible to believe it now, but a revolution had happened out there.

Anarchists flying the black flag in Paris, the demo in Grosvenor Square, Rupert Bear having sex in *Oz* magazine. It was like the battle of Jericho. All the walls were coming down.

It had begun with the music. He had started to hear it at school. Hendrix, the Doors, Janis Joplin. The Fish Cheer. You didn't even have to listen to it particularly, you could hear it everywhere. Human beings were coming back to life after years of hibernation and music was a celebration, a welcome to the restored dead. Gravity had relaxed its grip. People could stand tall.

But now that he had left school and was free to participate it was all over. The music was still pretty great, but everything else had changed. Everybody had sobered up. It was the morning after, and the world was just apologetic. A little embarrassed. Half of the Revolution's heroes were dead anyway. And a schism had split the People right down the middle. On the one hand there were the walking wounded, fluttering about the streets like litter after a parade, and then there were the profiteers, who were thriving on all that dead idealism like flies on shit.

Whatever, nostalgia was beside the point. He was feeling grim but he would have felt grim anyway. He had no money. His shirt stank. His socks stank. All the clothes in his chest of drawers were filthy. There was a car oil stain on his coat. The heels of his shoes were worn. His trouser legs, frayed from catching beneath the worn heels, had lost a half-moon of material at the back. And he had no job now, thanks to decimalisation. Of course he needed new clothes. In new clothes he would feel like a new man. How could he ask Christine to go out with him looking like this?

Christine was Danny's chick, not that he cared about that. But he had waited too long to ask her now and his nerve had gone. The question had assumed ridiculous importance. He was not up to it, obviously. How could he trust himself? He would be unable to speak, or he would say too much. His character was always playing tricks on him. Also, he knew nothing about girls. Robertson had told him that boys found out about these things in the playground, but in Martin's playground there had been no girls to practice on. The other boys were as ignorant about sex as he was. They were all freaks of nature.

Christine was gorgeous, definitely; a skinny little chick with a husky, sexy voice; he had more or less been able to make out her breasts beneath the thick layers of clothing the Edinburgh winter obliged her to wear and they seemed pretty reasonable. He liked her skin especially, even though he had only her face and hands to judge by. He wanted to see all of it, to lie with her naked and feel her skin next to his. The lightness of her would lift the weight from him that made his body feel as if it was full of mud, and lift the weight from his thoughts too. He pictured them together, in a state of post-lovemaking bliss. If it could only be that simple.

His estrangement from Taigh nan Òran had been slow but inevitable. He could blame Danny and Ray, but it wasn't really their fault. He had met them when he was still living at home, and bought dope from them, but no one had forced him. He had finished school and was just bored. Danny thought he was buying friendship really, and the dope was just an excuse. Whatever the case, he got a taste for it and started stealing money from Taigh nan Òran to buy it, and that was the final straw.

'Why didn't you ask me if you needed money?' his mother had asked sadly. 'That's what I don't understand.'

Robertson explained. 'It's quite simple, my dear Alberta. As the perspicacious Hazlitt once observed, the rogue is as much impelled by a craving for excitement as for material gain. Subterfuge, betrayal, low cunning are the virtues the rogue cultivates. Virtues sadly lacking in the performance of honest work.'

The following morning he had driven Martin to Newcastle Terrace, from one lifeless street to another near the city centre. It had been a fine day; thin snow sparkled on the bowling-green; along the street rows of windows shone in the northern dawn like little suns. Mrs Morrison, a shy woman in her sixties, had hovered at the doorway of the bedroom as Robertson checked the sheets, fingered surfaces for dust, tested the hotplate.

'My husband and I moved in here just after the war,' she explained, leading them through to a sitting-room crammed with china cabinets and bulbous Victorian furniture. 'He was from Harris. A very severe man.' She smiled proudly. 'Capable of enduring any hardship. Of course, he died nearly twenty years ago. He was planning to move into that bedroom on his sixty-fifth birthday, but he was gone before that.'

'And you've been renting it out since then?'

She nodded sadly and poured them tea. A regulator clock on the wall chimed dully.

'When we were married I used to sit in your seat, Mr Robertson.'

'Murdoch,' Martin said. 'Mr Robertson is my uncle.'

'Yes. And Edward sat where your uncle is sitting. That's Edward with me on that photograph.' She glanced at a frame on the mantelpiece, half obscured by a Capo di Monte figurine of a shepherdess. 'It was taken by a street photographer on the High Street, the very first day we came to Edinburgh. Edward didn't want to encourage the man, but I insisted we have a photograph of ourselves. He didn't approve of them, but it was still the war and what would I have done if anything had happened?'

The door burst open and a small wire-haired dog with a face like a lavatory brush propelled itself into the room, skidding to a halt on the polished floor by her chair. 'Teddy!' she cried, before turning to the two men. 'I hope you have no objection to animals,' she said.

'Surely that would be futile,' Robertson replied, peering amiably at the dog. 'They are ubiquitous.'

He had written Martin a cheque for the first month's rent and given him a little money to tide him over. After he had departed, and Martin was alone in his new room, he had gone to the open window and inhaled the first ecstatic, self-conscious breath of his new life.

He got a part-time job in a petrol station, bought a red lightbulb for his bedside lamp and on his nights off sat up late smoking hash, masturbating, reading poetry, his head filled with intoxicating dreams of decadent, erotic countries where tragic white exiles drank themselves to death, or went mad, or grew old before their time. He warmed himself on street corners with bottles of Doctor Collis Brown's Lung Tonic, drinking the mixture neat, or boiling off the ether and spooning out the sickly brown residue. He ate Tuinols and Nembutals and sodium amytals with

Danny or Ray, smoked hash in the Waverley station lavatory, returning home in the mid afternoon to fall asleep in his bedroom, waking up hungry or cold in the middle of the night, bewildered in the strange, silent flat. Winter wore on and he grew disenchanted with this life but consoled himself with the thought, 'at least I won't get old.'

As he stepped from his room, carrying his shoes to avoid attracting attention, Mrs Morrison surprised him in the hallway. She came slowly towards him, almost bowing, and spoke in an apologetic whisper. 'Ah, Martin.'

The shoes slipped from his hand and tumbled to the floor. 'Sorry,' he began.

'Sorry,' she replied.

They faced each other in silence.

'Ah yes,' he said. 'The rent. I'm just going to the bank.' He leaned down, retrieved his shoes and glanced at his watch. 'I'm just going now.'

The landlady took a further step towards him. 'You haven't seen my shepherdess, have you Martin?'

'Your shepherdess?'

'Yes, there were two. On the mantelpiece.'

'No. I don't remember a shepherdess.'

He opened the front door and backed out into the close, still in his socks, returning the landlady's wan smile and wishing with all his heart that he had money.

Chapter two

In the shelter of tall stone columns, on the steps of the Scottish National Gallery, a small, green-eyed girl, shivering inside a white plastic raincoat, sat with two men. The younger of them, a gaunt youth with rat brown hair, his body wrapped in an army-surplus greatcoat, picked dead skin from around his nails. Beside him, a red-haired man, smaller and more solidly built than his companion, watched with an ironic smile the crowds passing on Princes Street. Above their heads stony Queen Victoria stared resolutely towards the New Town. Black clouds accelerated over Calton Hill, throwing down gusts of rain.

The wind sharpened. The girl huddled against the small man as he pulled a ragged Mexican poncho around their shoulders. Their companion took a banjo from a case at his feet and began playing quietly, his fingers moving nimbly about the neck, despite the cold.

'I'm fucking starving,' the small man said.

'You're always starving, Danny,' the girl replied.

There was a lull in the volume of traffic along the pavement. An expression of boredom froze the pretty smile on her face. Her eyes wrinkled and she yawned. She was wondering what she was doing there, with these two sad cases, killing time when she could have been at home, having a decent tea with her mum. She looked at the pair in turn. Ray, the banjo-player, strummed with his eyes shut. She quite liked Ray, although he did not bear up well under her closer scrutiny. Both his appearance and his gestures betrayed a lack of conviction. Even his beard seemed parsimonious. Thin curls barely obscured a small, irresolute chin and miserly lips, from which a trail of drool was now slithering onto the banjo. He opened his eyes and glanced up. When his eyes met hers they darted away, as if a forthright look would reveal thoughts he preferred to keep to himself. What was it, she wondered, that made him so secretive?

She closed her eyes and listened to the banjo melody, a

sharp, metallic bird song echoing among the stone columns. The chilly wind seemed to evaporate as an image came to her mind of dry heat, sand, and waves falling on a bleached shoreline. Ray could play the banjo well, she knew that, but it struck her that the spirit which made the music was nothing to do with Ray, that trapped inside him somewhere was the ghost of a real musician, someone you couldn't see, you could only hear.

She turned away and buried her face in Danny's shoulder. He could be a tinker, she thought, the way he smells. Woodsmoke, mud and wine, animal sweat, like a horse's or a dog's. A wee animal. She laughed inwardly at this. Ray was all indoor odours, a cocktail of incense, stale fat and bleach, like the air of the close outside his flat. She trusted Danny more than Ray, simply because of his smell. But what was to become of him? He couldn't go on begging for ever. And he wouldn't always look adorable. In fact, he was already taking on that expression Ray had, a hunted, pathetic look. Martin's expression was different.

As she continued to reflect, Martin appeared. She had known him for some weeks, although she could not remember where they had met. In late winter she had begun to see him around in the cafés and streets between the art gallery and the station where she and her friends passed their interminable free time. They must have got into conversation at some point; after a while it was as if he'd always been there.

He intrigued her a little, with his antiquated English way of speaking, as if the world was a private joke he could laugh at with this funny vocabulary that was like a secret code. Gradually, however, he started using slang, imitating Ray mainly, calling them 'man', and referring to her as a 'chick'. His accent changed and the long words vanished. Sometimes he seemed to have no character at all, and was just a mirror for whoever he was around. At other times she wondered if he was patronising them with his newly adopted street patter. This was Danny's opinion, at least.

'Fuckin' *bourgeois gentilhomme!*' Danny had said, when they had first met Martin.

'What the fuck does that mean?' Ray had asked.

'Cold fish,' was all Danny would say.

Martin smiled up at them and climbed the steps. 'Wine anyone?' he said, passing Christine a paper bag and sitting down beside Ray.

'What is it?' Christine inquired. 'No Lanliq, I hope.'

'El Dorado, what else?' Ray said, pausing in his playing to peruse the label on the bottle. 'When I was in London we used to think people who drank this stuff were winos.'

'Well, don't have any then,' Christine said, pouring herself a capful and passing the bottle back to Martin.

'I'm not proud. It's OK. It keeps you warm, anyhow,' Ray said, grabbing it and taking a sip.

'How's things?'

'I got the sack,' Martin said.

'From the petrol station?'

'Yeah.'

'Drag.'

'Yeah.'

'What happened?' Christine said.

'The customers aren't used to the new money yet. Sometimes they give you double. Like fifty pence instead of five bob. But one guy came back a few minutes later. He complained to the manager that I ripped him off. So I got the sack.'

'Drag.' Ray said again.

'Yeah. And my rent's due.'

The sherry circulated. A gust of rain blew in Martin's face and he shivered.

'You'll have to go to the S.S.' Ray said.

'The S.S.?'

'The D.H.S.S.,' Ray said. 'The Nazis.'

'Ray can take you, he knows the way well enough,' Danny said.

'The arrogance of the self-employed,' Ray said.

Christine turned to Martin. 'What kind of clothes do you fancy anyway?'

He sniffed his armpits. 'At this point anything clean would do.'

She nudged him in the ribs and smiled. 'New gear will take

your mind off your money worries.'

Without warning Danny leaped to his feet and pursued a bustling man into the intensifying rain. They vanished into the crowd.

'Has he ever done any other kind of work?' Martin asked.

'He once tried to register at the dole office as a pedestrian,' Christine said.

'And he sells moody gear to students in pubs,' Ray said. 'Oregano and stuff like that. Course, half of them get stoned on it anyway.'

'He's a scary beggar, though.' Christine said.

'He'll follow that guy home if he doesn't give him any money. He never gives up.'

'Move in with him.' Martin said.

'Live with him!' Christine added.

'Get married maybe!' they said together, laughing.

Danny emerged from the crowd and climbed the steps breathlessly, waving a pound note.

'A fucking quid,' Ray cried. 'Ya beauty!'

'Fancy a Wimpy? I've got enough now.'

'The World's Greatest Beggar,' Christine said, tenderly stroking his hair.

Ray packed up his banjo and they made their way through the Princes Street traffic and up Hanover Street to the Wimpy bar, Martin bringing up the rear. By the time he entered the café, Danny and Ray had already squeezed into a booth beside a nervy, dark-eyed girl Martin assumed to be Carole.

'This is Carole,' Ray confirmed.

She brandished a handful of red fingernails like a weapon. Martin shook it carefully.

'Your pal has a handshake like a haddie,' she said.

'This is Martin,' Ray said.

'I didn't want to break them,' Martin explained.

'Y' cannae break these,' she said, clattering the nails on the Formica tabletop. 'There's enough varnish on them to stick a wing on an aeroplane.' She smiled myopically through a mask of kohl and pan stick.

Martin paused, thought her beautiful, blushed.

She returned his stare. 'Y'll ken me next time,' she said.

Their attention was distracted by a commotion: Danny scattering his change over the table. 'There's enough for five coffees, five Wimpys, and one chips, or five coffees, five chips, and one Wimpy,' he said.

'What about three Wimpys and two chips?' Ray said.

'Or three chips and two Wimpys,' Christine suggested.

'For fuck's sake!' Carole said.

'What's got more food value?' Ray asked.

'The wee cardboard plates,' Danny said.

'Chips give you energy,' Martin said.

'I've got some fucking bread!' Carole cried. 'Why don't we just have five of everything?'

There was a brief silence.

'Well, that's settled, then,' Christine said, as Carole accompanied Ray to the counter.

'So, who buys your clothes anyway?' Danny inquired, as Carole and Ray returned with the laden trays. 'Yer ma?'

'The coat's nice,' Carole said.

'I don't have any money for clothes,' Martin said.

'Don't pay any attention to him,' Christine said. 'Danny's a simple wee man, though his heart's in the right place.'

Danny nudged Ray in the ribs and winked. 'Aye! In my jeans!'

In the shoe shop, Carole contemplated the cherry red boot on her left foot and smiled up into the perspiring face of the shop assistant. A dozen left shoes lay scattered about her on the floor. 'What do you think?' She turned her foot back and forth.

'They look nice,' Martin said.

'I just don't know. Can I try the other one?'

She put it on and grimaced. 'I think they're too small. Can I try the next size up?'

Three or four pairs later she threw up her hands in exasperation and smiled at the exhausted salesgirl. 'I just can't make my mind up, hen.' She handed one pair to the girl. 'Can you keep these for me till tomorrow? I need to think about them.'

She gave the girl a name and hurried from the shop arm in arm with Martin. Ray and Danny emerged from the men's department and joined them outside. Back in the Wimpy bar Carole opened her coat and removed a pair of red patent boots.

'How did you do that?' Martin asked.

'Easy,' Carole said, ordering chips and coffee for the table.

'Saw her pinch a barrie fur coat from Jenner's once,' Danny said.

'Nearly wet myself when I saw the price,' Carole laughed. 'Eight hundred quid.'

'Took it right off the dummy and put it on,' Danny explained.

'Sold it for fifty quid,' Carole added. 'A real rip off.'

Ray laughed hoarsely. 'When I was in London,' he muttered, 'I had this great raccoon coat...'

'...and here's a pair for you, son,' Danny said, ignoring Ray and handing Martin a pair of Cuban heeled boots.

Martin protested, but Ray and Danny grabbed his legs and forcibly removed his old shoes.

'These are all right for golfing,' Ray said.

'But these are what chicks like, Martin,' Danny said, shoving the first boot half way on to his foot.

'Do they fit?' Carole asked.

'Of course they fit,' Danny said.

Martin pulled them on, stood up and walked unsteadily back and forth beside the table. 'These are great. I've always wanted boots like these.'

They ate in high spirits and returned outdoors. The sun came out and the day was almost warm.

An hour later Martin had new velvet flares and a gaily coloured Mexican poncho. 'Thanks very much,' he said to Carole, as the others stood about him, surveying his new ensemble.

'That's cool,' Ray said. 'Great strides, man.'

'You're welcome,' Carole said dully.

'We should celebrate,' Martin said. 'I think I've got enough for wine.'

He handed the shopping bag of his old clothes to Ray and

tottered away to an off-licence.

Conviviality ruled at first, but conversation died as the wine ran out. Ray played his banjo. Danny and Christine necked half-heartedly. The sky clouded over again and, in the dingy afternoon light, their faces acquired an ugly uraemic tinge. Ray lost interest. His playing meandered tunelessly.

They watched the crowds.

Christine yawned.

'I wonder what the time is,' Martin said.

'About half two,' Christine said.

'Christ, it feels later than that.'

Ray laid his banjo on its case and pulled a tobacco tin from his coat pocket. 'Shit!' He clicked his tongue at the empty tin.

Christine yawned again and nodded at Danny. 'I think we're taking a donner,' he said. 'Before the rain starts.' He pulled Christine to her feet.

'Oh, right.'

Carole stood also. She glanced at Ray. 'What are you doing?'

He ignored her and turned to Martin. 'We'll need to go to the S.S. if we're going.'

'You better had,' Christine said.

'Yeah. My landlady's freaking out.'

'Maybe see you tomorrow?'

'Yeah.'

Christine and Carole stepped to the pavement and linked arms. Danny jumped down behind them, pushed between them and took their hands, pulling them across the road towards the New Town. 'Good luck at the dole!' he shouted.

Martin picked up his bag of clothes as Ray packed away the banjo. They set off. He looked back as Danny and the girls rounded the corner into Hanover Street, and waved hopefully. The rain came on just as he and Ray reached a shelter.

'Got any bus fare?' Ray asked.

Martin found a few coins in his coat pocket. 'A shilling, and a few pence.'

'We'll get a busy one and go upstairs,' Ray said. 'We'll ask for a stop in the wrong direction. By the time the conductor gets to us we'll be nearly there.'

He knelt down, picked up a dog end from the floor of the shelter, lit it, and passed it to Martin. 'A bus stop is a good place for douts,' he said. 'People just light them up for a bit of warmth. Plus it makes the buses come quicker.' They exchanged the smoke. A bus approached. 'See what I mean?'

'What do they do at the S.S.?' Martin asked.

'They'll ask how much your rent is, then they send a visitor to your room,' Ray explained, as they clattered up the stairs to the top deck.

'I don't like lying to people,' Martin said. 'I told her I had a job.'

'You've got to start sometime,' Ray said. 'You're not a bairn any more.'

Ten minutes later they disembarked, crossed the road and pushed through a thick glass door into a bleak, airless room floored with disintegrating linoleum and lit by two dim tube lights. Two dozen chairs, arranged in rows, faced a caged-in counter. At the end of each row a pillar ashtray overflowed with cigarette ends and empty crisp packets. From the shadows behind the counter, ashen-faced clerks peered like neglected animals. The air was thick with stale smoke.

As Ray and Martin entered, a young woman with a baby was whispering intently to a face behind the grille. Martin and Ray found two seats next to an ashtray. Ray pulled out his tobacco tin, rolled himself a cigarette from the dog ends he had collected at the bus stop and passed the tin to Martin.

Suddenly, the young woman turned away from the counter, tears rolling down her face. She clutched the baby to her roughly, and rushed from the office.

Ray lit his cigarette and coughed. Martin paused before lighting up and looked around the office: only half a dozen people were before them in the queue, but he had a feeling they might all wait there for ever for their turn. All appeared to have accepted the possibility. Two older men, a couple, a young girl, and a single man in his late twenties sat with heads bowed or staring emptily at the counter. The old men smoked. One read a newspaper. The girl glanced periodically at her watch, ignoring a large clock on the wall beside the counter.

As Martin lit his smoke the doors flew open and the mother reappeared, strode in, high heels echoing in the hushed office, and thrust the baby on to the counter.

'You look after it then!' she screamed at the clerk. 'I cannae!' She turned away, pushed through the doors and disappeared.

The baby lay sleeping on the counter. There were vague movements and murmurs from the shadows behind the grille. The people waiting in the queue watched the baby for a while then lost interest. The old man turned the page of his paper and began reading again. The girl glanced at her watch and sighed theatrically.

'Next!' said a disembodied voice.

Returning home, outside the gallery, Ray gave Martin a Mandrax. They walked across Princes Street and up Hanover Street. After a hundred and fifty yards Martin fell asleep on his feet and landed face down on the pavement in front of the Wimpy bar. Ray helped him to his feet and dusted him off. 'You better come home with me,' he said. 'You can't afford to lose that nice place of yours.'

Chapter three

Ray led him through a maze of alleyways and back courts to a tenement near the railway line. The bitter smell of bleach hung in the air. 'Eric is God!' was scrawled in biro on the wall. They climbed to the first floor. Martin shivered and rubbed his hands briskly as Ray unlocked the door, pushed several times with his shoulder and squeezed inside. An odour of decay drifted from the room.

'The whole place is rotting,' Ray said, 'You can't open the door any more than this.'

Martin pushed in behind him and pulled the door shut. Ray was standing by a tiled hearth, rubbing his hands before an unlit gas fire. Damp walls hung with drooping Dayglo posters of Jimi Hendrix, the Doors, Jefferson Airplane. Above the fireplace a trouserless man with a Groucho Marx moustache peered down at them from a toilet. An ornate brass bed occupied an alcove to the left, beneath the outside stairwell. The kitchen sink overlooked a scrap of couch-grass between the building and the street. A passing train rattled the window. On the wall above the cooker a lopsided kitchen cabinet hung by a single nail. The only seat was an inverted plastic milk crate beside the fire, jammed under a flimsy coffee table. Martin leaned down and picked up a London tourist brochure from a pile scattered about the hearth.

'Got that shilling?'

Martin took a ten pence piece from his pocket and stood by the fire, thumbing through the brochure as Ray disappeared into the toilet; a moment later the coin clicked in the meter and gas hissed from the fire.

'It's dangerous in there. The walls are sinking into the floor,' Ray explained as he returned. 'One day me and the bog are going to fall through on to the neighbours.' He pulled a silver lighter from his jeans' pocket, lit a ring on the cooker, then knelt down and lit the fire. 'At least I can screw the money back when I leave,' he said. 'You should have seen the place I had in London, man. Central heating, security phone. Never seemed to be able to get back on my feet after I got out of prison though.'

'You were in prison.'

'Yeh, in Pentonville. Done for sus, like everyone else in Pentonville.' He grinned. 'Got picked up in the Dilly. They took me to the cop shop and put me in this room. A wee bit later, the sergeant comes in with a ring of car keys. "These are yours, son," he said. And that was it.' He pointed to the bed. 'Sit down. It's either there or the milk crate.'

He went to the sink, filled a kettle and put it on the stove. 'Still,' he laughed, 'at least it wasn't fucking Wandsworth.'

He followed Martin's eyes as his friend appraised the room. 'I got this place from a guy called Gaz – "The Gentleman Bank Robber", they called him in the papers. He screwed a bank in Wick or some teuchtar place up there, dressed up like a dog's dinner in a nice suit and a bowler hat. A posh guy, too, Gaz was. Anyway, he walked in and asked in a nice, polite voice if they wouldn't mind awfully filling a bag with money for him, and handing it over.' He turned off the gas under the boiling water and emptied a handful of tea from a caddy directly into the kettle. 'Of course, they caught him almost the same day. He gave them too much time to look at him. The only way to rob a bank is to scare the shit out of everyone. Use lots of weapons and that, so nobody wants to make eye contact.' He handed Martin a mug and took a sip from his own.

Martin gratefully wrapped his hands around it to warm them. Despite the fire it seemed to him that the cold and damp in the flat had a personality of its own, hovering like a dismal guest in the corner.

'We ought to nip out and nick some biscuits,' Ray suggested. 'There's a wee shop just down the street.'

Martin showed no signs of wanting to move. 'What happened to him?'

'Who?'

'Gaz.'

'Cancer. He died about six months ago.' A flash of silver landed on the carpet by Martin's feet. 'He gave me this lighter.

Dunhill. Lights first time every time. Flash that in the right place and you can get in anywhere.'

They sipped their tea in silence. Martin was almost asleep, the nearly full mug slipping slowly from his grasp. Ray chuckled quietly. 'He met this Yankee bank robber in the nick once. You know what they do in America?'

Martin shrugged, his eyelids sinking inexorably as the growing warmth from the fire compounded the effects of the Mandrax.

'They wear pink shoes! He said he'd try it the next time.' He examined Martin's face for a reaction.

'See, they wear pink shoes because when the cops come afterwards that's the one thing everyone in the bank remembers. 'Oh, yes, officer, he was wearing pink shoes!' And they forget everything else.'

He peered sadly into his mug. 'Gaz was never into violence, you see. He just wanted a bit of bread so he and his old lady could have a holiday.' He looked up. The mug lay overturned on the floor, Martin snored quietly on the bed.

Martin woke briefly during the night and found the room empty, the fire still on, a red lightbulb glowing on a Mateus bottle lamp on the coffee table. A plume of smoke rose from a stick of incense jammed into the wall beside his head. He dozed off again almost immediately, and was woken by someone shaking him. The meter had run out; a damp chill had sunk into his bones as he slept. He raised his head and peered over the edge of the bed. There were other people in the room now, most of whom were lying on the floor, as if they had dragged down by excessive gravity. He rolled over and reached into his bag of discarded clothes for his coat, took off the poncho, put on the coat, folded the poncho into a pillow and leaned back with his head propped against the record player.

'I've got some downers,' Ray said. He pulled a syringe from inside his coat.

'Oh, I don't think so. I don't know about needles.'

'It's nothing, man. You just get off quicker.'

Martin looked around the room. Danny and Christine peered at him from under a coat on the floor.

'These rooms are aye cold. Morph is better, but this stuff keeps you warm too.'

'Well.' Martin rubbed his hands together. 'I suppose you never know until you try.'

Danny and Christine joined them as Ray opened the caps and mixed the contents with water. Danny rolled up the sleeve of Martin's coat and grabbed him tightly around the arm.

'Look at those veins!' he said, tapping a pulsing blue line in Martin's forearm.

'A born junkie!' Ray said.

Christine watched as Ray inserted the needle then pumped the blood in and out of the works. 'You're right,' Martin said. 'It is warm.' He smiled, then became dimly aware of Christine's sharp, unsympathetic inspection.

'Well, he's away,' she said, lying back on the floor and pulling the coat over her.

'We should be blood brothers,' Ray said, after a long silence. Martin, euphoric and anaesthetised, watched as Ray cut a two-inch wound on his arm with a razor sharp penknife, another on his own, and pressed the two together, watching a thin trail of blood trickle down into the palm of his hand. 'Your blood in mine, mine in yours,' he said. Martin noticed Ray's arm was covered in similar scars.

'You should wash it,' Danny said, getting to his feet, pulling the coat from Christine, then lying back on the bed. 'They can go bad. And fuck knows what's in his blood.'

Martin wobbled to his feet and went to the sink.

'You have to be careful who you fix up with too, and keep it clean, or you can get abscesses.'

'Downers are worse for that because of all the chalk they mix them up with,' Ray said. 'Remember big Frank? Lost both his arms and legs because of gangrene from abscesses.'

'You're joking,' Martin muttered, scrubbing his arm furiously.

'Aye,' Danny added, 'but he did get a job at the Buroo as a paperweight.'

Martin fell back suddenly on to the cold carpet, laughing woozily, wrapping himself in his coat.

'Play another song, Ray,' Danny said. 'Play the *Gravel Walks*; play that one about the carpet.'

Ray picked up the banjo from the floor in front of the extinguished fire, plucked a chord, and sang in a throaty, soulful tenor.

My carpet is a friend to me,
I sense superiority
Whenever I walk upon
Axminster or Wilton!

A fatigued, half-intoxicated giggle came from the bed.

My ceiling is an enemy
A friend my ceiling cannot be
While my carpet clings just like a leech
My ceiling I can never reach!

From the bed, Danny sang along with the last verse.

My walls, I'd say, are in between
Seldom heard, but often seen
Often seen, but seldom washed
If they fell down, I'd soon be squashed!

When Martin awoke, Ray was dozing with his head against the bed, clutching the banjo between his legs. Bird song scratched at dawn light behind the kitchen curtain. A milk float hummed at the corner of the street, bottles knocking on a neighbouring doorstep.

'Are you awake, Martin?'

A pair of green eyes gazed down at him.

'Where's Danny?'

'He's away. Left hours ago,' Christine said.

'You didn't go with him?'

'Where? He sleeps under the bridge at Lothian Road.' She smiled. 'You going home?'

'It's Sunday,' he said. 'I'm going to see my mother. I haven't seen her for weeks. That's if I can get upright. I think my body's seized up.'

She took his hand and pulled him into a sitting position. 'It's awful cold in here.'

He rubbed her cold hands between his own, then picked up his bag of clothes as she dragged him to his feet. He changed back into the still-damp poncho, and together they negotiated a path through the obstructions to the door. Ray turned over and spoke sharply in his sleep. 'Sorry! Sorry! Sorry!'

'What's he dreaming about?' Martin said, leaning down to pull a blanket over the sleeping youth.

They walked down the broken cement path. Dew glittered on the couch-grass lawn and evaporated in the warm sunlight.

'You didn't say much last night,' he said.

'Couldn't get a word in,' she said smiling, 'with your mutual admiration society.'

'What do you mean?'

'Nothing.' She looked him up and down. 'What will your ma say about your new clothes?'

Martin regarded himself disconsolately. 'This gear already looks old.'

He followed her towards the main road.

'Maybe I could come and see you later?' she said.

'That would be great,' he said. 'Come around ten. I'll be back by then.'

Chapter four

The first leaves of the year shone in the roadside trees, along passing avenues, in parks and gardens. Between buildings, blue hills, visible at the horizon, hovered in mist. It was a two hour walk from Ray's flat to Lowther Avenue, a meandering, cul-de-sac hidden behind the main road. A sharp breeze was blowing through the cherry trees which lined the avenue and the air was filled with flying blossom. Long gardens, visible between high stone gateposts, were uniform and orderly. Shrubbery tumbled over stone walls; on others, broken bottle glass deterred intruders. Taigh nan Òran lay at the end of the avenue, a rambling sandstone villa, blackened by smoky Edinburgh air and draped in wintry clematis.

The rain of the day before had soaked into the legs of Martin's flares and the still-damp poncho exuded a strange, fishy odour. He huddled inside the poncho like a refugee in a Red Cross blanket, hobbled down the driveway, entered the porch and continued into a narrow, oak-panelled corridor. The floorboards jumped as he walked. The hallway always reminded him of the entrance to an eccentric museum. One side was decorated with arrangements of deerskin shields, crossed assegais, ebony nobkerris, daggers and hunting spears, and on the other little portraits of strangers' ancestors, acquired by his grandfather over the years, peered out from elaborate gold frames, lips and eyes floating in the gloom.

At the end of the corridor, he pushed through a heavy door and into the kitchen. A Rayburn glowed against the far wall, a kettle simmered on the hob. Alberta was sitting at the bare oak table, reading a detective novel. She frowned as he entered.

'I saw you coming down the driveway,' she said. 'Are they new shoes? The way you're walking, you look like one of those women with rickets.'

He sat down at the table, threw down his bag of clothes and took off his boots.

'It's warm in here,' he said, rubbing his feet.

'It's such a luxury,' she said. 'When we were children, the house was always freezing. If I was cold your grandfather told me to go for a walk.' She laughed mournfully. 'It's not got any better. Your uncle thinks it's extravagant to have the Rayburn on all day. He says the poor have to do without heat, so why shouldn't we? But I find Edinburgh so cold. Mother did as well.' She stood up and went to the kitchen cupboard, opened a drawer, took out a knife and fork, laid a place at the table, then cut and buttered some bread, which she placed on a plate from the dresser.

'Do you ever hear from her?'

'Melibee does from time to time,' she said, breaking a pair of eggs into a frying pan on the Rayburn. 'She's living in a place called Don Mills. She said it was even colder there, but at least it wasn't Lewis.'

'Why didn't she stay in Edinburgh?'

Alberta shrugged. 'When she came back from Lewis she felt as if she didn't belong in Edinburgh any more. Your grandparents didn't get on very well.'

Before the war, Martin's grandfather, Malcolm Robertson, had built a cottage on the west coast of Lewis with the intention of retiring to the island. Alberta and her brother had spent some years there when they were children, and they had taken Martin there during the school holidays.

'Why Canada?'

'I think because it was beyond the pale. "The colonies", you know. Your grandfather always talked about it as if everyone rode around in oxcarts or lived in wigwams. She probably went there to annoy him.'

She wiped her hands on a tea towel and sat down opposite him.

'So you lost a mother as well as a husband.'

'And your granddad too,' she said. 'Very careless, wasn't I?'

'That must have been hard.'

'It was harder for Melibee. He was always more soft-hearted than me.'

'Soft-hearted!?'

'Oh yes. He's terribly soft-hearted. He used to pray every day for her to come back. When she didn't, I think it rather put him off God. It certainly put him off your grandfather. Anyway,' she went on, 'how's the job? What was it? Petrol station?'

'I'm not doing it any more,' he said.

'Why not?'

'It was boring,'

'I don't understand you. Most men your age can't wait to get out and make something of themselves. But you're always moaning about your job – or you're complaining about having no money. Why can't you be more practical?'

'Practical! Where the fuck would I have learned to be practical?'

'Don't use that language with me. You're not with your new friends now.'

He muttered an apology. 'Well anyway,' he went on, 'you see all these people who are twenty years older than me doing exactly the same rubbish job they did on the day they started. What's the point of being alive if you can't do something exceptional?'

Alberta scooped the eggs from the frying pan on to the plate, and set it down roughly on the table. 'Your uncle may be a dreamer, but he's paid the bills since we came here. Your education, which you seemed determined to waste, and everything else. He's willing to pay you too, if you want to work.'

'He wants me to work with him? Doing what?'

'Well, I don't know, exactly. But you needn't sound so surprised. He doesn't like to see you wasting your talent.'

'What talent? Besides, I can't take any of that stuff seriously. It's all just stories isn't it?'

'Everything is just a story, Martin. And if you don't want to work with him you'll have to find something better than petrol stations. You're not stupid.'

'I can take care of myself.'

'You'll have to, it doesn't matter whether you can,' she said.

Martin wiped up a smear of egg with his last piece of bread.

'Well, that should keep you going until dinner,' Alberta said. 'I have work to do.'

'Where is he?'

'Having a bath,' she said, shutting the door behind her.

Martin washed his dish and went outdoors. Behind the kitchen a vegetable patch led to a pond overgrown with weeds. Beyond, a derelict apple orchard bordered a hillside, where rhododendrons grew in the shelter of a high stone wall; behind the wall, a row of elms divided the city's edge from farmland. He walked up the hill, pushed through a tangle of undergrowth and into an overgrown bivouac he had first constructed when he came to Taigh nan Òran. He lay down on the rough earth, lit a succession of cigarettes, gazed up at the sky, smoked and thought.

An hour later Alberta appeared at the kitchen door in rubber boots, carrying a trowel and a watering can. She skirted the pond and made her way to her 'Provençal' garden near the pond, knelt down and began weeding in a thick clump of rosemary. Martin watched her for several minutes then extinguished his cigarette, extricated himself from the undergrowth and walked down the hill to join her, crouching beside her on the grass.

'Melibee wanted me to get rid of this.' She nodded at the shrubbery.

'Why's that?'

'Some superstition about women ruling a house where there's rosemary in the garden. Although I suppose he might have been joking. I can't always tell. He used to spin the most ridiculous yarns.' She began to chuckle. 'You know when he was a student, he tried to organise a group of students to take a bus to Berwick and pee over the border to commemorate the signing of the Act of Union. He called it the "Micturate on England Group".'

A breeze rustled the lawn and skimmed over the pond. She brushed soil from her dress and shivered. A scent of rosemary hovered about her.

'I buried a bird here,' he said. 'In a glass jar. You never found it?'

'No.'

'I used to dig it up now and then to watch it decompose,' Martin said.

'You were an odd child.'

'I could never work out how the maggots got in,' Martin went on. 'The jar was airtight.'

Alberta smiled absent-mindedly and continued weeding.

'The only other explanation is that they were there all the time,' Martin went on. 'It's funny that. Are they in us, do you think? Just waiting?'

Alberta sighed. 'Are you coming to Lewis this year?' she asked.

'No, I felt like doing something different.'

'Like begging on the art gallery steps?'

'How did you know that?'

'I was on the bus one day. I was going to get off. There's a Pissarro picture of a river in there I like to look at sometimes. Then I saw you with your new friends.'

He was surprised by the contemptuous expression on her face.

'Nice people, are they?'

'Yes. They are nice people. They're not like us, of course. Not nice like us,' Martin replied, scornfully.

'Well, he'll be disappointed. It's become an institution for him, the three of us going there in the school holidays. I think he finds it easier to be human up there. He can relax – it's where he feels at home.'

Martin remembered. After a few days at the cottage, Melibee Robertson did relax. It was as if the starch had run out of his suit. He became spontaneous, less menacing. They'd go for walks together, and his uncle would become invigorated by the motion of walking. He would launch into endless lectures on the local history, the quality of the peat, the local birds and plants, all the time bewildering Martin with philosophical questions until his head clanged like a belltower with incomprehensible theories. Even when he grew older he could never be sure if his uncle's obsessions were serious or facetious or simply mad. Their walks usually ended with him giving his uncle the slip and fleeing to the beach or over the hill to his hideout on the sheiling, leaving the bemused Robertson to return to the cottage alone.

'Yes. It's lovely up there,' Martin conceded, 'but there's nothing to do.'

'You used to love swimming. I don't know how you could stand the water. It was so cold.'

Swimming was about the only thing he had learned at school which interested him. Within an hour of arriving at the cottage he would be in the water, gliding from rock to rock in the frigid surf. Alberta worried about his obsession with the sea, although she was impressed by his ability to stay submerged for long periods of time. Robertson approved however, and bought Martin a pair of goggles and a snorkel. He told Alberta that the boy was preparing himself for a life underwater, and it was best for him to be properly equipped. The snorkel came in useful in other ways too. For most of his childhood Martin had been tormented by nightmares. Sometimes he would wake up during the night and see ghosts in his room. At first he had hoped that one of them might turn out to be his father, but the phantoms would vanish before he could pluck up the courage to ask them who they were. To help him sleep, he hit on the idea of taking the snorkel to bed with him, in order to breathe beneath the blankets, but his imagination still filled the room with spirits and sleep only came as dawn appeared at the window. On some mornings, when he awoke, his ears would fill with a rushing sound, like the roaring of the sea, and he would find himself floating between the dreaming and the waking world; on one occasion, disembodied and drifting through the night sky, stars flashing around him; on another, paralysed and suffocating inside an impenetrable lead box. When this happened, he would dress quickly and rush to the sea. Once immersed, the memory of the dreams would vanish and he could relax, kick himself away from a rock, through the sea wrack towards the open sea. Sometimes, he would simply jump from a rock and crouch on the stones at the bottom, breathing through the snorkel, watching the distorted flash of birds passing by overhead.

'I just lost interest,' he said.

'Well, I know all about losing interest,' Alberta said, and went back to digging.

Martin watched her. She hardly seemed old, he thought. No grey hair yet. But at that moment he could hardly picture her being interested in something. Of course she didn't have to be interested. Since they had come from England all she did was work in the garden and do the cooking. They were all living off the money his grandfather had made.

The study window opened. Scratchy fiddle music blared across the lawn. Alberta wiped the trowel on the grass. The sun was setting, and the shadows from the elm trees at the top of the garden stretched over the lawn. She groaned as she got to her feet. 'Well,' she said in a jolly fashion, 'it's nearly supper time. Are you staying?'

He picked up the watering can and doused the newly weeded shrubbery as Alberta watched. 'It smells nice, this garden,' he said.

She smiled. They walked back together to the house.

They parted company at the stairs as Martin went to the bathroom to wash. The room was still hot, the walls running with condensation after his uncle's bath, the air filled with the medicinal aromas of Robertson's shaving cream and skin tonic. There was little indication of Alberta's presence in the room, no distinctive smells, a toothbrush in a glass, an earring on the shelf above the sink, but otherwise, no personal items. In fact there was little to show for her presence anywhere in the house, apart from a kind of silence that seemed to emanate from her. Martin remembered when they'd first arrived from England, when he was eight, both his father and grandfather dead. The day after their arrival they went to Malcolm Robertson's funeral, and his uncle Melibee had given a speech that Martin hadn't understood. As he later found out there was nothing unusual in that, Robertson always spoke in speeches. Afterwards his uncle and mother, who hadn't seen each other for fifteen years, sat in the kitchen and talked incessantly for two or three days. Martin watched them from his bivouac. He tried to eavesdrop but picked up only the odd phrase here and there. For much of the time his mother wept, leaning over the table, Robertson's ruined hands clasped in hers.

Then, after that initial burst of communication they lapsed into silence, and that was what Martin remembered about his childhood in Taigh nan Òran. A silence that seemed to be a kind of conversation between his mother and his uncle, interrupted periodically by a speech.

He wiped the mirror over the basin and looked at his reflection. Robertson's bone-handled razor was lying open on the glass shelf beneath the mirror. He lifted it to the level of his eyes, opened the blade, and ran his thumb along the edge, unexpectedly drawing a line of blood to the skin. He stepped back a pace and brandished the weapon at his reflection. 'I'm gonnae cut ye!' he said in an unconvincing Scottish accent. Dissatisfied, he attempted American. 'I'm gonna cut your troat!' he snarled, then hurriedly shut the razor, ran his thumb under the tap, and hurried downstairs, disconcerted by a chill at the back of his neck.

As he entered the dining-room, Alberta was serving dinner. Robertson was at the far end of the table with the window behind him, casting a tweed shadow over the meal. Alberta's arm moved mechanically back and forth from a tureen of potatoes. Robertson carved and served slices from a small roast. The three began to eat.

'Perhaps you will introduce me,' Robertson said, after a few moments' silence, 'to the foreign gentleman who has joined us for dinner this evening.' He peered over the table at Martin. 'Ah, Martin,' he said, 'my apologies.' He lifted a loaded fork to his mouth. 'And what have you done with your other clothes?'

'Pass the mustard,' Alberta said, frowning at Martin.

'Perhaps I can speculate,' Robertson continued. 'During your perambulations you encountered one of those Argentinian gentlemen – a guano, is it? – with the fresh smell of the pampas in his hair.'

'I still have them,' Martin said.

Robertson paused, and looked at him with a puzzled expression. 'A student of bovine husbandry perhaps,' he went on, 'recently arrived to complete his education at the University.' He took another mouthful of food. 'He engaged you in conversation, confided in you his alarm at the incongruity of his Latin attire, which though appropriate for the wide plains of his native land, now appeared to him unduly flamboyant, when contrasted with the more sober mode favoured in our own city.' He rested his knife and fork on his plate and continued. 'And, ever ready as you are to assist those in distress, you suggested to him an exchange – your own hand-lasted brogues for his ill-fitting cowboy boots, a Shetland Island cardigan for his rudely woven blanket, and your gabardine trousers for those extraordinary items you are wearing now.' He looked up and smiled blandly.

'I still have them,' Martin said again.

'In this way, you suggested, he would be free to begin a new life in a civilised country, free from the odium accorded the sartorial excesses of those in foreign garb.'

'Have you finished?' Alberta said, getting to her feet. Robertson and Martin nodded. She collected the plates and vanished through the dining-room door.

'Otherwise, how would you have obtained them? You have no money, as you are always reminding us. What possible explanation can there be?'

Martin looked down at his feet and said nothing.

'Mmmm?' said Robertson.

'That's exactly what happened,' Martin said.

'As I suspected,' Robertson replied. He turned to face the door as Alberta returned with the dessert. 'It seems my theory was correct,' he said.

'Really.' Alberta nodded, banging down a bowl of bread and butter pudding on the table in front of him.

'However, Martin,' Robertson continued, 'I must admonish you to discontinue the practice of exchanging your clothing with every indigent foreigner you encounter. Judging from previous commerce, you will in no time be completely denuded by your wily acquaintances.' He smiled blandly across the table. 'I cannot begin to contemplate the effect on your mother should she encounter you on the street clad only in sandals and dhoti, for example, after another of these ill-conceived transactions.'

Alberta looked up from her plate and dropped her spoon on the table. Robertson looked at her quizzically. 'All this wit gets a little wearing,' she said, standing up and collecting the dishes.

Robertson turned to Martin as the door closed.

'You do realise ...' he waved his hand to indicate the room, '... that this is not the Real World?' He stood up slowly, put down his napkin, walked around the table, and stopped behind Martin, resting his hands on his nephew's shoulders. 'I hope you enjoyed your childhood, Martin.'

His grip tightened. Martin tried to stand up, but found his upward movement restrained with surprising force.

'These are wonderful days!' Robertson said. 'Remarkable times! You are about to leave the womb that has been your home. Walk upright, as it were. At last the time has come! Henceforth you must survive on your own wits, such as they are. No longer can you rely on other people to buy your clothes,' he tugged at Martin's poncho, 'put food in your belly,' he leaned over and poked him softly in the stomach, 'or listen with rapt attention to every whimsical opinion, complaint, or ill-conceived intellection that your empty head can produce. Things can change with surprising speed. There may be no more money tomorrow, for example. What will your feckless generation do then? Great men, such as your grandfather, pillaged the world to create wealth for this tiny little island. Now all those poor savages have tired of fattening us up, all the little, fat, spoiled children of the west who can think of nothing better to do with their money than spend it on toys and narcotics while complaining incessantly about their petty and miserable lives.'

Martin had not expected this diatribe. His face reddened, and his hands clenched. 'You should be glad I'm who I am!' he said. 'You should be grateful I don't just laugh at your ridiculous ideas like everyone else. Everybody laughs at you. Everybody thinks you're ridiculous!'

'Really?' Robertson said, removing his hands from Martin's

shoulders and standing back from the table. 'Well, I'm sure they do. And I'm sure they're right.' He went back to his chair and sat contemplating his hands with a melancholy expression.

'And it's "gaucho",' Martin said, 'not "guano".'

The hall clock struck seven. Neither moved. They sat in silence for several minutes.

'What were you writing this afternoon?' Martin said eventually.

'Some notes for this evening's meeting,' Robertson replied genially, as if his tirade had never occurred.

'How did it go?'

'It all goes rather astray, theologically speaking. I doubt if your grandfather would approve. I don't share Calvin's contempt for human beings. My father was such a pious man, and my ideas are somewhat out of step with orthodox views. And, of course, I have difficulty in making myself understood.'

'Mother says not many people come.'

'We've had a lean year or two. These days there is a taste for the exotic. Every swami east of Suez has set up an ashram here, and it's not easy to compete with the spicy aromas and inscrutable philosophies they go in for. All I have to offer is a technique of contemplation, and the public demands wonderment. To be honest with you,' he smiled oddly, 'I'm not a great believer in religion.'

When he was younger Martin had taken up Robertson's 'contemplation practice', sitting cross-legged on the study floor with the others in the group, watching, as instructed, the endless flux of emotions and thoughts swirling about in his mind. He had believed, or at least hoped, that one day he would attain the Realisation of Natural Ephemera, which Robertson assured his followers, was the first step towards reclaiming the True Human Heritage. He even took part in the winter meetings his uncle held at the pond, the group scattered about on the bank, wrapped in blankets, and contemplating the formation or disintegration of ice on the water. However, as he grew older, his uncle's attempts to lead them to this ideal world began to strike him as ridiculous, the sad desperation of an old, failed man.

'I used to enjoy it,' Martin said.

'How long is it now? Since you last joined us?'

'Five years. I don't know.'

Robertson propped his elbows on the table and tapped his lips thoughtfully with his good fingers.

'A younger man might vitalise us,' he said. 'I would like it if you would work with me. You could make some suggestions. They might even be implemented.'

'What would I do? Sell tickets? Make sandwiches?'

Robertson looked up at him. A flicker of fear seemed to dart across his face.

'I'm sorry,' Martin said.

From the garden came the muted sound of bird song, and the rhythmic, metallic ring of Alberta's trowel in the flowerbed. Martin said nothing. The doorbell rang. Robertson got to his feet. 'Would you care to join this evening's gathering?' he asked.

Martin followed his uncle to the drawing room. He went to the piano that stood half concealed in an alcove beside the fireplace, sat down on the stool and waited as Robertson answered the door. During the following minutes the bell rang a number of times and soon the room was filled with a disparate collection of men and two women in early middle age, who huddled together on the couch.

Robertson entered with a laden tea tray and set it down on the carpet in front of his desk. The evening had grown cool, and the large room was chilly. He lit the fire in the grate, and after the tea was served, the group edged closer to the hearth, chatting together and now and then, laughing.

'Haven't seen you for a while,' a young man said, bringing Martin a cup of tea. 'Why don't you come over by the fire?'

'I'm fine where I am,' he replied.

'I can't tell you what a difference your uncle's teachings have made to us,' the young man said. 'He really is a remarkable man.'

'What sort of difference?'

'I'm so much happier now. So much more confident. I tell

you, finding some people to talk about real things with, it's been a godsend.'

'I thought you looked happier before. I hardly recognised you.'

'Oh, no. Not at all. I was deluded before. Caught up in distractions. I suppose I did take some pleasure in passing fancies, but now I'm getting down to the root of things. I feel so much more of a person.'

'Funny,' Martin said.

'Funny?'

'Yes. You seemed happier in the past.'

'Well, of course, once you start becoming aware of other people, of the amount of suffering in the world, happiness does take on a different flavour.'

'The flavour of misery?' Martin suggested.

The young man's face seemed to collapse from within.

'You don't know,' he said, retreating towards the others. 'You don't know what it's worth not to be lonely.'

Regretting his curt tone, Martin tried to think of something friendly to say, but the young man had already taken refuge in the shelter of the group.

Martin remained in the shadows, drinking his tea, watching Robertson and the others. The light from the blazing fire seemed to expand into the shadowy parts of the room, enveloping the group in a dream-like warmth. As Martin watched they relaxed, lapsed into contented but alert silences, their fearfulness dissipated.

Robertson stood up and switched on the lamp on his desk. Behind him a dim reflection of the light appeared in the french windows. He folded his arms, looked carefully at each member of the group in turn, and began to speak. 'I have passed my life inside buildings constructed generations ago by men unknown to me, which have remained virtually unchanged since I was born. Once I have vacated these premises there will be no evidence of my having used them, and they will doubtless outlive me by many more generations, until my entire clan dissipates into an oblivion of impotence and intermarriage.'

Martin's mind wandered, lulled by the sonority of

Robertson's voice, past the gathering in the room, to the garden. The sky had cleared; swallows played in the blue dusk, their tiny, electronic cries echoing against the stone walls of the house as they swept past. He tried to follow the path of each bird as it darted up into the sky, but they moved too quickly, melting together and splitting apart, sometimes seeming to vanish altogether.

His awareness was drawn back to the room by a change in the pitch of Robertson's voice. Beads of sweat clung to his uncle's forehead, and his eyebrows seethed with energy. He seemed to be making a great effort to remain calm while apparently battling against a surge of barely controllable physical vitality.

'I ask myself,' Robertson was saying, his teeth almost clenched, 'what will have been the consequence of my life, of all our lives here, the endlessly decomposing contents of this impermeable history of matter? Simply to have maintained the structures and edifices within which we are imprisoned; the houseproud caretakers of a cathedral which is itself a God?'

He looked to the window and out into the garden. The chime of Alberta's trowel echoed in the twilight as it struck a stone in the flowerbed. He walked awkwardly around the desk to face his audience. 'Does this thought never strike you?' he said. 'You recollect the most significant moments of your life, you remember vividly exactly where you were standing, the view, the weather, the other person present if you were with another person, at these moments you cannot forget, when you were filled with love, or anger, and it seemed as if all the energy of the universe was concentrated on that very spot. And now, when you remember those places, where the most important events of your life took place, there is not a trace of you anywhere. There is not a trace of the person you loved or hated with such fervour. The wind continues to blow, the sun shines, the rain falls, the furniture may even be in exactly the same position, but as for you – there is not a sign.

'The place you occupied is empty. And now, for example, in this room, you will stand up, you will move an arm or stretch your legs, you will be going home, the room will be tidied, dusted, the teacups cleared away, and there will be nothing left of you. And there is no amount of commitment that you can bring to being here now that will alter that fact.' He sat down, as if almost surprised by his own words.

Martin began to experience an unpleasant feeling of dislocation, vertigo. His mouth became dry, and his forehead felt clammy.

'So how is it possible that we can be dust like this, and yet love one another?' Robertson continued. 'Are we not perpetual ghosts, disintegrating and dematerialising at every moment of our lives? And yet, is love not real?'

Two or three heads nodded in agreement, but Martin stood up abruptly, muttered a few words, which seemed to go unheard by the others, and rushed from the room. He fetched his boots and his bag of discarded clothing from the kitchen, barged through the kitchen door, pushing past Alberta who was returning indoors, out into the garden, past the study window, up the driveway and into the street.

The moon had risen and a lone planet stood in the sky, as still as a headlight on a distant road. He half ran to the main road and, without waiting for a bus, hobbled towards the city.

Chapter five

When he turned the corner into Newcastle Terrace, Christine was waiting for him, her rain-wet coat a welcoming light in the doorway of the close.

'I brought you these,' she said, handing him a brown bag as he unlocked the door. 'It was Carole's idea. We went shopping today, if you know what I mean.'

He opened the bag as they climbed the stairs and examined two new paperback books, a French edition of Baudelaire's poetry and a copy of *On The Road* by Jack Kerouac.

Mrs Morrison's head appeared from the sitting-room door as he showed Christine into his room.

'You'll mind the time, Martin,' she said.

Christine stepped past him, sat on the bed and looked about. Martin closed the door, threw down the books and his bag of clothes beside her and filled the kettle at the washbasin. Still unnerved by Robertson's lecture, he found it difficult to concentrate, feeling as if he needed two brains, one to unravel his uncle's Mysteries, the other to respond to Christine's presence. He took off his poncho and threw it over a chair.

'I wasn't sure if this was the right place. Ray told me the number, but you never know,' Christine said.

'He's been here a couple of times. He was probably stoned. I should have told you the address. Sorry.'

'Your landlady seems like a nice old soul.'

'She's OK,' Martin said.

'I wish I had my own place.'

'You live with your parents?'

'Aye, except when Danny and I stay at Ray's. But I'm going to do nursing next year so maybe I'll get my own place then.'

'Nursing?'

'I'm not stupid you know.'

She bounced up and down on the bed. They were both nervous.

A cloud of steam swept up the wall. Martin washed two mugs in the basin and took a packet of teabags from the mantelpiece. From the street below they heard two staccato voices and the sound of breaking glass.

'There goes someone's evening,' Martin said.

Christine stood up and walked to the window. She looked down into the street, her solemn face profiled in street-light.

'How's your scar?' she asked.

'My scar?'

'Aye. Your blood brother scar.'

He rolled up his sleeve. 'I must have been more stoned than I thought.' He surveyed his arm. 'It seems all right. At least he didn't cut through a vein.'

'Blood brothers!' she said. 'What a lot of nonsense.'

'Well, if you're going to be a nurse, you can give me medical attention if it goes septic.'

'I expect nurses have better things to do,' she said. 'Sometimes they get folk with real things wrong with them.'

'I suppose it was rather stupid.' He filled the mugs, picked up a cigarette pack from the mantelpiece, and joined her at the window.

'Look at those poor old souls,' she said.

Below, the owners of the broken bottle were kneeling on the pavement gloomily observing a pool of evaporating whisky. Martin offered Christine a cigarette, lit a match, his hand shaking involuntarily as she cupped her fingers around the flame and inhaled. 'Your hands always that cold?' she said, and smiled.

A trembling bass voice rose from the street, audible through the open window. 'You can't turn back the clock, Bill.'

'That would be great, eh?'

Martin and Christine gazed down at the two men.

Bill was staring morosely at the pavement, reconsidering. 'Although, I don't know,' he said. 'There are so many things I fucking regret I'd spend the rest of my life trying to sort all the damage I did in the past. I'd be going round in circles for ever.' He sat back on his heels and rubbed his chin.

'He's like my dad,' Christine said, taking a sip from her cup.

Bill began to cry noisily. He fumbled in the pocket of his coat and removed a red and white polka dot handkerchief. 'You know who gave me this, Chic?' he said, waving the handkerchief in his friend's face. 'Ma. You remember her, my ma, don't you, Chic?' Chic nodded as Bill rose slowly to his feet, brushing bottle glass from the knees of his trousers. 'There's nobody like your mother, Chic,' he said, burying his face in the handkerchief.

Martin laughed cynically as Chic gripped Bill under the arms and leaned him against a lamppost. 'I think my dad was a boozer,' he said.

Chic lit a cigarette in the shelter of the doorway and patted Bill tenderly on the shoulder. 'Get a grip, Bill,' he said.

'I don't have any milk,' Martin apologised.

'No biscuits?'

'No biscuits. Sorry.'

She moved towards him and took a drag from her cigarette. They watched Bill and Chic make their way up the street.

'Take off your coat if you like.'

Christine returned to the bed, removed the mac and sat down, clasping it on her knees. 'Do you like this dress?' she said, standing up again, laying the coat on the bed and turning round slowly. 'Carole picked it up for me today. Though you can see too much of my legs,' she said, sitting down quickly. 'I'm embarrassed.'

'You've got nice legs,' he said, irritated immediately by his feeble compliment.

Christine, too, seemed disconcerted. 'Carole's really generous,' she replied quickly. 'She gives away everything she pinches. And she's always looking for stuff that someone might like. I keep telling her that she doesn't have to give me things, I'll still be her friend.'

Martin nodded seriously. 'What about these books? Why is she giving them to me?'

'Must think you need something to read.'

He picked up a paperback from the bed. 'This one's in French. I don't speak French.'

She took the book from him and chose a page at random.

' *"Ne cherchez pas mon coeur,"* ' she read, ' *"Les bêtes l'ont mangé."* That's easy, "Don't look for my heart, the beasts have eaten it," ... Did you not learn French in school?'

'I didn't learn anything at school.'

'Oh-ho. Ignorant and proud!'

Martin looked away. 'How long have you known Carole?'

'You're barking up the wrong tree there.'

'What do you mean?'

'It was obvious you fancied her. She's beautiful, isn't she? Eyes like an Arab bird. And her hair. Wish I had hair like that. Not my teenybopper look. I look like a crow that's been out in the rain.'

'I think you're beautiful, Christine.'

'Don't be daft.'

'Anyway, why did you say I'm barking up the wrong tree?'

'Well, she's in a bit of trouble right now. She's been seeing Ray but now she's pregnant.'

'Pregnant?'

'Aye. She's not his girlfriend, really. It's just ... one night she stayed over with me and Danny, and there was just the four of us at Ray's flat. It's a shame. She felt sorry for him, I suppose. She doesn't usually do things like that.'

They sat in silence, drinking the cold dregs of their tea. Christine flopped back on the bed, bounced back up again and looked about the room. 'It's a really nice place. It's so quiet. I bet it's bright here in the daytime.'

The silence lengthened.

'I'd hate to end up like that,' she said. 'Like those two old codgers. Staring out of a bottle ... Bit like my dad. You said your dad drank?'

'Yeah – at least, until he killed himself. Mum never talks about him much, except to say what a great guy he was. But I think he did drink a bit.'

Christine became still. Beside her, Martin could feel the warmth of her body, hear her heartbeat. He became aware that all her attention was on him. The silence that had punctuated their conversation, the constant reminder of his awkwardness, his inability to relax with her, took on a new intensity.

'Your dad killed himself?'

'Yeah. Sorry. I shouldn't have mentioned it.'

'Why not?'

'Well, it's a bit of a downer, isn't it?'

Christine frowned at him.

'When did it happen?'

'Before I was born.'

'You never knew him.'

'No.'

'You must have a feeling for him, though. Have you got photos?'

'Yes I've seen some photographs, but supposedly they don't look like him. He was a journalist. He was very dapper, wore expensive clothes. My mother did then, too. He had a sports car, and they used to drive all over the South of England – that's where they lived, going to horse races, the Grand Prix. They lived by the sea, on the seafront in Worthing. Something happened to him in the war. He got a fright or something, that changed him. My mother told me it was like some sort of contamination in the house. He had nightmares. Although, I have nightmares.'

'What happened?'

Martin realised that a momentum had taken over now and although he had no desire to go on, the story would tell itself. 'Before the war, he had been a flight engineer, you know, for an airline. He took the car one morning, when my mother was still in bed. They'd had a few falling-outs, I think. One time he was drunk he came in and pissed all over the floor. I mean, that wasn't what he was like, that's what he became, because of whatever had happened to him. My mother says he was a really great guy, generous, really good fun. Everyone liked him.' He paused, patted his trouser pockets. 'I wish I had a cigarette, but they're all gone.'

Christine rested her hand on his knee, but said nothing.

'There used to be an old airport at Croydon, before the one at Heathrow. There were flying clubs that still used it. And no security, I suppose. They found the car the next morning outside the fence; there were all these cigarette butts lying beside it, as if he'd been smoking for hours, sitting there, smoking and thinking. Anyway, someone from the airport said they'd seen him strolling out on the tarmac, and hadn't thought much of it. He knew his way around there, so he would have looked casual. Someone had just started up an old Rapide, I think they said it was a Rapide, one of those old planes. He just threw away the fag, strolled up to the plane and walked into the propeller.'

'God.'

'Yeah. That was how flying people killed themselves in those days. Must have given the poor guy in the plane a turn. They don't do that now of course. Now they've got jets. You'd need a ladder.' He laughed uncomfortably.

Christine smiled. 'Do you want to cry?'

'Why should I want to cry?'

'Well, it's a sad story isn't it?'

'It's done now,' he said. 'No point in crying.' He took a deep breath. 'Anyway, that was that. *Sin agad e ma tha*, as they say in Lewis. Then, when I was eight we moved here to stay with my uncle.'

'What's he like?'

'He's totally mad. He started this institute – the Institute for Spiritual Regeneration. I've just been to one of his meetings, but I can't handle them. He's quite intense. He had some sort of vision at sea, apparently, although he never talks about it. He used to be a musician before he lost his fingers.'

'He lost his fingers?'

'Yeah. He got frostbite.'

'What did he play?'

'Accordion. Supposedly he was one of the best players in the Hebrides. But then he had this accident, and he couldn't play any more. So he started a religion. My mother cried when she saw his hands.'

'Lucky family.'

'Yeah. Really. Well, we were all right for money. My grandfather made a lot of money building bridges.'

'But now your uncle's given you the boot?'

'He's all right. He got me this room. It's not his fault I didn't feel like working. I would have thrown me out too.'

A few moments of silence followed, before Christine spoke. 'Mind you,' she said, as if the idea had been preying on her mind, 'Carole's taste isn't that great. I hate to say it, but that stuff she got for you really doesn't suit you.'

'What doesn't?'

'That poncho, for one thing. They look really manky after you've worn them for a few days.'

'Don't you like the boots? I've always wanted boots like these.'

'Aye. They're OK, I suppose.'

'More tea?'

'Aye.'

He boiled the kettle and refilled their mugs. Then he remembered a small lump of hash he had hidden in a drawer and offered her some, constructing a makeshift pipe from the cigarette packet's silver paper. After a couple of draws the pipe disintegrated; a red hot coal fell to the floor and burned a hole in the carpet. The street outside grew quiet. They heard Mrs Morrison in the hall, Teddy's tail banging against the wall, the old woman muttering to the dog, the click of a light switch and a door closing.

'It's cold in here,' Christine said. 'Can you not close the window?'

'The thing is, the room smells a bit with the window closed.'

'It can't be worse than Ray's.'

'And it's raining again,' he said. 'I like to hear the rain.'

She shrugged.

'How long have you and Danny been going out?' he asked.

'Oh no,' she said, glancing at her watch. 'I'd forgotten. I was supposed to meet him. Well, it's too late now.'

'What would he think about you being here?'

'He'll be sad probably, but he won't be angry.'

'You're going to tell him?'

She looked at him oddly. 'You can't lie to your friends, can you? You went to a posh school, didn't you? I suppose when you go to those places you get funny ideas. Didn't you ever have any friends?'

'Well, I didn't really fit in where I was. If I wasn't afraid of someone, they were usually afraid of me. And my family doesn't go in much for friends.'

'You had no mates at all?'

'Sort of. Sometimes. I don't keep in touch with anyone I went to school with. I never thought much about it. I never thought it was strange to feel strange. I just thought I was odd, I suppose, and everyone else was more or less normal.'

'It's like my mum says,' Christine said. 'It's no wonder they're Tories when you see how they treat each other.'

Martin picked up his empty mug from the floor and took a pointless sip.

'I've known Danny since we were at school,' she said.

'It's not serious though? You and him?'

'He's a friend. He's never faithful to me. All he ever talks about is capturing some new bird. But he's mostly front. I don't know what he'll do when I leave home. He's into politics. Wants to be a bomber. He's got this pal in London in the Angry Brigade. He went to their office once. It was under the Tory Party headquarters in Camden. He was so impressed! Now he's got all these pictures on his bedroom wall of Danny the Red, and Rudy, and the Bader-Meinhof gang, like they were pop stars.' She looked sadly at the floor. 'Permanent damage,' she said. 'Like Ray, I suppose. They're wee liars, really. Him and Ray. Lie to themselves all the time. You know that, don't you?'

'I don't think so,' Martin said.

'Well, Danny would never be a bomber. He'd just like to be *somebody*, but he couldn't hurt anyone. And as for Ray.' She laughed. 'It's terrible.'

'What is?'

'You know what Danny and I call him?'

'No.'

'Don't tell anyone. Don't tell Ray.'

'No.'

'Mr Shabby,' she said.

'Mr Shabby?'

'The way he looks. Like he's a tramp. An apprentice tramp.'

'There's nothing wrong with being a tramp,' Martin said. 'I wouldn't mind being a tramp myself.'

'Well, if Carole keeps getting your clothes ... Still, you've all got your wee dreams, haven't you?'

'What dreams?'

'It's like you look at all those old men out there and you think they never had dreams themselves.'

'Who are you talking about?'

'You boys. Always dreaming for something impossible. Ray wants to be a big-time drug dealer, but he's not clever enough and he doesn't have the nerve. And Danny wants to be a bomber, except he doesn't want to hurt anyone.'

'And what about me?'

'Your dreams are so impossible, you just pretend you're no' interested in anything. You do crappy jobs and hang about the street even though you don't belong there. It's stupid. Plenty of people don't have any choice about doing crappy jobs. But you really want to be Prime Minister, or a Nobel Prize winner or something, so you just hang about with your nose in the air as if you don't want to do anything at all, rather than find out what you could do and end up disappointed. It wouldn't do to find out you were just ordinary.'

'I'm not like that,' he said indignantly. 'And anyway, what's the point of being ordinary? There are millions of ordinary people already. You might as well kill yourself.'

'You wouldn't do that, would you?'

His outburst had embarrassed him. He laughed unconvincingly. 'Kill myself? Of course not. One in the family's enough. But I could never be a nurse, or some job like that. Clean up people's shit or wash dead bodies, and all that. And hospitals are so depressing.'

'Not if you're sick,' she said. 'They're not nearly so depressing if you're sick.'

He put his arm awkwardly around her shoulders. She rested her head against him. The dull scent of perfume and cigarette smoke drifted around him.

'Do you want to know what happens to you when you die?' she said, putting her face up to his and leering theatrically.

'Not really.'

She leaned over him and eyed him with an evil grin, a slender forefinger slicing his throat like an imaginary knife. 'First,' she said, running her nail down his chest, 'they cut you open and take out all your insides, stuff them into poly bags and sew them back in.' She pushed him back on the bed and held him down with a hand on his chest. 'Then,' she marked further incisions with her nail, 'they make a cut in your scalp at the back of the skull and peel the skin off, so your face turns inside out like a rubber mask. Then someone saws off the top of your skull, takes out your brain, dissects it and puts it back in again. Then they stick your face back on.'

She was now lying on top of him, her feet off the floor. He felt her heart beating through the light dress. He reached up and stroked her face, then her breast, and kissed her on the lips.

'What's wrong?' she said. 'You look worried.'

'I don't know how to behave with girls.'

He heard a shoe fall. His free hand slid down to her waist. Beneath his fingers, the hem of her dress, bare skin, knickers.

'I've got a sensitive bum,' she said, kissing his ear and raising her behind as his fingers slipped under the elastic. 'Can I stay the night? I didn't realise it was so late.'

He raised her dress and turned her over on the bed, hand inside her pants, slipping between her buttocks. Cold fingers unzipped his trousers and darted inside. She held the tip of his penis between her thumb and fingers, pulling softly as he came, laughing, her tongue in his ear, as Martin stroked her breast.

'Oh,' he said.

'Can I stay the night, then?' she said.

'Sorry,' he said. She put her finger over his lips and took his hand between her legs. He unbuttoned the top of her dress and kissed her breasts. She stroked him through his wet underpants. 'It was so quick,' he said.

'I knew you were a virgin,' she said, laughing. 'I could tell by the way you walk.'

'I'll put the light out,' he said. 'The toilet is just across the hall. Don't make any noise, or I'll get flung out.'

She left the room and returned a few minutes later without flushing the lavatory. He followed. When he returned the bedside light was extinguished and the room, bathed in street-light, swarmed with shadows. Her skinny silhouette slipped from the shadow of her dress and she stood naked at the window, gazing thoughtfully at her breasts. She got into his bed, drawing back the covers beside her. He climbed in beside her and pulled the sheets over their heads, kissed and stroked her. He felt as if an audience that had been watching him all evening had vanished. Amorous green eyes glittered in the dark; her skin flashed beneath his fingers like an electric current. Cool fingers slid between his legs and he shuddered with pleasure.

Chapter six

He was woken by a high sweet voice singing in Italian, and thought he was dreaming.

'It's OK,' Christine said. 'The old dear's gone out with her dug.' She leaned over the bed and kissed him on the lips.

'Who was that singing?'

'Tetrazzini,' she said, giggling as he reached under the covers and put his hand up her dress.

'You forgot to put your knickers on.'

She fell on top of him and they made love, Christine pulling away and stroking his penis as he ejaculated. 'Want to get me pregnant?' She leaned over and nipped him with her teeth. 'You've gone all red.'

'I'm not used to such forward women,' he said.

'You're not used to any women.' She fell back beside him on the bed. 'It's a lovely room this, in the day. I knew it would be.'

Sunlight poured in at the window, a sparkling haze swam lazily above their heads.

'Where did you learn to sing like that?'

'It's in our blood,' she said. 'Papes. My daddy calls me Tetrazzini. His wee Tetrazzini. That was *Sempre Libera – Always Free.*' She giggled. 'Well, you didn't have to pay.'

'Where are you going? Do you have to go?'

'Back to Glasgow for the day. Explain myself to my mum.' She jumped from the bed, picked up her knickers and pulled them on, put on her coat, and sat down beside him on the bed.

'Why don't I come home with you?'

'I don't want you coming to my place,' she said.

'Why's that?'

'It's not what you'd be used to.'

'You don't know what I'm used to.'

She looked at him. 'I'll come back again tonight, if you like. Meet you at the Diamond Club up on Lothian Road. Don't wear that poncho. Wear a jacket and a white shirt. They've got black-light that make you glow in the dark. It's dead romantic.'

'Great,' he said.

She kissed him again and was gone.

He jumped from the bed and hurried to the window to watch her as she half ran from the close into the street. She turned once and looked up into the sun, waving blindly at his window. His infatuation with Carole had vanished. He could hardly remember what she looked like. He leaped around his room, playing an imaginary guitar solo, punched his arms in the air, fell back on the bed, shouting under his breath, 'Fuck! That was great!' to his invisible audience. A few minutes later he was asleep.

He was woken an hour later by a knock at the door. Mrs Morrison stood in the hallway, staring anxiously towards the front room. Teddy peered up at him from under her skirt, his tail banging against the hall stand behind him.

'I think I must have put too many fire lighters in. There seems to be something wrong with the fire.' She pointed vaguely towards the sitting-room door. 'Perhaps you could have a look at it, Martin.'

He followed her along the hall and into the sitting-room. Flames curled over the mantelpiece, varnish bubbling and peeling from the mahogany surround. He ran to the kitchen and returned with a wet towel, removed the accessible coals from the grate with fire tongs and held the towel over the fireplace until the flames subsided.

'The chimney needs to be swept,' he said. 'I might be able to do it myself, if I had the brush.'

'Perhaps we could make some arrangement about the rent,' she said, 'if you're sure you know how to do it. It might be rather dangerous. Although, there is a flat roof I believe. I have a stepladder you can get up there with,' she added helpfully.

She disappeared from the room, returned with her purse, and gave him a five pound note for the rental of a brush.

He walked to the art gallery, smiling indiscriminately at passers-by. Behind the gallery the castle stood like a giant's lair against a haze of coral clouds that floated at the edge of the city. On the steep grass bank beneath the rock, families strolled and lovers rolled together under the trees. Martin felt like an initiate. Nothing could impede his progress now, he thought. All objects of desire had become attainable; he had finally made contact with life and was discovering possibilities for himself everywhere. Yet somewhere in the back of his mind a thin cloud of uncertainty drifted and he could not identify the cause. Perhaps something Christine had said the night before? He put the problem aside and focused his mind instead on the unfamiliar sensation of happiness.

Ray was crouched on the gallery steps, rolling a cigarette. 'What happened to you?' he said, glancing up. 'You look like you've just had a good shag.'

Martin laughed and waved the five pound note in the air. 'Fancy a drink?' he said.

'Never say no to a wee bevvy,' Ray replied.

An hour later they climbed through the trap door above the Newcastle Terrace stairwell with a rented chimney brush, two cans of lager and a bundle of extensions. They lay on the roof with their backs to the chimney, smoking cigarettes and drinking. During the morning the sky had clouded over and now a cool wind, wet with impending rain, blew up the street, numbing their hands as they smoked.

'You know all about this, do you, Martin?' Ray inquired sceptically.

'I think it's pretty simple. You shove the brush down and it clears all the soot out.'

'It's a wonder everyone doesn't do their own lum if it's that easy.'

'It's dirty work,' Martin said.

'Oh, aye,' Ray said. 'But for who?'

Martin stood up, stubbed out his cigarette and connected the brush to an extension. Ray assisted him and together they inserted it into the chimney, then shoved it down.

'Seems to be going in fine,' Martin said.

'Aye. I just have this feeling there must be more to it than this.'

As they reached the end of the first extension, they attached another and continued pushing.

'Perhaps we ought to push it up and down a few times to loosen the soot,' Ray suggested.

'That seems reasonable,' Martin said.

They continued with this procedure as each extension was added. After several minutes the brush came to a halt.

'It's jammed,' Martin said.

'Aye,' agreed Ray.

They sat on their heels on the wet roof and lit cigarettes. Ray handed Martin his can of lager. 'There's a wee bit left.'

They gazed silently at the protruding extension, which waved merrily back and forth in the freshening breeze.

'Of course you get birds' nests and all kinds of rubbish in these lums,' Ray said. 'It'll be something like that.'

'Yes,' Martin said. 'That'll be what's making the chimney smoke.'

'I suppose if we pull it up a bit then give it a good shove.'

'That should budge it.' Martin nodded.

They finished the cigarettes, drained the can and resumed their work. As Ray had anticipated, by withdrawing the brush two or three feet and ramming it with redoubled force down the chimney, the obstruction was removed and the brush continued its smooth course. 'This is getting me excited,' leered Ray.

A few minutes later the brush jammed for a second time. They applied a similar remedy and freed it once more.

'By my calculations,' Martin said, 'we've easily enough length to have reached the fireplace. Let's go and have a look.'

'Aye,' said Ray. He rubbed his hands together briskly. 'It's getting cold up here.'

'We can have some tea downstairs.'

Ray was the first to climb down through the skylight. Martin followed a moment later. As he stepped on to the ladder he was surprised to see Mrs Morrison waiting for them, Teddy sitting between her feet, their faces obscured beneath a layer of soot.

'Martin,' she said, apologetically, 'I'm so glad you decided to come down.'

She led them downstairs, Martin's heart sinking. Behind him Ray's laughter echoed in the tiled close. In the front room the china cabinet lay on its side, its shattered contents strewn across the carpet. A thick layer of soot covered the furniture and a muddy trail from the fireplace marked the serpentine progress of the brush across the carpet and up the wall, where it had come to rest about four feet from the floor. Ray and Martin lifted the cabinet back on to its feet and surveyed the damage.

'I'm terribly sorry, Martin. I tried to shout up, but I suppose you couldn't hear me. Teddy was barking too, weren't you Teddy?' She leaned over and patted the ebonised brush head of the dog from which beady eyes glared ferociously.

Martin looked hopelessly around the room. His assistant had vanished. Cruel laughter could be heard from the hall. The landlady appeared not to notice. He walked over and picked up a few pieces of china from the carpet and tried fitting them together before handing the fragments to Mrs Morrison and helping her to the armchair by the fire, where she sat down heavily amid a cloud of soot. He hurriedly dismantled the brush, pulling the remaining extensions down the chimney, and rushed out through the open front door and down the stairs to the street, catching Ray as he disappeared around a corner.

Ray had stopped to rest against a lamppost and was laughing nastily as Martin watched, leaning on the chimney brush and glaring moodily at his friend. 'It's not that funny, Ray,' he said.

Ray disengaged himself from the lamppost, wiping his eyes. 'Of course it's funny. Dotty old dear.'

Martin slid to his heels with his back against a neighbour's wall. Ray sat down beside him and rolled a cigarette.

'You were the one who said it would be simple,' Ray said. 'Anyway, no use crying over spilt milk.' He smiled again. 'Let's get some dope. My mate Moscow always has good dope. And wait till you see his drum. It's barrie.' He stood up and tugged at Martin's arm. Martin resisted however, and instead arranged to meet Ray later at the Diamond Club.

Martin returned the chimney brush to the rental shop and walked aimlessly through the wet, twilit streets. He found a pound note in his pocket and bought a tube of glue. An hour later he entered a pub on the High Street across the road from the Heart of Midlothian. An incompatible mixture of tourists and old local men eyed each other across the bar. His exultant morning mood had dissipated into vague panic and he wondered what he would have to do to feel as alive all the time as he had that morning with Christine, or even for brief moments that afternoon on the roof with Ray, bracing himself against the sharp north breeze. He looked about him, contemplating the people in the pub. His impressions were sour and uncharitable. All he could see in them was ugliness, emptiness, weakness. The old working men, who in moments of humanity he admired and romanticised now seemed despicable. Their eyes, weak and watery with alcohol, sentimentality, self-pity; their pinched lips, bitter and disappointed. As for the tourists, they were even worse; oblivious to the misery around them, their vanity and self-satisfaction concealed atavistic, violent souls – a psychopathic indifference to the defeated world through which they came and went unscathed.

He abandoned his drink and walked outside. Night had fallen and the High Street was at its most picturesque. Rusty light glowed on the cobblestones leading up to the castle, the shadows, crevices, pediments and ancient, irregular stones of St Giles and the surrounding buildings sparkled as if in a film set. The old world, of thieves, beggars, resurrection men, dissipated lords, executioners, mobs, febrile children, disease, luxury, became almost tangible, as if locked in the stones were a million voices that whispered all the secrets of the past. He stopped in a doorway and watched the passers-by. A kind of terror rose up inside him, a fear that if he forgot what hope was like, or was unable to re-create it, he would die by surprise one day, and his own voice would be sealed up in the stones, along with all the other anonymous dead voices.

He returned to Mrs Morrison's and before setting off for the Diamond Club, passed the early evening in the sitting-room, assembling broken china. Most of the damage was irreparable. The old lady and the dog, taciturn and enigmatic, watched him work.

'I suppose it seemed like such fun,' Mrs Morrison said, as she went to the kitchen to make tea. Martin finished restoring an arm to a figurine of a ballerina and put it on the blackened mantelpiece to dry.

'Nothing is fun,' he told Teddy melodramatically, laughing ironically as the ballerina's arm slipped slowly down her torso, suspended for a moment in its descent by a shrinking thread of drying glue, and fell, shattering on the hearth tiles.

Chapter seven

He descended the stairs into throbbing, amniotic darkness, brushed by the doorman, through heavy double doors into the Diamond Club. Poplin shirts and polyester dresses glowed in black-light, the air hot and heavy with perfume and alcohol. Girls milling by the packed dance floor chewed gum, imitating the mannerisms of tired women; groups of boys jostled dancing couples and scanned the crowd for possible sex or violence. Martin drew into himself and made his way forward, aiming for an imaginary point in the distance, a yard beyond the next shoulder. Ray was waiting at the bar, Carole behind him, chewing gum revolving between shiny lips. The disembodied face of Christine hovered beside her, a smile brightening as he pushed through the crowd. On stage a band in black improvised a rock-and-roll raga. An erotic shiver ran up his spine, as if he'd been plugged into a grid.

'Two Carlsberg Specials.' Ray ordered the beer as Martin leaned over Carole's shoulder and kissed Christine.

Ray turned and handed Martin his drink. As he did so, several couples fled abruptly from the dance floor, pushing through the crowd at the bar. Like the last block in a set of tumbling dominoes Martin bore the accumulated momentum of their retreat. He threw up an arm and a graceful rainbow of lager illuminated by bar lights fell, miraculously intact, into his coat sleeve. In the gloom fists were flying; white shirt-cuffs flashed in the black-lit darkness. A girl's scream cut through the music. Two boys, one bleeding from a cut above his shirt collar, were being dragged from the floor by doormen.

The dancers reassembled, the fracas absorbed by sound and movement. Martin put down his empty glass on the bar, shook out his sleeve.

The four friends moved away a little from the dance floor.

'That was Bendy,' Ray said.

'Bendy?'

'Aye,' Carole said. 'Bendy skelped the boy. He's the leader of Mental Drylaw. That's him with the red hair.'

Martin peered through the crowd at a stubby red-haired youth in a shining suit, smiling broadly in the midst of a group of admirers.

'He's radge,' Carole said.

'Radge?'

She spun a crimson fingernail by her ear. 'Crazy Horse. Belongs in the bin if you ask me.'

'Should I congratulate you?' Martin said to Ray, nodding at Carole.

Ray patted the girl's belly and shrugged.

'Immaculate conception, so help me God,' Carole muttered. 'I'd read about it in books, but I never dreamed it could happen tae me.'

The club was becoming more crowded, the heat and noise intensifying. The girls retired to the toilets.

'I didn't realise Carole was your girlfriend,' Martin said.

'She's not my regular bird. Just some Humpty-Dumpty now and then.'

'Oh.'

'Aye. A right adventurous cow she is too. Never had a bird do some of the things she does. Stuck her tongue up my arse once. It was fucking great.'

Martin bought himself a replacement pint, and a vodka and orange for Christine. The girls returned, Carole leading, elbowing her way vigorously through the growing crowd. Behind her, irritated drinkers wiped beer from their jackets and glared after her.

''See fucking students …' she said.

'Thanks for the books,' Martin said.

'You're welcome, I'm sure. Are they all right, then?'

'I read a bit of the Jack Kerouac book. It looks good.'

Carole turned to Ray. 'No dancing?'

'Nah.' He turned his attention to the stage.

She redirected the question to Martin.

'I'm not much good at dancing.'

'You just have to be good at enjoying it,' Carole said, taking too large a swig from her glass, spilling a mouthful down her dress. She giggled, and a blush rose into her cheeks as she reached into her bag for a cigarette.

'She's nervous,' Christine whispered in Martin's ear.

'About being pregnant?'

'She's all front. And Ray isn't going to do anything, is he?'

'About the baby?'

'Aye.'

'Probably not.'

Ray turned back. 'Have you ever seen this place after a bust?' he said, resting his beer glass precariously on Christine's shoulder. 'There's usually about a hundred quid deals on the floor afterwards.'

'That's where he gets all his dope,' Carole snorted.

Martin finished his beer and put the glass down at his feet. 'Maybe we should be leaving.'

Christine nodded.

'Come back to my place,' Ray said. 'I've got some grass. Durban Poison.' He put his arm around Carole's waist. 'Cheer us up, eh?'

As if someone had switched off the magic, the music stopped and the lights came on. An amp hummed loudly from the stage before it too was silenced. The bell for last call rang out. As Martin bought a quarter bottle of vodka at the bar Christine appeared at his shoulder. 'We shouldn't go there,' she said. 'I've got a feeling.'

Martin kissed her and behind her Ray, grinning, raised his glass in a salute.

Christine looked back at Ray and Carole. 'We could just go to your place. I'd rather be with you.'

Martin smiled as if not having heard her, took her hand and pushed through the crowds to the door. A youth he had seen with Bendy jostled him, muttering malevolently. Fear crept through him.

'Want to fight?' the youth asked.

'No thanks.'

'Fair enough. Fair enough,' the boy said, raising his open palms into the air.

They walked out into a cool night. Light snow fell and congested streets filled with singing, shouting, the smell of perfume, alcohol, fried fish and vinegar. Crowds of youths filed past. Timid pedestrians moved from the pavement into gutters and shop doorways; darting eyes, alert and hungry, gleamed from furtive, amber faces.

They caught a bus to Ray's flat. Alone on the top deck the couples talked about nothing; loud singing downstairs terminated abruptly. The bus crawled along Easter Road. Tenements closed in around them. Martin looked through dead curtains at children sleeping, lightless, empty rooms, solitary men sitting on beds. 'It's sad that people have to live like that,' he said.

'Like what?' Christine followed his pointing thumb in the direction of the tenement windows. 'What's sad about it?' she said. 'Sad they're not rich, you mean? Or just sad you have to see them as you're passing through.'

'That's not what I meant.'

'They can take care of themselves. It's boys like you who need to look out.'

She turned away, then glanced back, smiling. 'No, you're right, I suppose. It is a bit sad. You don't have to live like that, but you want to. I don't understand it. You with your nice house to go back to.'

'It's a phase I'm going through,' he said.

'Aye, it will be.'

A group of four boys boarded the bus, rushed up the stairs and sat at the front, brooding and silent. A chill descended. Martin spoke quietly to Christine, about nothing in particular, concentrating all his attention on her.

'Nearly there,' Ray said, looking round as the stop approached.

As he spoke, one of the boys shouted something and leaped to his feet, pointing out of the window. His companions peered down into the street then stood up and ran back to the stairs. In the fisheye mirror Martin saw them jumping from the platform as the bus slowed down. Ray reached up and rang the bell. The others followed him down the stairs.

As they assembled on the platform, Martin looked back up the dimly-lit street. Two of the boys stopped to pick up a pair of empty milk bottles from a doorway. Further away Martin could make out the silhouette of a man beneath a street-light. As the boys reached him he turned and raised his arm over his head. The bus stopped and the two couples disembarked. They all looked back up the street. The first boy reached the man. Wielded with determination, the first milk bottle hit him hard on the temple. He turned away, lowering his hand to his forehead as the second boy struck him a hard blow on the crown of his head. The man's legs buckled and he fell face first into the road. Neither of the heavy bottles had broken. One of the boys looked back down the street to where Martin and the others were still standing. He tugged at a friend's sleeve and nodded in their direction.

'Let's go,' said Ray.

Martin grabbed Christine's hand and they all began to run, the boys following about two hundred feet behind.

Ray led the way. After a few moments Martin lost his grip on Christine's hand. Carole caught up with Ray, and together they accelerated through the maze of dark lanes and back courts. A thin layer of wet snow now covered the ground. Christine stumbled over a cobblestone and fell behind. Martin heard her call his name. Ray and Carole vanished through an open doorway into a dark close and he found himself alone. In the empty back court a row of dustbins leaned against a low midden wall. High above his head a tuneless voice sang behind an amber window and fell silent. He heard shouting and the rush of approaching footsteps.

He grabbed a dustbin lid and held it up as a shield, then ran a little further, heard his name again, more faintly. Christine appeared around the corner of the alley a few yards behind him, her face illuminated by a light from the close opposite. He ducked behind the midden wall, still clutching the dustbin lid, and squatted among a pile of wet rubbish and mashed vegetables. Through a hole in the brickwork he watched the girl searching desperately for an escape route. She looked across to the open close and began to run towards it. Martin almost called her name, but the four boys appeared around the corner. The two leaders still carried the milk bottles and as they rounded the corner one smashed the end off his bottle against the wall. They quickly caught up with the girl and surrounded her, pushing her back against the wall a few yards from Martin's hiding place. She and the boys stood together, all breathing heavily.

'Where's your mates?' asked one of the boys.

She laughed humourlessly. 'They've gone.'

'We'll do you then,' another said.

'One of them your boyfriend?'

She did not reply.

'Well, he's a wanker.'

'Let's get on with it,' said the boy with the broken bottle, grabbing her by the throat and pushing her head back against the bricks.

'On you go, then,' his friend said sarcastically.

'I'm pregnant,' Christine said. 'You're right hard men, you are. Four of you and one pregnant woman.'

'Do her anyway,' said the throttling boy.

'Your girlfriends would really be proud of you, no?' Christine said, 'if they could see you now.'

Martin peered through the hole in the wall. The boy with the bottle tightened his grip around her throat. Her voice dissolved in a strangled wheeze. The boy brought the jagged edge of the bottle up to her throat and headbutted her on the nose.

'I'm sorry,' she gasped.

'Forget it,' the first boy said, brushing his friend's arm away.

'Leave her alone,' said another.

'She's a nice lassie,' said the first, turning to Christine. 'Your boyfriend? Is it his kid?' He pulled his friend's hand away from her throat. 'I hope yer no gonna marry the yellow bastard.'

Christine looked back at him steadily.

'Go,' he said.

She paused, rubbing her throat. 'Thank you,' she said.

Behind the first boy, the second began pushing towards her. The first put up an arm to intercept him. 'Go!' he shouted.

She turned and ran, past the midden, into the darkness.

The boys hovered disconsolately in the lane.

'You should have asked her for a fucking lumber,' one said.

There was the sound of glass smashing against a wall, then silence. Martin closed his eyes and sank down into the foetid mud of the midden, burying his head in his beer-soaked sleeve.

Twenty minutes later he heard Ray calling his name. He looked up over the midden wall.

'You all right?'

'I'm fine,' Martin said. 'Where's Christine?'

'She's all right. She's at the flat. Good job she told them she was pregnant.'

Martin followed Ray from the lane, brushing wet mud and congealed rubbish from his trousers.

'She's not is she?' Ray asked.

'What?'

'Pregnant?'

'Not as far as I know,' Martin said.

'No,' Ray said. 'She's not stupid. Not like some chicks.'

'Carole ran pretty quick for a pregnant woman.'

'Oh, yeah, she's got a good turn of speed. She gets plenty of exercise with her shoplifting and that. Best thing to do anyway. Live to fight another day, eh?' He looked at Martin curiously. 'Fear does strange things to a man,' he said, screwing up his face in a poor imitation of Edward G. Robinson.

Christine looked up at him as he walked through the door of Ray's flat, the welcome in her eyes extinguished. 'Where did you get to?'

'I got lost.' He knelt down and ran his hand over her bruised forehead. A thin trail of dried blood still lingered on her upper lip.

'Yes,' she said.

No one in the room spoke.

'Well, I think we should get back,' he said.

'You go on,' Christine said. 'I'll be along in a while.'

'That's OK,' said Martin. 'I'll wait.'

'No,' Christine said. 'You go.'

Martin looked around the room. The others stared back at him without speaking. 'OK, then,' he said. 'You'll be along in a bit?'

He sat in the chair by the window and watched a grey dawn come up over the street, heard the first morning bird calls, milk bottles clattering on the step below, a neighbour's car starting. He made a pot of tea and waited, without drinking, until the pot grew cold. As the ground-floor doors opened along the street and footsteps sounded he opened the window and leaned over the ledge, expecting to see Christine. He fell asleep and woke a few hours later, washed his face at the sink, wandered back and forth between the door and the window, lay on the bed, breathing in Christine's smell on the pillow. 'What could I have done, for Christ's sake?' he asked himself, sliding to the floor beside his bed. From there he watched the sky grow dark, the street-light come on, heard a door open in the hall, the landlady making her way to the lavatory, Teddy's tail banging against the wall.

She knocked on the door. When he did not reply, she shuffled away. He heard the click of the hall light, listened to the flow of traffic fading in the street outside, a few shouts from a neighbouring road. He knelt down on the carpet and pulled his coat up over his head in case anyone heard the shuddering grief in his throat.

He passed the following day in a state of lassitude, rising early after a dull sleep, searching amid sweat and stale smoke for Christine's evaporating scent in the pillow, washing lethargically and slipping from the house, walking empty, metallic streets where melting snow slid under his feet. In the afternoon, staring dumbly in a bookshop window, he thought he saw Christine's reflection. He turned and rushed after a blonde head as it vanished into an adjacent street, but when he reached the corner no one in the crowd of pedestrians resembled her. After that he saw her everywhere, climbing on buses, darting into shops, even once in the passenger seat of a car. He ran after it, almost catching up with it at traffic lights, watching it pull away as the lights changed. Despite all this he avoided the art gallery and when one morning, he saw her walking towards him, he turned rapidly, dodged into a doorway and waited until she had passed, feeling as if a molten stone had lodged in his belly.

Chapter eight

The summer came. Robertson and Alberta departed for Lewis. During their absence Martin visited Taigh nan Òran, sat by the pond beneath Robertson's beech tree, walked in the fields, smoked cigarettes in his overgrown bivouac. The house was locked, but Alberta had left him the key. He wandered through the cool rooms, sat on his old bed and watched the blackbirds and sparrows hopping about the garden, read passages from the Bible in the wash stand, passed an afternoon in the study trying, unsuccessfully, to break into Robertson's desk, pursuing all these activities as if he might unearth a vital secret, either in the form of documentary evidence or through osmosis. It was as if he hoped the house might speak to him, like a spirit from beyond the grave. Robertson's personality, which had certainly cast a spell, or at least a cloud, over the house, had something ghost-like about it, and he always seemed to speak in such an anachronistic way, as if the dead were his intended audience. Now, as Martin wandered through the rooms, his conviction grew that over the years of contact with the solitary Robertson, and later with his mother, the household furnishings might have become imbued with vital information he could extract telepathically, if he could only attune his mind to their enigmatic language. And even though he gained no realisation during his weeks alone in the empty house, he felt quite at home there, stimulated; sometimes it seemed that by contrast with Taigh nan Òran, the city was lifeless and uninhabited.

He was returning to Mrs Morrison's one wet morning in the early autumn, when he saw Ray walking up the street towards him, wiping rain from his eyes and smiling furtively. Not having seen him for several weeks, Martin was struck suddenly by the precarious nature of his friend's life, as if only luck stood between him and summary annihilation. 'I haven't seen you lately,' he said.

'Been hiding?' Ray asked.

'No. Working. I got another job.'

Ray squinted at him. 'Fancy scoring some dope?' he said. 'I was just on my way to Moscow's. Got a little business to do with him.' He winked and patted his woollen shoulder bag. 'And you look like you could do with some cheering up. I told you about Moscow. He'll have something.'

They walked across the city and arrived an hour later in a short street occupied by an overgrown vacant lot and a solitary Georgian townhouse. Black clouds fulminated in a watery blue sky. Although it was already mid-morning a few lights could still be seen inside the building. Ray hopped up the wide stone steps to the front door, buzzed the intercom and waited. A voice answered and he cackled nervously into the speaker. The door opened on to a broad vestibule with a pillar at each side, half concealing two leather sofas set in mirrored recesses against each wall.

'What did I tell you?' he said, waving proprietorially towards a wide, carpeted staircase. 'Even real flowers, man.' He indicated a Chinese vase filled with lilies on a table at the foot of a staircase.

They heard a voice overhead. Martin looked up but saw only a pair of hands resting on the top floor banister. He followed Ray's breathless ascent up five flights of stairs to the dealer's flat.

'I brought a friend,' Ray explained to a tall, thin man of about thirty standing by the door.

The dealer eyed Martin suspiciously. 'That's a unique concept, Ray,' he said. He stood aside as Ray brushed by him. 'Know him well, do you?' he asked Martin, waving him in courteously.

He closed the door and led them along a newly painted hallway into an elegant drawing room. High windows overlooked a spacious garden five floors below, a thick carpet covered the floor from wall to wall, and cushions with Oriental silk covers were scattered before the fireplace in which a pair of cherry logs blazed merrily. The room was sparsely furnished. A walnut bookcase stood against the wall adjacent to the fireplace, and beside it stood an unplugged Spiderman pinball machine. A sleek Bang and Olufsen stereo rested on a coffee table beneath the window.

'Moscow,' Ray said.

The dealer nodded at Martin.

'Miserable day,' Ray added, rubbing his hands together.

'Is it a quid deal, Ray?' Moscow said, without waiting to hear Martin's name.

'Just a minute,' Ray said. 'I think I can do better than that. I've been carrying this bloody thing around for weeks.' He reached into his bag and produced a Capo di Monte figurine of a rosy-cheeked shepherdess. 'How much will you give me for this?'

The dealer took the figurine and glanced at it briefly before handing it back. 'I'm not a pawnbroker, Ray.'

Martin watched Ray stuff the figurine back into his pocket. 'That looks like Mrs Morrison's,' he said.

'Oh dear,' Moscow said, 'it's not even yours, Ray.'

He pointed at the stereo. 'Put on a record. I'll be back in a minute.'

Ray shuffled over to the window and stared uncomprehendingly at the record player.

'I don't know how to work this.' He smiled nervously at Martin. 'I'm afraid I might break it.'

Martin stared at him for a few moments then went through the selection of records in the bookshelf.

The dealer returned with an uncut slab of Afghani hashish and threw it ostentatiously on the carpet. It gleamed like shoe leather in the firelight. 'Want me to cut a quid deal off this for you, Ray?' he asked. 'I've only got an old set of Pesolas to weigh it with. I wouldn't want to rip you off, man.'

Ray looked downcast. Moscow reached in the pocket of his jeans and pulled out a ball of silver paper which he slipped into Ray's hand, slapping him fraternally on the shoulder. 'Cheer up, mate. Roll up some of this and I'll make some tea.'

'What's this like?' Martin asked, holding up a Hot Club of Paris sleeve.

'Django Reinhardt, Stephan Grappelli. Brilliant.' Moscow left the room and returned a few minutes later with a pot of maté tea, three cups and a plate of cake on a tray. Ray had unpeeled Moscow's gift. Inside the silver paper Ray had found a lump of sticky black hashish, and was now constructing a joint.

'How's the chest?' Moscow inquired, as they waited for the tea to infuse.

'Can't complain. A bit sore in the damp.'

'You should take better care of yourself. You haven't got the physique for street life, Ray. You ought to get an indoor job.' The dealer's laconic laugh blended strangely with Ray's cackle.

Ray completed the spliff and lit up. He disappeared briefly in a cloud of smoke, then reappeared, his bright red face contorted in a cough. 'Good shit, man,' he said, complacently.

'Makes you really paranoid too, Ray.' Moscow turned to Martin. 'Known him long?'

'A few months,' Martin replied.

'And you're still talking to him?'

'Very funny,' Ray said.

Moscow smiled pleasantly at Martin, took the spliff from Ray and passed it to him.

They consumed the tea and cake in silence. A violent gust rattled the windows, logs crackled in the fireplace.

'Miserable day,' Ray said again.

'This guitar player's amazing,' Martin said, taking a puff of the joint and passing it to Moscow.

'He only had two fingers,' Moscow said. 'Lost the others trying to save his guitar from a fire. He was a gypsy.'

'Two fingers!'

'That's all you need, eh, Ray?' Moscow said. 'Enough to smoke a fag, enough to feel up a chick, and tell someone to fuck off.'

'Yeah.' Ray laughed and rose stiffly to his feet. 'I can't go on sitting like this. You ought to invest in a chair.'

'Have you been selling drugs for a long time?' Martin asked Moscow, who stared at him without answering. Twining his fingers together nervously Martin stretched and yawned. Moscow continued to observe him thoughtfully. Eventually he said, 'No point in being in a city without money. You might as well be a gardener or something if you're not interested in money.' He spat on his finger and dabbed the end of the joint. 'I don't sell morph or downers, only hash and stimulants. Downers are just a way for the Government to keep people in their place.'

'You sound like Danny,' Ray said. 'Where's the toilet? I've forgotten.'

Moscow stood up and accompanied Ray to the hall, returning a moment later. 'I mean, take the Vietnam War, for example. The Yanks send all the spades from the ghettos to the Golden Triangle, stuff Fort Knox full of junk and get the guys who aren't killed or driven crazy strung out on smack. That certainly put paid to political unrest in America.' He nodded towards the door. 'What do you think of him, then? Make a good cartoon character, yeah?'

Martin recalled Ray's Mr Shabby nickname.

'He's a nice bloke,' he said.

'Oh, yes, he's a nice bloke,' Moscow said, smiling to himself, 'though I probably wouldn't pick him for my role model.' He leaned back luxuriously on the carpet and took a deep draw from the joint. 'Mind you, I wouldn't mind living in America. The weather's better isn't it? And they like to see you doing well. They like successful people.'

'Money isn't everything,' Martin said.

The dealer poured them each another cup of tea, and thought about this for a while. 'Think that up yourself, did you?' he said.

Martin tried unsuccessfully to think of a reply.

'People here want you to fail,' Moscow said. 'That's what keeps the country together, mate. Defeat and failure. If you want to make something of yourself it's like you're betraying your birthright. I mean look at the heroes they pick for themselves. William Wallace, for example. A total wanker. Everything he did turned to shite.'

'He won the battle of Bannockburn.'

'Yeah. That must have been a great consolation to him when they were cutting his balls off and pulling his guts out.'

The record finished. Moscow got up slowly and walked over to the stereo. 'People here revel in poverty. They're proud of it. It doesn't make sense to me. I suppose when you're always a victim you don't have any responsibilities.'

'Perhaps people are only poor because they share what they have. Poor people aren't as lonely as rich people.'

Moscow switched off the record player, returned the record to its sleeve, put another log on the fire and sat down again on the floor. 'You think so? Poor people aren't as lonely as rich people?' He stared intently at Martin. 'That's a new one on me.'

Once more Martin could think of nothing to say.

Ray came back into the room. 'You can't live on icing alone,' he said. 'Yeah,' Moscow laughed, 'Let them eat icing. I like it, Ray. I like it.' He handed Martin the record. 'You like this?'

'Yes, but ...'

'Take it.' He rerolled the remainder of the lump of hash in the silver paper and gave it to Martin.

'How much?' he asked.

'No charge,' Moscow said. 'Just don't come back.' He stood up. 'Nothing personal, mate,' he added. 'Really ... I just have enough friends already.' He led them to the door, opened it and waited at the threshold. As Ray passed, he rested his hand on his shoulder. 'Give him the ornament, Ray.'

Ray took the figurine from his pocket and gave it to Martin.

'It's the sheep you've got to watch out for, mate,' Moscow said, smiling fraternally at Martin. 'You know where you are with the wolves.'

Ray had already reached the stairs. Moscow put his hand on Martin's arm. 'You want to get out of here, mate, before it sucks the life out of you.'

Martin looked at him for a moment then followed Ray to the stairs.

'Have a nice life,' Moscow said, closing the door.

'Big-headed bastard,' Ray muttered as they reached the street. They stood by the door, Ray staring sadly at the ground. 'Still, I wouldn't mind having his gaff.'

The sky was clearing and a mist of evaporating rain rose about their ankles in the warm sunlight.

'I'm sorry about the ornament,' he said. 'I didn't know you then. I thought you were some straight.'

Martin smiled. 'Take the hash, Ray.'

Ray's face brightened suddenly. 'Why don't we go to Dunoon?'

'Dunoon?'

'Yeah. Go fishing. It's beautiful down there on the Clyde. Have a few cans on the ferry. Smoke this dope.'

'I'm knackered, Ray. I've been up all night.'

'I've got just the thing for that.' Ray pulled a small bottle of yellow pills from his pocket. He handed them to Martin, took the figurine and the record and stuffed them into his bag.

'That's settled, then,' he said, sniggering oddly.

Chapter nine

The train followed a winding path among canyons of tenements to the widening Clyde, past clamorous shipyards where the shells of growing ships swarmed with men and the iridescent flash of oxyacetylene. As they boarded the ferry to Dunoon, crisp white clouds slipped off distant hills into a bleached blue sky. In the empty saloon Martin bought them pints and lay back on a bench, staring out of a porthole at the sky. They arrived in Dunoon in the early afternoon. Bright sunlight illuminated the small town; sharp blue light reflected from the windows of shops and houses. Pennants fluttered on the esplanade flagpoles. A scattering of the previous year's dead leaves scratched along the pavement. The day was warm.

They walked to a windowless coffee bar. Red-lit paintings of bullfighters, maracas, castanets and nets filled with plastic starfish hung from red mock-adobe walls. A ghostly, mascaraed face floated out of the dark.

'That's a rip-off,' Martin said, as he paid for the coffees.

'Costa Clyde, costa fortune!' the girl said, dematerialising into the gloom.

Martin laughed half-heartedly. 'I wonder how many times she's said that.'

'Aye. Probably her only joke,' Ray agreed.

Martin leaned back on the squeaking red vinyl and stretched his arms over the back of the booth, admiring himself in the tinted mirror behind Ray's bench. 'Nice legs though,' he said.

They walked back to the pier and caught another ferry across the Holy Loch to the village of Blairmore. The sky clouded over and the air grew cooler as the wind rose. They stood on deck for the short trip, huddled in the lee of the funnel, and watched a submarine cross the ferry's bow on its way to the American dry dock. Two more nestled at the side of the nearby mother ship like piglets at a sow's udder. Racing yachts undulated on blind grey water. A dozen CND demonstrators paced by the navy pier at Sandbank.

Ray waved towards the pier. 'Danny and I used to come here fishing some weekends, then go looking for chicks at the Borough Hall dance on Saturday night. He hated the Yanks. Him and Moscow both have this thing about Yanks. Don't know why. They seem OK to me. They used to sell us these big bottles of Jim Beam from the PX. And their music's good. But Danny used to stand on the beach and shout at the sailors on the dry dock, telling them to desert or go home, or worse, depending on what kind of mood he was in.' He cupped his hands around his mouth and shouted, 'Yankees Go Home!' in the direction of the ship, then nudged Martin in the ribs. 'Come on!' he said. 'Every bit helps.'

'I thought you liked them,' Martin said, half laughing. 'Anyway, they won't hear us from here, the wind's too strong now.' Nevertheless, he imitated Ray, and they continued to shout impotently into the wind until the ferry rounded the peninsula, and the ship, the dry dock and the submarines vanished from view.

As the ferry cruised along the Firth, Ray pointed over the water to a bland horizon. 'At night you can see the Glasgow lights from here. It's like the city's on fire,' he said. 'And the shipyards. And there's Cove. Another wee village like this. And back there's the big Cloch lighthouse. Sometimes we'd stay at the hotel and the light used to flash on the wall all night, and when it was foggy you could hear it groaning like a sea monster.'

The engine changed pitch and the ferry drifted towards the pier. The sky had cleared again, and the wind died as they entered the bay. The single village street seemed deserted. A middle-aged couple waited on the pier. On a hill behind the village a house was on fire. Flames leaped from upstairs windows and curled over the roof. Beside the village street, and all over the hill gorse was blooming and the scent of coconut and smoke drifted down towards them. They disembarked and walked up to a shop, bought a fishing line, loitered on the street to watch the fire, then returned to the pier as the ferry departed. At Ray's suggestion, Martin climbed down a barnacle-encrusted ladder and tore away a handful of mussels from the piles for bait.

Ray bashed open a shell with the heel of his shoe and showed Martin how to bait the line. 'You put the little black bit on the hook and use the orange part for a lure.' Martin fiddled distastefully with the mussel and hook as he watched. Then he tied the line to a pile and they walked back up the pier, bought two sliders and a can of pale ale from the shop. As he lifted the can to his lips, Martin tasted with pleasure the salty aroma of sea life on his fingers. They paused at the roadside as a Pontiac coupé with a chrome shark's nose rumbled by, an American petty officer at the wheel. Beside him, a woman with bleached hair was lighting a cigarette, and from the back seat two young girls stared at them with studied indifference. He looked back to the hill. A disconsolate family stood in the garden staring up at a smouldering, gutted house. In the distance they could hear the ringing of an approaching fire engine. They returned to the pier.

'Did you see that car?'

'The Yankee car?'

'Yeah.'

'Daft,' Ray said. 'Big cars like that on these wee roads.'

'I thought it was great,' Martin said. 'You need big roads for those cars.'

The line was bobbing about in the water. Martin reeled in a tiny brown fish with sharp dorsal fins and a monstrous head.

'Cobbler,' Ray said. 'Don't use your hands.' He rested his foot on the squirming fish as Martin twisted the hook from its mouth.

'We could have it on toast,' he said. 'I'm quite peckish.'

'You can't eat that,' Ray said, flipping it off the pier with the toe of his shoe. 'It's a shite-fish. Try again. Maybe we'll get a flounder.'

He baited the hook and they sat down on the pier's edge, watching a long white ship glide slowly along the far shore as the sun began a slow descent over the hills. Martin thought of

Robertson, and his vanished grandmother, and waved.

'You've got something,' Ray said.

The line was heavy, but still. A limp orange starfish broke the surface of the water as the line broke. Together they watched it sink back into the murk of the river.

'Well, you couldn't have eaten that either,' Ray said. 'Poor thing. Spending the rest of its life with a hook and a foot of line in its gob.'

They stared sadly into the water.

After an hour Martin grew restless. The tide turned. Sewage pipes and rocks sprouted from the water. The rocky beach sang with the exhalations of stranded creatures, the popping and gurgling of draining tide pools and dehydrating shells. They tied the line to the ladder and walked along the shore, hopping over barnacled sewage pipes, beached jellyfish and slimy, algae-encrusted rocks. They sat down beneath a sheltered overhang beneath the shore road. Ray took out his tobacco and Moscow's hash, rolled a joint and a cigarette. 'You want another pill?' he asked.

'No thanks,' Martin said, lying back against a low rock.

Ray lit the joint and passed it to him.

'I think I'd rather just have a cigarette,' Martin said. 'Your hand's shaking,' he added.

'Just cold,' Ray said. He passed Martin the cigarette, then lay back on the beach and took a long draw from the joint, shifting uncomfortably on the stones, finally coming to rest with his leg touching Martin's.

Martin smoked casually, although something of Ray's uneasiness seemed to be infecting him. After a few moments, he sat up.

Suddenly, Ray was at his shoulder, his hands resting on Martin's cheeks. He kissed his forehead and began to stroke his hair.

'It's all right,' Martin said, patting his shoulder.

Ray kissed his lips and Martin felt his hand slide between his legs. Terror gripped him as he waited to see how his body would respond to Ray's caresses. 'It's all right,' he said again.

'Do you like that?'

'No.'

Ray remained silent and continued rubbing his hand softly against Martin's crotch and kissing his hair, his cheek, his lips.

After a few minutes he took away his hand and sat forward, folding his arms over his knees and staring bleakly out at the river. 'The thing about being a homosexual,' he said, 'is that you can't be. You can be any fucking thing you like but a poof. Christine and Danny, they'd forgive me anything, but being a poof is something you've got to keep to yourself.'

'You didn't do this when you were here with Danny?'

'You must be joking. He'd have cut my balls off.'

They lapsed into silence. A herring gull hovered on the wind a few feet from the shore then lowered its huge rubber feet on to a rock at the water's edge.

'I didn't know,' Martin said.

'I thought you were all at it at public school.'

'It wasn't really a public school I went to. Anyway, at my school it was mainly wanking. We did have one boy who liked beating the younger boys but everyone thought he was a bit odd. Anyway, I thought you got Carole pregnant.'

'Oh, I fuck lassies too,' Ray said.

'How is Carole, anyway?'

'She had the kid. Premature.'

'I think you're wrong about Christine and Danny,' Martin said.

'You don't understand what it's like,' Ray said. 'If you think it's so easy how come you were so relieved to find you didn't like it?' He picked up the extinguished joint from a stone beside him and relit it.

'I suppose we should start heading back anyway,' Martin said, after some minutes' silence. 'There's a ferry coming now.'

The sun fell towards the sea in the west and darkness crept over the sky. The current spun by and an animated breeze hurled thin white waves against the ferry's side. They stood on deck and watched the passing of a shipwreck mast swirling in a whirlpool at the edge of the harbour as they passed Dunoon.

They parted company at Waverley station.

'You won't tell anyone?' Ray said, handing Martin the shepherdess and the Hot Club record.

'Course not.' And thought, Moscow was right, I've got to get out of here.

Chapter ten

A few days later, he found a note slipped beneath his door. Alberta and Robertson had returned to Taigh nan Òran.

The following morning he phoned his mother.

'I hate the phone,' she said. 'Talking on the phone always reminds me of your Dad.'

'Dad?'

'Yes. I used to wait by the phone. Literally, stand by it and wait for him to ring.'

'When was that?'

'When we first met. He was working at the paper. "Living in sin." That's why your grandfather wouldn't let us come home when your dad died. We had to wait. I hated him, but then he got old and suffered too. Everyone suffered. What was the point?'

'I keep thinking I'll finally meet him sometime.'

'Your dad?'

'Yes. Funny. I suppose I think he must be alive somewhere.'

'I thought of phoning you from Lewis,' Alberta said. 'I was hoping you'd come up. These days, I wait for you to phone but you never do.'

Martin could hear rain battering at the Taigh nan Òran sitting-room window.

'Robertson is going back up tomorrow. He wants you to go with him. Mr McRitchie died. The funeral is today in Bernaray. His wife's too old to look after the cottage now, so he has to pack up. He's thinking of selling it.'

'Mr McRitchie … who taught you music?'

'Yes.'

'I'm sorry,' he said, but the line had gone dead.

He arrived at Taigh nan Òran in the late afternoon.

'How's Uncle?'

Alberta took his hand and held it. 'Why don't you look in on him? He's in the study. Dinner won't be ready for a wee bit.'

She walked away to the kitchen as Martin went along to the study, knocked lightly on the door and turned the handle.

Robertson was leaning back in his chair, facing the window. His journal lay open on the desk. A fiddle record played quietly. He appeared not to hear Martin enter, and muttered something indecipherable. Martin sat down without speaking. After some minutes of near silence, Robertson swivelled round in his chair. 'Martin,' he said brightly. 'It's a fine afternoon.'

'Fine? It's cold.'

'Is it?' Robertson glanced out of the window. The sky had cleared to a watery blue. A flame of sunlight ignited on the window. 'How are things?' he said.

'I'm not sure.'

'No. To be honest I was rather worried about you after our last meeting. You left abruptly.'

A flock of blue tits whirled by the window.

'I brought you a record,' Martin said, pulling the Hot Club disc from his coat.

Robertson leaned across the desk and took the gift, perusing it with polite interest. 'Ah yes,' he nodded, 'Grappelli. Magnificent player. I saw him many years ago at the Usher Hall.'

'Apparently the guitar player only had two fingers,' Martin said.

Robertson looked at him strangely. It seemed to Martin that he was about to say something unpleasant, but instead put the record on the desk and faced the window. 'I like to sit here in the evenings,' he said. 'It's like a little diorama. Not a real world at all. I suppose it reminds me of Lewis. It's deserted. It's not easy to find somewhere to go, these days, that isn't overcrowded with people and all their hubbub.'

The music ended. He stood up, pushed his chair under the desk, went to the turntable and removed the stylus from the record. 'We missed you this year. It wasn't quite the same without you. I would appreciate your company on this trip.'

'I was sorry to hear about Mr McRitchie. You've known him a long time, haven't you?'

Robertson nodded. 'He was my guru Martin, as they say nowadays. He taught me how to put my feet on the earth.'

'He taught you how to play the accordion?'

'That's right, and his wife taught your mother to sing.'

'Mum doesn't sing much now.'

'No. But you should have heard her then. My word.' A spark of joy flashed in his eyes. He returned to his chair and resumed his watch of the garden. 'I know you have other things to occupy your mind,' he said, as if concluding an interview, 'but I thought you might not mind a day or two away from the city.'

Chapter eleven

They crossed the Minch on a cold and eerie morning, the sky cloudless but dark, the water smooth. Robertson sat at the stern of the ferry writing in a notebook as Martin wandered restlessly from the cafeteria to the deck railings and back, carrying cups of tea and staring into the black murk of the swell. A fulmar floated in the slipstream behind the funnel, flapping its stiff little wings from time to time like an automaton. As soon as the land appeared Martin realised he had not expected to see it again. In the two years since he had last visited the island, it had been transformed in his mind into a mythical country.

The sky brightened; evanescent light flowed out of the horizon and over the sea towards him; the shine of the approaching land, radiant beneath the vast, lucid sky, lifted his spirits. He leaned on the rail and stared towards the approaching land, absorbed in a kind of forgotten bliss.

They reached the cottage in the late afternoon. Black-faced sheep grazed on the slope by the shore. A warm wind blew over still, yellow countryside. Beyond, the Atlantic attenuated into distant sky. Cuchulain, the McRitchies' collie, met them in the lane, pale eyes, hyperopic from a life spent gazing into space, staring up at them as they pushed open the front door.

'Absence is a sort of presence, if you see what I mean,' Robertson said as they entered the lounge.

Martin, preoccupied, hardly heard his uncle speak. He picked up a newspaper from a pile at the hearth, rolled it up, stuffed it into the grate, and went outside to the peat stack. When he returned Robertson had not moved. He lit the fire, went to the kitchen and filled the kettle.

'No one will buy it, of course,' Robertson said. 'No one stays here any more.' He pointed vaguely up the track. 'There are two empty houses up there already. The old people die and no one wants them.' He sat down heavily in an armchair beside the fire.

Martin went up the narrow stairs to his old bedroom. He looked out of the window. Weightless light shone over the fields; clover bloomed on the cliff tops. To the south, a jagged horizon of prehistoric blue hills evaporated into the sky and sea. Behind him, through the window at the west of the house, the sun exploded at the edge of the sea, bathing the room in an unworldly pink light. He stood at the window for a few minutes and watched a group of crofters and their dogs ambling up the slopes to the cottages by the main road.

When he returned downstairs he found Robertson standing at the open door watching Cuchulain, supine in the long grass. 'There should be some tins in the kitchen, if you're hungry,' he said.

'I'll make something,' Martin said. 'I've had some practice.'

He opened a tin of ravioli from the kitchen cupboard and heated it in a pot over the open fire. They ate in silence at the table by the window. After finishing the food Martin lit a cigarette and watched a faint star appearing in the half-lit Eastern sky.

Robertson stood up and went to the cabinet beside the fireplace, turned the key in the glass door and looked thoughtfully at an array of memorabilia from his time at sea, a trilobite from Yosemite, a soapstone elephant seal, a Chinese puzzle box, a leather-bound blackjack from Baltimore. 'Do you remember this device, Martin?' he said, removing a 3-D viewfinder. 'You used to find it most diverting, I recall. I don't know where all the pictures have got to.'

Martin nodded as Robertson replaced it carefully and took down an old pair of field glasses. They went outside and in turn looked out at the sea and the Harris hills to the south.

Robertson's hands were trembling as he passed the binoculars to Martin. 'It's cold this evening,' he said, shoving his hands awkwardly into his trouser pockets.

Martin lifted the glasses to his eyes. 'It's a huge sky here.'

A thin Islamic moon rose over the water, its reflection dividing the sea from horizon to shore. Clouds hovered at the edge of the sea.

'When a man dies up here, a universe vanishes,' Robertson said, 'a language, a nation, everything that makes him unique. Of course, in this part of the world a nation is dying too. Optimists give the Gaelic language one hundred years. No one will notice, I expect. Gods and faiths vanishing. Life getting smaller.'

They walked around the cottage and followed the track across the field to the low cliff edge. Sea pinks shivered in a breeze; the smell of sea wrack and clover hung in the air about them. Phosphorescent waves splashed indifferently among the stones.

Robertson sat down on a mound of grass, plucked a marram stalk and sucked it pensively. The chewing of invisible sheep echoed from the fields around them.

'I've been thinking about your future,' he said. 'I began to wonder what might become of you. At one time you expressed an interest in travel, and it occurred to me that you might benefit from a change of scene. You seem to consume your environment at an alarming speed. You lose interest quickly. A bit like your mother. You're an extremely impatient person.

'I thought I'd buy you a return aeroplane ticket to Toronto. It is many years since I was last in Canada, and Toronto was by no means my favourite city, but I believe it might be your most effective starting place. Perhaps you might even find your grandmother there. I will augment this with ten pounds in cash, which should provide you with food and shelter for the first day or so. After that you will be on your own, free, of course, to return immediately or at any time thereafter that suits you.'

'I'm sorry,' Martin said, 'but I can't imagine doing what you do.'

'No.' Robertson sighed. 'I've been telling stories for so long,' he said, 'sometimes I forget that's what they are.'

'You think they're stories?' Martin said, surprised. 'I thought you believed them.'

'Of course I believe them.'

'But, you said, they're stories.'

Robertson looked at Martin curiously. 'Martin. Supposing the police asked you to give them a description of someone. What would you tell them?'

'I don't know. Their height, clothes, I suppose, that sort of thing.'

Robertson seemed pleased with this response. 'But would that tell them what this person was like? What they dreamed about? Who they hated?'

'They wouldn't be interested in that. No, they wouldn't know what kind of person they were. '

'There you are, you see. This is what I do. I describe the clothes the world is wearing. Just because it's true doesn't mean anything. I can't really tell anyone what the world is like. Goodness knows, it's a complete mystery to me.'

They fell silent.

'I've made a mess of everything,' Martin said suddenly.

'Well, I wouldn't take it too seriously,' Robertson replied. 'You're not that important, and neither are your mistakes.'

'I'm important to myself!' Martin said.

'Indeed,' Robertson averred. 'And also to your mother and me. But we in the middle-class always take ourselves too seriously. It's a habit we've acquired during our evolution. This idea that we're responsible for everything. Not only for the temporal world, but for the spiritual world as well. We seem to think it's our duty to keep telling people that everything will be all right in the end. We're the officer class. We're the only people with any moral fibre, and the troops will go to pieces without us to buck them up.'

'I don't feel like that at all. I feel exactly the opposite,' Martin said. 'If it was only the officer class I couldn't stand it. I would go to pieces. I went to school with them. Most of them don't even know anything's wrong. It's the people who get their hands dirty who have the most courage. We just sit back and make judgements all the time about everything.'

'You're very harsh, Martin,' Robertson said. 'Without myths, what would be the point? It would be just an animal existence. And who else is going to make these myths but well-educated people like me with time on their hands?'

And for the first time since Martin had met his uncle,

Robertson laughed out loud.

'Oh dear,' he said. He wiped his eyes on his coat sleeve, and stood up. Martin also got to his feet, and they stood for a few minutes looking out at the sea.

'It's chilly. You'd better keep your window shut,' Robertson said, as they walked back up the path to the cottage. 'You can hang your hat on the moon.'

Ruby light fluttered at the cottage window. Martin chose half a dozen peats from the stack by the house, held the door open for Robertson, and followed him into the sitting-room. The room swarmed with firelight. A moth tapped at the window.

'Does my suggestion appeal to you?'

'Yes,' Martin said, laying the peats on the hearth and stirring up the dying fire. 'Oh, yes.'

He stirred the ashes until the fire was nearly dead, said goodnight and left Robertson alone. He went up to his old room and lay down, fully dressed on the cool, damp bed. He fell asleep quickly but was woken in the middle of the night by a storm wind battering at the windows, and the white coated figure of Christine fleeing through a labyrinth of alleyways as he pursued her futilely, his feet immobilised in a quagmire of rotting vegetables.

Early in the morning he found a paper bag by the door containing four eggs and two thick oatcakes.

'Mrs McRitchie,' Robertson muttered in explanation.

He lit the fire and boiled the eggs in the kettle. They ate at the table, watching the stars dim as the sky lightened.

Martin finished his breakfast and removed a cigarette packet from the pocket of his jeans.

'I'd really rather you didn't smoke in here,' Robertson said tersely. His relaxed manner of the previous evening had dissipated. He seemed tense and rancorous.

'What was Canada like?' Martin said, putting away the cigarettes.

'A dreadful place. Unruly people, many of foreign extraction. An extraordinarily cold place. Zero degrees on the Kelvin scale for much of the year.' He sniffed pompously. 'However, it has to be said that the countryside abounds in scenery of great magnificence.'

'I'd always wondered about going there,' Martin said. 'It's supposed to be the land of opportunity, isn't it?'

Robertson looked at him thoughtfully. 'It is not a country for malingerers, Martin. The streets of its cities are littered with the dead bodies of its unproductive citizens. In fact, I believe Polynesia would suit your temperament better. I understand that there one can survive entirely on coconuts, and even a roof over one's head is thought by the natives to be a vulgar ostentation.'

'I don't have anything against working,' Martin said irritably.

'Ah,' Robertson replied.

'I just don't want to work my whole life for nothing. You have to have fun as you go along.'

'And are you having fun now?' Robertson leaned back in his chair and folded his hands behind his head.

Martin shrugged, stood up, went outside for a smoke.

They stayed at the cottage for two days. Martin wandered along the shore and up over the moorland, casually bidding farewell to the empire of rocks, hiding places and vast panoramas he had possessed there as a child. From time to time a shadow crept over the day even when the sky was cloudless. He found it difficult to tell if the chill in the air originated in an imperceptible breeze blowing off the sea or in his own mind. As he sat watching the sea on the first afternoon, memories came flooding back to him of his childhood visits to the cottage and of his fascination with the sea's moods; how in the winter, stirred up by westerly gales, the violent green of the mid-ocean battered against the cliff so loudly he could hear it in the cottage, while on summer days the swell lapped indolently among the pale rocks and out at sea the water darkened from aquamarine to indigo, an occasional crimson wave appearing in the distance, as if blood were seeping up from a wounded animal below the surface.

On the second evening, Robertson, who had been reluctant to remove any of his belongings, made a random selection of clothes, books and chairs from the kitchen that would fit conveniently into the boot and the back seat of the Humber. At four am they were woken by Mrs McRitchie's knock at the door. She invited them into her cottage for breakfast, and gave them a packet of sandwiches and a Thermos of coffee for the trip. 'Murdo won't be needing it now,' she said.

They ate in silence, in a kitchen that smelt of wild flowers, dried fish and peat, while the old woman, wrapped in grief, mechanically arranged kindling in the unlit range.

'He's buried at Bernaray,' she said to Robertson as they were leaving. 'I'm sorry you couldn't come.' She disappeared into the back room and returned with a large black case, bound with twine.

'Murdo was a great admirer of your talent,' she said. 'He told me when he saw your hands after your accident that he felt as if he'd lost a child. He'd want you to have this back.'

'My accordion?' Robertson said. He reached out for the case as if relieving another of a burden, rather than wanting the gift. He and Martin walked outside into a faint dawn. He squeezed the case into the back seat of the car. The door closed as they turned to say goodbye.

Dying wind whistled in the grass. As they drove away, a thin plume of smoke appeared from the cottage chimney. All the fields were black. The buttercups had vanished. Already lights were coming on in the cottages by the road. On a fencepost the thin legs of a blackbird struggled briefly in the throat of a herring gull, and vanished. Cuchulain's head appeared from the roadside grass, his pale, intelligent, blind eyes followed their departure until the car reached the summit of the hill and submerged beneath the grass horizon.

Chapter twelve

They arrived back at Taigh nan Òran after lunch. Martin helped unload the car, stuffed a chicken pie from the fridge into his coat pocket, left the house and caught a bus into the city.

When he arrived at Ray's flat, he could hear a record playing inside. He rang the bell and waited while Ray dragged open the door. On the carpet before the single bar fire were scattered tourist brochures depicting Beefeaters, Tower Bridge, the Houses of Parliament, Pearly Kings and Queens and guardsmen wearing bearskins. Ray's banjo case sat on the floor beside the milk crate. A packet of Embassy cigarettes lay open on the ledge above the fireplace. The alarm clock had stopped. Ray reached into a pile of clothes on the bed and pulled out a can of lager, which he opened and handed to Martin. Martin produced the pie. 'Hungry?'

'Fucking starving!' they said together.

Martin gave him ten pence for the meter.

'At least I can screw the fucking thing when I leave,' Ray said. 'Get my money back.' He fed the meter, went to the cooker and lit the overhead grill, turned on the oven and put the chicken pie inside. He removed a packet of Weetabix, a saucer of butter and a sugar bowl from the cupboard by the sink, spread butter on four of the Weetabix, sprinkled sugar over them and put them under the grill.

They looked at each other for a few moments, as if trying to read each other's expression.

'Yeah,' Martin said quietly. 'Well, everything's fine.'

The Weetabix was toasted in a moment.

'We'll have to have the dessert first,' Ray said.

They gobbled it down and sat in silence drinking beer and waiting impatiently for the smell of cooking chicken.

'How long do these pies take?' Ray muttered.

Martin stared down at the empty beer can in his hands. Ray stood up, rubbed his hands together and picked up the cigarette packet from the ledge above the fireplace. He removed the two remaining cigarettes, crumpled the packet and threw it on to the tiled hearth. He put one cigarette in his mouth and held out the other to Martin.

'I'm going to Canada,' Martin said. Silence buzzed in his ears. The chilly song of a robin echoed from the street, a rainbow arpeggio sparkling in the dusk.

'Oh, aye.'

'My uncle can get me in. My granny lives there, not that I've ever …'

'Ah,' Ray said, withdrawing the cigarette.

'There's more opportunity over there …'

'Aye,' Ray said. 'There will be.' He balanced Martin's cigarette on the edge of the hearth and lit his own. 'I was thinking of going to London for a bit,' he said. 'You don't fancy coming?'

'No,' Martin said. 'It'll be the same there.'

'Don't be daft. There's a lot more going on in London. The UFO Club, and all that. I bet I could get things going in no time. I still have connections there.'

Martin said nothing.

Ray smoked his cigarette. The room filled with the warm smell of baking chicken. Steam condensed on the window. Ray leaned back and opened the oven door. 'I think the main course is ready now.' He reached in and pulled out the foil pie tin with his bare hands, dropping it on the hearth between them. He stood up, walked over to the sink and returned with two saucers. Upending the foil tin, he slid his thumbnail around the edge. The pie fell, with ominous heaviness into one of the saucers. He broke it open, and handed half to Martin. 'It's still half frozen.'

'I'll write you when I get things going in Canada. You could come over.'

'Aye.' Ray smiled, wrapping the room around him like a shell.

Martin nibbled at the warm circumference of his pie and stared fixedly at a point between his feet. 'Do you fancy playing a song?' he said.

Ray reached over to the banjo case and lifted the lid,

wheezing a soft laugh. The instrument's neck lay folded over the drum, snapped in half.

'What happened?' Martin leaned over the case and lifted out the neck.

'I got into an argument with one of the waitresses at Wimpy's. I was playing a tune. A couple of heavies threw me down the steps.'

'Heavies? In Wimpy's?'

'The manager. A wee nyaff and a big cook.'

'That's fucking ridiculous,' Martin said.

'Aye. Well, I'd been thinking of packing it in anyway. It's not a tragedy,' Ray said. 'No need to look so shocked.' He laughed quietly. 'A guy stopped his car in the middle of the street and said he'd be my witness. Nice bloke. Said he'd go to court for me and everything, if I wanted to sue them.'

'So? Are you going to?'

Ray closed the case and looked at him with an amused expression.

'People like us would never get anywhere in court.'

'What do you mean? Everybody has rights.'

'Aye,' said Ray, 'that'll be right.'

'I'll write from Canada,' Martin said again, a few minutes later, as the door closed behind him.

He wandered aimlessly across the city, through back streets where his breathing was the loudest sound. His footsteps echoed on the pavement, giving him substance. The transition of seasons had taken place. Dead leaves littered the pavement, few remained in the trees. He stopped at St Mary's Cathedral: in the churchyard, beech and elm leaves smouldered in unattended piles between the gravestones; wisps of smoke floated at shoulder height in the crisp autumn air. He pushed open the carved door and walked in. The church was almost empty. Above the nave a graphically impaled Christ stared hopelessly at heaven. Martin's head rang from the scale of silence; footfalls echoed up into the arches, every movement stirred up a gust of air, sweeping over cold stone slabs, the building a well of stillness, preserved like the last water in the world.

He sat down in a pew and tried vainly to conjure up an elevated thought to match the splendour of the building. He felt the momentum of an ungraspable faith sweeping about him, a history of aspiration and belief that he could not experience, but that humiliated him somehow; as if the building itself was accusing him of some obscure philosophical crime, of neglect, or cowardice, or indolence. He jumped to his feet and rushed out into the sunlit, noisy street, and hurried down a hill towards Dean Village. Children played in a schoolyard. He leaned on a bridge abutment in the shadow of incongruous turreted Bohemian buildings glowing crimson in the dusk, smoked a cigarette, and looked up, following a vapour trail converging behind a jet in the cool blue sky. He walked up Dean Path and into the sunlight, climbed over a wall, slid down a wooded embankment to a weir, sat in the sun, sheltered from the freshening breeze, and watched the rush of water, thinking nothing. At nightfall starlings gathered overhead, flung up like little scars of black ink on cold blue canvas. Exuberant songs from another dimension vanished in the cold dusk.

After several hours wandering he arrived at the city centre. The wind whistled up Princes Street, humming through his clothes like ice in the rigging of a trawler. He looked about him at the dull, heavy faces of passers-by. The world around him seemed as remote and predatory as the North Sea. He felt afraid, as if the city was lying in wait for him to lose his hold and tumble overboard.

Later, a self-appointed night-watchman, a half-bottle of Monte Cristo in his pocket, he patrolled the city as it retired for the night. He walked for hours through New Town streets, watching curtains drawn, bedroom lights going out, snooping in at basement windows, the warm reception rooms of private hotels, straightening his deportment as occasional police cars passed. At three in the morning in a bakery in the Canongate, he bought hot bread rolls to eat with the sherry on Arthur's Seat. From the hill he watched the sunrise gleam on city windows, heard the traffic start up, a last bat whirling home in the twilight, starlings chattering in the new day's sky as the farmyard smell of hops wafted up from the brewery at the foot of the crag.

'One down, one to go,' he muttered to himself, stumbling down the hill through heavy dew drenched bog grass towards the station.

Chapter thirteen

He leaned back in his seat and peered through the grimy window of the Glasgow train at a melancholy railwayman pushing a tiny cardboard box on a freight cart along the platform. The atmosphere was airless and heavy with hot diesel fumes, as if the compartment was about to burst into flames. Across the aisle a girl methodically painted her nails.

Christine's family lived in a housing scheme in the east of the city. As the bus made its way east, city centre activity dissolved into claustrophobic streets squeezed among Victorian railyards and factories, terraced rows of grey, postwar villas, windowless pubs and condemned tenements, and into open ground where brown pebbledash villas stretched along wide, shopless avenues. He felt as if he were entering another country; sickly, unsentimental faces proliferated in the bus as the city dwellers disembarked. He sat on the top deck in a cloud of dead smoke, listening to animated conversations about illnesses and surgical procedures undergone by the other passengers. Fatigue made him alert to the vivid grey world passing by, of streets with few cars, buildings that seemed to have grown up organically from the clay, windows broken, boarded up or covered with wire, lichen green patches of damp rising up two floors, here and there an incongruous rose garden blooming in the drab surroundings like an illuminated manuscript.

He disembarked on a long street divided by a grass verge, stopped an old man walking a dog to ask directions, and walked up over an embankment towards the scheme. Children rode by on bicycles or stopped and leaned on handlebars to watch him enigmatically. In the distance a roar from the Parkhead Jungle rose into a bright autumn sky, tall white clouds towering like the Himalayas over the long river valley. Two boys of about eleven years old played football on grey scrubgrass at the front of the house. Across the street half a dozen schoolgirls lounged on swings beside a gravelled football pitch. They stopped as Martin passed and lit cigarettes, watching him silently as he pushed through the broken gate and walked up the path. The front door was open and the sounds of clattering dishes and acrimonious conversation came from within. A man in his twenties leaned in the open doorway smoking a cigarette, watching the footballers with a disenchanted expression. He called Christine's name, as if Martin had been expected, and stepped aside without glancing at him. Christine came slowly to the door, wiping her hands on a dishtowel.

'What are you doing here?' She looked back into the house.

'I don't know. I got your address from Ray. I just wanted to see you.'

'I told you not to come here. I could have met you somewhere.'

Martin turned away indecisively. 'I wanted to say goodbye. I'm leaving for Canada next week.'

'Just wait a minute.' She went back into the house and returned wearing the white vinyl coat. 'I'll walk you to the bus stop.'

From the next street the dissonant chime of *The Blue Danube* played from an ice cream van. The girls leaped off the swings, stubbed out their cigarettes and ran off down the street, bare legs and fluttering skirts dancing weightlessly through the wind-dust like the bodies of little birds.

They strolled up the narrow street and back across the grass embankment to the main road. A chilly wind blowing up the hill from the river cut through their coats. Instinctively he took her hand and rubbed it between his own. 'I could have been a better friend to you.'

'You've been a good pal to me, Martin. We had a good time.'

They walked for a while in silence.

'So. You've decided to Go West to make your fortune?'

'Yes. I'm kind of fed up here. I feel sort of boxed in. I fancy the big spaces they have there. You can go for thousands of miles along the same road.'

'Sounds all right.'

He imagined she was about to say something else, but changed her mind.

They stopped in the silent avenue and watched the low, grey

clouds gusting down the valley, gulls squealing overhead in a chaos of breezes. He glanced down and grabbed Christine by the wrist. 'Come with me,' he said. She tried to tug her arm away but he maintained his grip. 'Come with me!' he said again.

She jerked her arm away and rubbed her wrist. 'You're daft. To Canada?'

He looked along the empty road, and around him at the grey housing blocks. 'You're not going to stay here all your life?'

She followed his glance for a moment, considered with equanimity the tumbling clouds, the grey houses, a dog sniffing aimlessly among dead leaves on the embankment, the branches rising and falling in the damp wind. 'What's wrong with it?' she said.

'It would be great,' he replied lamely. 'An adventure. You've always liked adventure. Imagine being somewhere completely different. You'd feel like a different person!'

'You don't like me the way I am,' she said, half smiling, 'I see.'

'No,' he said, feeling the thread of his argument unravelling. 'I wouldn't want to go there with anyone else. It's just that … How else can you have your own life? A life you choose for yourself, make for yourself? You can't have that staying in the place you were brought up.'

She pulled back the sleeve of her coat and checked her watch. 'I've got to be getting back.'

'But come with me. I'll get the money for you.'

'You're daft, Martin,' she said. A bus appeared at the end of the avenue, a cloud of black exhaust drifting into the air as it accelerated up the hill towards them. 'You can write me. Tell me all your adventures.'

The bus came to a stop and the door banged open. She leaned up and kissed him, pulled her coat around her, folded her arms and walked quickly away. He put his foot on the step and turned to watch her. 'Are you getting on or not?' he heard the driver say.

'Come with me!' he shouted at the white dot vanishing over the embankment.

As the bus pulled away she turned at the brow of the hill and waved.

It was dark by the time the bus reached George Square. He climbed on to the head of a stone lion in the shade of the City Chambers building and watched crowds of football fans running by to the station. Above his head Gothic Victorian crags and precipices loomed against the night sky. The terrain would have made an ideal habitat for baboons, he thought, laughing to himself as he pictured tribes of unruly apes hurling refuse down on the people below. Two large policemen spotted him on the lion's head and dragged him off to a police box in the centre of the square as he struggled ineffectually to extricate himself. 'I won't escape,' he said, honourable and obsequious as Alec Guinness in a war film, 'but just let go of me!'

The busies secured him more tightly. By the time they reached the police box he was crying uncontrollably. They released their grip and he sank to his knees, weeping.

'For God's Sake, son, we just need to ask a couple of questions.'

Martin sat snivelling into his hands, unable to reply. Eventually they abandoned their interrogation, locked the door of the police box, and marched across the square to intervene in a fight breaking out between rival fans.

He boarded the train. The first compartment was a sea of blue scarves and red faces. The air was weighty with song and the smell of beer. Martin sat beside a small, terrified family, a husband and wife and five-year-old son, and together they huddled into their seats, stared hopelessly at their own reflections in the window, avoiding eye contact with the fans in the opposite booth.

Oh, the Pope's so Young And Beeeoooootifulll
At the Age of Ninety-Four
But on the Twelfth he Hanged Hisself
With the Sash My Father Wore!
Fuck The Pope!!

His companions left the train at Falkirk. A web-like silence fell over the compartment in which Martin's nerves fluttered like a trapped insect. Deprived of the family's protective neutrality he was exposed. The singing began again and as the train pulled away he stood up and made his way to the adjacent compartment. He opened the door into a sea of wild green, blinding and bilious in amber train light.

> *Roamin' in the Gloamin'*
> *With a Shamrock in My Hand*
> *Roamin' in the Gloamin'*
> *With St Patrick's Fenian Band …*

He found an empty seat beside another covered in vomit. A sour looking civilian opposite eyed Martin aggressively. 'You'd think there were enough arseholes in Glasgow already without importing these bastards from Edinburgh,' he said, fearlessly.

Around them, a subdued wheezing sound expanded into laughter punctuated by squirting beer foam, breaking wind, coughing.

> *And when the music stops*
> *For King Billy and John Knox*
> *I'll be glad to be a Roamin' Catholic!*
> *Fuck the Queen!!!*

'I wouldn't mind, mind you,' said an old voice from the seat behind him.

'Wouldn't mind what?' replied another.

'I wouldn't mind doing something else on a Saturday.'

Chapter fourteen

Martin was irritably stuffing clothes into an old leather suitcase. Alberta sat on the bed and watched him pack. 'It's very sudden,' she said. 'How long are you going for?'

'Just a few weeks. I'll be back for Christmas.'

She sighed and looked about the room. 'Do you remember when we first came here?'

'Not really,' Martin said, rifling impatiently through the case, then turning it over and emptying the contents on to the bed. 'Where did I put the bloody ticket?'

Alberta went to the door, removed his coat from the hook and handed it to him. 'Everything's in here. Money, ticket, passport. I told you.'

He thanked her, threw the coat on to the bed and his clothes back into the case.

'You don't remember at all?'

'I remember his fingers. Gave me the willies.'

'I don't know where else we could have gone. It hasn't been so bad, has it?'

He opened the wardrobe door and foraged on his knees among a pile of papers and belongings. 'Where are my books?'

Alberta smiled. 'You can always get more.'

From his coat pocket he took a half bottle of whisky, which he buried among his clothes. He closed the lid. Alberta pushed down as he snapped the locks. She left the room for a moment, then returned carrying a nut-coloured fedora which she offered him. 'It was your father's,' she said.

Martin tried it on, surveying himself in the dressingtable mirror.

'It's a good fit,' she said. 'I thought you might like something of his. You have a big head too.'

'Yes.'

'You look like him in that hat,' she said.

They went down to the kitchen. Robertson joined them and they sat together at the table drinking coffee. Alberta finished first, went to the sink, ran her cup beneath the tap and went to the door. Light rain brushed the window, a gust rattled the glass. 'I hope it's not too bumpy on the plane,' she said, as she left the room.

Martin and Robertson floated like fish in the silence.

'So you didn't like Canada when you went?'

'All told, it was not an edifying experience.'

'Oh.'

'They're rough and unready people, Martin. Much like yourself.'

'Oh?'

'I wish you would stop saying, "Oh" like that. It makes our conversation sound like a sea shanty.'

'I'm sorry about the money for Mrs Morrison.'

'Aye.'

'Even so, she seemed sorry to see me go. Her dog was nice.'

'They're not like us over there,' Robertson continued, taking Martin's cup with his own to the sink, 'although, the people do speak a form of English in many places. And they are not malevolent people.' He took a pocket watch from his waistcoat and glanced at it. 'There's something I want you to see.'

He left the room, and returned with a collapsing photograph album. He sat down beside Martin and opened it on the table. 'I wonder if you have ever seen these photographs of your mother when she was young?'

He leafed slowly through a series of tiny snapshots with white, castellated borders. Two tall thin children, a boy of about fourteen and a girl two years older, stared obliquely at the camera. They were holding hands. The girl's expression was determined and ill-tempered, the boy's timid. Their eyes were hidden in shadow, which lent their faces a kind of ghostly anonymity, as if they belonged to another century and could no longer be alive.

'Alberta was much more adventurous than I,' Robertson said. 'I don't quite know what happened to her. There doesn't seem to be anything I can do about it. She seems to have lost her spirit somehow, since your father's death.' He glanced at Martin. 'Or mislaid it, perhaps?'

'I've seen them before. They're nice.'

'Nice,' Robertson repeated. 'A word from the Old French, signifying stupidity and ignorance. Surely a harsh judgement.' He closed the album.

'She's not coming to the airport.' Martin said.

'She doesn't like farewells. Women are sentimental creatures, even if they are more practical than us.' His expression was sombre. 'Still ...' he brightened, '... perhaps when you're in Canada, an idea may strike you as to how her spirits might be restored. I'm sorry to say that she blames herself for what happened to your father. Of course, neither of us knew him. But her attitude is typical of the egoism that runs in our family. It's unthinkable to her that your father was quite capable of being unhappy without any help from her. People kill themselves all the time and they never give a thought to how long people have to go on paying for it.'

Martin could think of nothing to say, yet he experienced a futile urge to come to his unknown father's defence.

Alberta did not appear again, and seemed to have left the house. Martin looked back and caught a last glimpse of the garden as the Humber paused at the gate.

'Of course, you must try to be careful,' Robertson said, almost casually, as the car pulled into the road, 'that in your anxiety not to be like me you end up like your mother.'

At the bus station he took a bottle of malt whisky from the glove compartment. 'They're fond of whisky, over there,' he said, as they waited by the luggage door. 'Although they are not overly particular about the quality. Still, it might be useful as currency.'

'Like chocolate?'

'Exactly. Like chocolate.'

Once, when Martin was leaving for boarding school Robertson had given him a bar of chocolate, and told him; 'At school, a rudimentary skill at sports is often necessary for one's survival. However, if you have no aptitude for games, chocolate can be a useful unit of currency.'

Martin smiled at the memory. 'Do you remember that story about Captain Jones you gave me when I left for school?'

'Ah, yes. Do you still have it?'

'I don't know. That was such a great story. I told it to the boys and pretended I'd made it up.'

'Well, I have another for you.' He reached into his overcoat and handed Martin a long manila envelope. 'It's to remind you of the North. Who knows? Perhaps we'll never go there again.'

They faced each other awkwardly; an explosion of exhaust behind them signalled the bus's imminent departure.

'Well, it's time you got on.'

Martin put the whisky bottle down by the bus door. Robertson reached out his hand. Lying on his palm was his pocket watch. 'A Hamilton,' he said. 'My father's. An excellent timepiece.' He followed the moving second hand with the stub of his ring finger. 'Your watch is like a bank statement,' he observed portentously. 'Look at it now and then, and observe your shrinking assets.' He handed it to Martin, put his arms stiffly around his shoulders and embraced him, then turned and walked away without looking back.

'Good luck with the Institute!' Martin said feebly, his voice carried away by the wind.

The smell of aviation fuel drifted over the grey morning Tarmac as he stepped off the bus, shivered with the crowd by the luggage doors waiting for his suitcase. He stared across the road from the terminal. Between Nissen huts and low cement office blocks aerials revolved, and a windsock like an elephant's trunk floated in the breeze. Behind the buildings tail planes as tall as ships, emblazoned with exotic symbols from every part of the world, passed by. The sun broke through unravelling cumulus. A transatlantic plane, wings gleaming, vanished into brilliant cloud, leaving in its wake a rose scrawl of vapour.

His spirits rose. In his imagination the tunnel of parsimonious light that had illuminated his life was bursting open, revealing open skies, open roads, magnetic cities, the world of the future.

When the world was formed, a great Stone Woman fell from the sky and landed on the mainland. She was very beautiful, had skin like pearl and hair as dark as the sea. And, as befits a creature from the depths, she had no eyes.

For a long time she stumbled and crawled over the rocky ground in search of food and shelter. She ripped up rocks and great swathes of turf, and built herself a blackhouse as high as Suilvein.

Not long afterwards there came a giant composed entirely of glass. Spat from the sun he had drifted through space, cooling, and searching for a companion. Floating over Sutherland he saw the Stone Woman in her blackhouse, howling at the invisible world.

The Glass Giant fell to earth and shattered all over Sutherland.

The Stone Woman took two shards of glass from his body and pressed them to her forehead. Instantly she could see everything in the Glass Giant's memory.

Maddened by this gift, she pulled the blackhouse down around her head and rolled back and forth over the hills and meadows, through the gorse and into the bogs until she and the blackhouse had become one great, stony skin. Then she lay down exhausted. The sun came out and dried her into a rock.

Moss and lichen covered the rock, birds watched from it.

A tribe passed that way and stopped to rest. They set up camp on the rock and soon began to hear a voice as deep as a sea current, coming from inside.

'You may know where you're going,' the voice said, 'but you've forgotten where you began. The end cannot be seen from the beginning, nor the beginning from the end. So who makes the journey?'

The tribe, who liked insoluble riddles, thought about this for a long time.

Then the voice recounted the entire history of the world and concluded with the instruction that the tribe should take their hatchets and smash the rock to pieces.

The voice said: 'Every splinter will contain the story of one life. When you meet again you will put the rock back together and complete the world.'

Many years passed. The tribe died out. The stones were mislaid, lost in battle, hidden for safekeeping, traded, sold, thrown into the sea.

Now no one can remember what happened, where they came from, why they set out, or where they intended to go when they left.

The story of the world is smashed into a million pieces and scattered everywhere. Despite this, wherever you go today you will find fools picking up stones, holding them to their ears, and muttering: 'Is this mine? ... is this my story?'

Part two

Chapter fifteen

The traffic in all lanes cruised at a steady sixty. Through the driver's window Martin saw a stream of vehicles making for the horizon. He pictured a gargantuan road-laying machine somewhere ahead of them, discharging asphalt, factory buildings, signposts and entire cities, the localities of his future. The road rose over a hill and the lakeshore appeared, bank towers gleaming in a chemical red sky. They passed carnival grounds and streets of red painted triplex apartments. Elderly men in striped bowling shirts drank beer on porches and fat, baby-faced women, thighs undulating in tiny elasticised shorts, pushed strollers through autumnal streets. Spray painted slogans on the corrugated roofs and walls of demolition sites and industrial parks advertised the Canadian National Party.

The bus pulled off the freeway into a sharp turn, back under the freeway and up into the centre of town. It sped along a stately boulevard wrapped in imperious stone insurance buildings, traffic lanes divided by flower-beds, splashing fountains and statues of forgotten civic dignitaries. The few pedestrians in sight resembled figures placed in an architect's model of a titanic city of the future, to give the illusion of life.

At the bus station families and itinerants clustered by the magazine stand and in the coffee shop. The sky clouded over and a light drizzle fell on Bay Street. Martin found an empty table in the coffee shop and drank his first cup of Canadian coffee. Two youths in denim jackets and jeans stopped at his table. They looked him over in a friendly fashion and conferred briefly. 'You wanna buy some weed?'

'No thanks.'

'Ten bucks a lid. Good stuff. Oaxacan Gold.'

They were interrupted by an older man, listening at the next table. 'Yeah, man, he looks like he was born yesterday.'

'Come again?'

'Well, I know if I wanted to score some Oaxacan Gold the first place I'd try would be the coffee shop at the goddamned bus station.'

'What are you? The Ombudsman?' one of the youths said testily.

'Where's a good cheap place to stay?' Martin asked no one in particular.

'Seaton House is cheap,' one youth replied. 'I don't know about good. But it's upstairs from the welfare office.'

'How do I get there?'

The youth got to his feet. Martin picked up his case and followed him into the street. The rain had stopped and a haze rose from the hot road.

'Where are you from?'

'Scotland.'

'Och, hoots mon!' He reached into his jacket pocket and handed Martin a joint. 'Welcome to Marlboro Country, dude,' he said. 'Have a doob.'

Martin thanked him and put it in his coat pocket.

'Seaton House ain't great. But they give you breakfast and a sandwich for the day. You got to watch your valuables, though.' He pointed to the street which led to the hostel. 'It ain't far. You can walk in ten minutes.'

'Well, thanks,' Martin said.

'Later,' said his guide.

The other youth and the Ombudsman glanced at him through the window and nodded.

Curiosity led him north for a few blocks, past the hostel street to a busy corner where he stopped to rest, his hand frozen into a bloodless claw around the suitcase handle, his mind numb with fatigue. An enervated girl in a long print frock sold home-made candles from a stand. He stared blankly at the fairytale castles, mushrooms, lurid demons, Elvis Presley busts, and mounted policemen with wicks protruding from their hats. 'You made all these yourself?'

A wan smile flickered over the girl. There was a delicatessen on the corner. He left the case beside the candle stand and bought himself and the girl a takeout coffee, then walked west, precariously balancing the polystyrene cup under his coat, to a park bathed in sunlight. He lay down in the shade, his head resting against the peeling trunk of a silver birch. Joggers circumambulated the park on a thin running track, faces pinched and rubicund; beyond them traffic sped round a loop of road, the noise muffled among the trees. He drank the coffee and slumbered, waking an hour later as the sun set, the half-full cup of coffee still upright in his hand.

Artificially refreshed, he set off again in search of the hostel, clutching in his exhaustion a dull nugget of determination to find a bed.

It was dark when he reached Seaton House. He was too late and all the beds were occupied for the night. The warden directed him to a student hotel a block away. He found it and checked in as it started to rain. Fifteen dollars for the night – and after that? Ten dollars to begin a new life. He strolled downstairs to the restaurant, ordered a hamburger and coffee, sat alone at a table facing the street and watched long, iridescent cars cruise by in the rain. He considered exploring the city, but had no idea where to go. The atmosphere was inert. The streets visible from the hotel offered few clues – empty office buildings, rows of brittle yellow lights along empty streets. Sirens whined in the dark; two teenage girls in shorts stopped on the pavement outside the window. He stared obsessively at their behinds.

He left the coffee shop by the street door, and glancing along the street, caught a glimpse of bright lights, heard the muffled hubbub of accelerating cars and human activity. In five minutes he had arrived at the main street. In both directions a line of neon signs advertised restaurants, record stores and body-rub parlours. The pavements crowded with teenagers, a soft sea of breasts and buttocks. Older people with the faces of worried larvae scuttled by in the shadows. Groups of young men leaned from cars, shouting at girls, or simmered mysteriously behind dark glasses and tinted windows. He walked south for a block, stopping to look at pornographic magazines in a shop beside the Celestial Massage

Institute. Browsers of all ages pored hungrily over them and Martin felt comfortably anonymous until leaving the store, when his eyes met those of a girl standing in the doorway of the body-rub parlour. She smiled, but he hurried off into the crowd, embarrassed, wanting to apologise for his thoughts.

He walked round the block and returned to his hotel room, took off his clothes, turned on the TV, showered and lay on the bed. He fell asleep instantly and woke once in the middle of the night to empty his bladder and turn off Bela Lugosi.

Chapter sixteen

He rose early the next morning, packed his suitcase and checked out immediately. Walking south past old wood-framed pawnshops he came to a small park in the grounds of a church. It was well provided with benches. On each one a derelict wrapped in blankets or a thick coat came to life as edgy sunlight rose above the buildings, cutting tree-shaped shadows on the dewy grass. Businessmen passing on their way to work were assailed by tired cries of derision. An elderly black woman sat bolt upright on her bench, carefully straightened her coat lapels and exclaimed in a loud voice, 'I live in a mansion! And I have a car, which is driven by a chauffeur!'

He bought the fattest available newspaper from a vending machine and staggered with his suitcase into another coffee shop overlooking the park, where a hand-written sign in the door advertised: 'Eat Here or We Both Starve'. He took a seat by the window, stuffed the suitcase under the table, ordered a coffee and scanned the rooms to rent in the classified section. From time to time he squinted at the sunlit street and watched the faces of passengers, passing by in clattering streetcars. He finished the coffee and counted his money; he needed twenty dollars for a room.

He paid the bill, folded up the classified section, retrieved his suitcase and walked back across the park, resting by the window of the biggest pawnshop, gazing in at wedding rings, cameras, electric guitars, watches. He pushed open the heavy glass door and stopped in the dark, cool interior. On wooden panelling at the back of the shop a sign indicating the loan department led him into a corridor with open booths on one side, divided by small partitions. There were already half a dozen people waiting. He took a large plastic number from a box on the wall and found a booth as far from the other customers as possible. Removing Robertson's watch from his coat pocket he laid it on the counter next to his number. Someone entered the booth next to his and his body tensed as if he were bracing for a fight. He leaned over the counter and watched the melancholy assistants writing out tickets and haggling with customers.

A sad old man in a dusty grey suit served him. 'Is it a loan?'

Martin nodded.

'How much do you want?'

He hesitated. 'It's a good watch,' he said. 'A Hamilton. My father gave it to me.'

The old man sighed.

'Fifty dollars,' Martin said.

'Fifty dollars?' The old man picked up the watch and looked at it sceptically before shuffling off to the back of the shop. Martin watched him hopefully. An Indian in the neighbouring booth stuck his head around the partition and looked at him inquiringly. 'Jeez. What a place, eh?'

Martin laughed weakly.

'You never see one of these places going out of business. Sometimes I reckon I was put here on earth just to carry money between the welfare office, the pawnshop, the liquor store and the racetrack.'

The old man returned, holding out the watch in the palm of his hand. 'Twenty-five is the best I can do.'

'That's a damn fine watch,' said the Indian.

'Not even thirty?'

'Twenty-five is the best I can do,' the old man repeated. 'It's easier to redeem when you get less,' he added, by way of consolation.

Martin gave the student hotel as his address, stuffed the ticket and the twenty-five dollars into his back pocket, said goodbye to the Indian and left the pawnshop. He walked across the street into the park. The benches had been vacated. He sat down to read the classified section again. He didn't know where any of the streets were. There were two hundred rooms to rent. He took out his pen and wrote down a few numbers. The sun was rising in the sky and the day was growing warm. Sweat gathered on his forehead and he took off his coat. A light breeze blew through the park, flapping the paper from his hand. It scudded over the wet grass towards the road. He picked up his coat and suitcase and ran after it, retrieved the classified section, and set off in search of a phone.

The first number he called was answered by an old woman with an Eastern European accent. She gave him directions to the street and told him which streetcar to catch, but by the time he had put down the phone and written her address on the newspaper, he had forgotten the names of the other streets, and only recalled that his destination was west of downtown.

'It isn't far,' she had said.

It was approaching midday and he had already grown tired by the time he had walked six long blocks through the city centre. He walked up University Avenue, pausing to rest every few hundred feet. The sun beat down and carrying his coat made his load heavier and more cumbersome, so he put it back on. At the corner of University and College Street he stopped a policeman. 'Excuse me. How far is Dufferin Street?'

The policeman looked at him, then turned and walked away, laughing.

'Which way is Dufferin Street?' Martin repeated, but his mouth and throat were dry and hardly any sound came out. A passing woman pointed west and hurried away.

For two hours he tramped westward, stopping the occasional pedestrian for directions, finally arriving at a narrow street where a cooler breeze rustled through maple trees. The noise of traffic from the main street faded. He came to a tall, blood-red brick house with a sign indicating a room to rent hanging from a nail on a tree in the yard. He opened the short wire gate and walked up the path. The shadows of trees waved over the wooden porch floor. A late cicada buzzed overhead on the telephone wire; there was a muffled sound of dishes being washed and small children playing on neighbouring porches.

He rang the doorbell. After several minutes the door opened and an old Chinese man in shirtsleeves and shorts looked out at him.

'I'm here about the room to rent.'

The old man squinted at him irascibly.

'You have a room to rent?' Martin repeated, half turning and pointing to the sign on the tree.

'Ah,' the old man smiled, 'room.'

'Yes. Is it still available? Could I see it?'

Without replying the old man went back into the house, leaving the door ajar. He returned a moment later, still smiling. 'Only renting to Chinese people.'

'What?'

'Only for Chinese people.'

Martin stared at him. The Chinese man edged back into the house.

'Plenty other house.' He waved his arm in the direction of the world.

Martin retreated down the path and out into the street. He pulled the paper from his pocket and checked the address. The number he was looking for was next door.

A tiny old woman dressed in black peered at him anxiously for several seconds before unlatching the screen door. 'You here about the room?'

'Is it still available?'

She smiled. Little teeth glittered in a pretty mouth. She held open the door. 'Just leave that there.' She pointed to his suitcase and indicated a space beside an antique coat rack . 'Looks like you just got off the boat.'

She turned and led him into the house, through a high panelled hallway to a dining-room filled with antique furniture, the smell of cooking stew and fresh air. Despite the warm weather, gusts of hot stale air blew from a vent by the dining-room door. The subterranean rumble of a furnace in the basement could be heard through the floor. 'Sit down.' She indicated a dining chair by an open window. 'Would you like coffee? You look tired.'

He nodded, his mouth too dry to speak.

She brought him the coffee and sat down across the table from him, her hands folded demurely in her lap, watching him drink. 'There are two rooms. One on the top floor overlooking the street. It's eighteen dollars a week. First and last. The other is smaller, at the back of the house. It's bright, though. Sun shines in all day.'

'How much is that one?'

'Fourteen a week. First and last.' She thought for a moment. 'You on welfare?'

'No.'

'You're not from here, are you?'

'No. I just arrived.'

'English?'

'Scottish. More or less.'

'What kind of work do you do?'

'I'm an artist.'

'Oh yes.'

'Where are you from?' Martin asked.

'Poland.'

'How long have you been here?'

She ignored the question. 'You need welfare? You have money for the rent?'

He wondered if the truth would disqualify him as a tenant.

'If you have enough for a week, you can go to the welfare office tomorrow and give me the rest when you get your cheque.'

She stood up. 'I'll show you the rooms anyway. Then you can make up your mind.'

He followed her out into the hall. With a dignified air she led him up two flights of narrow, carpeted stairs, squeezing by a wardrobe on the landing, and up a third covered with loose linoleum, which clattered as they climbed. As they reached the top of the house Martin smelt cooking oil and detergent. The sticky, claustrophobic heat intensified. He stopped to remove his coat. She turned a corner and led him along an even narrower passageway with a single door at the end. Beside the door he noticed a fist sized hole in the plaster. She pulled out a small key pouch. A three foot crack ran down the grain of the thin pine door.

'It gets real dry in here when the furnace is on. No good for wood.'

'Why is the furnace on now?' he asked.

'It comes on automatic,' she replied, without elaborating.

She unlocked the door and stood aside to let him in. 'This room has its own bathroom. You share the kitchen with the other tenants.'

The room was crowded with furniture: a high, ebonised oak bedstead, the headboard jammed under a sloping ceiling; beside it, a small desk with broken drawers beneath a dormer window, and on the left hand wall next to the bathroom door, a chest of drawers, painted white. He walked over to the window and looked down through the branches of a maple tree into the street. 'It's nice,' he said.

'A real artist's room,' she agreed.

'So, it's OK with you if I give you a week now and the rest tomorrow?'

'You don't want to see the other room?'

He looked at the other room. 'It's nice and bright. But I like having my own bathroom.'

'Beggars can't be choosers,' the old woman said as she led him back downstairs.

'That's true.'

She looked back up at him with a smile that seemed to Martin almost seductive. 'You take it. But you give me the second week's rent tomorrow.'

He pulled a twenty dollar bill from his pocket and gave it to her. 'You might as well keep the two bucks for next week.'

'You're damn right,' she said, without acrimony. 'You wait here. I'll bring you a receipt.'

When she returned with it she handed him two keys, one for his room, one for the front door. 'You can come and go as you please. But no girls in the room after midnight. And no noise either.' She looked at Martin's battered suitcase as he retrieved it from behind the front door. 'And I expect you need bed linen, don't you?'

She followed him back up the stairs, pausing on the second floor to unlock the wardrobe and take out a pair of sheets. They returned to his room, and as Martin put down his suitcase to unlock the door he looked up at the hole in the plaster. 'What are the other people who live here like?'

'Very nice people. Very quiet,' she replied quickly.

He opened the door, put down the suitcase again, took the sheets and looked at the signature on the receipt.

'Thanks very much, Mrs Dombrowski. I'll get the rest of the money tomorrow.'

'You'll have to get up early. Five o'clock. Any later is too late.'

She turned to go.

'Five o'clock?'

'For free money? It's not so bad. Or maybe you'd like it better if they brought it over?'

'Five o'clock is fine. I usually stay up that late.'

The old woman looked at him without smiling. 'When you get the money, bury a little change in the garden.'

'I beg your pardon?'

'Then you won't forget where you've been. If you want to remember a place, bury money there.'

Martin nodded politely.

'You remember where people are buried, don't you? Well money's the same.' She nodded towards the window. 'There's a coffee shop just up the street, if you're hungry. They sell good piroghies there. Don't forget to lock up when you go out. Not that there's anything wrong with the people here,' she added defensively.

'I think I'm going to sleep for a while,' Martin said. He looked back into the room, which was now filled with evening sunlight. 'It's a lovely day.'

'It's getting cold,' Mrs Dombrowski said, turning her back and tapping away along the passageway.

Martin took a packet of cigarettes from his coat pocket, threw his suitcase, the coat and the sheets on the bed, then closed the door. He went to the window and leaned out over the ledge, scanning the street. Finishing the smoke, he flicked the butt into the upper branches of the maple and watched the disintegrating spark plummet through the tree to the garden. Suddenly exhausted, he returned to the bed, pushed aside the suitcase, removed his shoes and lay down.

Some hours later he was woken by a pang of extreme hunger, the sound of a woman screaming and a man shouting. The room was dark. A mat of dim yellow light illuminated the floor beneath his door. He stood up, put on his shoes and coat, locked the door behind him and walked along the corridor to the kitchen. The door of the room opposite slammed shut. From inside he heard a woman sobbing.

A young man in a T-shirt and jeans was sitting at the kitchen table, staring intently at a plate of pork chops. In his right hand he gripped a fork, while his left toyed with two sticks of polished black wood joined by a short length of chain. He appeared not to notice Martin's arrival.

'Goddamnit, Elaine!' the young man shouted, without looking up. 'I gave you money for steaks, and what's this crap?'

A muffled reply came from the room.

Martin remained motionless on the threshold. Without warning the man looked directly at him, as if catching an animal in a rifle sight. Involuntarily Martin retreated a step and nearly fell backwards down the stairs. He steadied himself against the banister. 'Hello,' he said.

Without replying the young man pushed his chair away from the table and stood up. He advanced across the kitchen, only coming to a stop when their feet were almost touching. Without blinking, he gazed steadily at Martin, the *nunchaku* sticks dangling from his left hand. A cold smile assembled itself on his face. He raised his hand with the heel pointing towards Martin's shoulder. 'Hi, man.'

Martin held out his hand tentatively. The young man stuffed the sticks into his jeans' pocket and grabbed him by the wrist. 'No man. Like this.' He demonstrated his handshake. 'Jimmy,' he said. 'Crazy Jimmy, because I killed a cop.'

'Ah,' Martin said.

'Well, what's your name, buddy?'

'Martin,' he replied, nervously. 'But my friends call me … Martin.'

'Well, they would do, wouldn't they,' Jimmy replied, 'if that's your fucking name.' He pointed over at the table and shouted unexpectedly.

'You're just in time for pork chops, Martin!'

Another muffled sob came from the bedroom.

'You moving in the room down the hall?'

'Yes, that's right.'

'Take a look at this.'

He led Martin over to the electric cooker. Two frying pans sat side by side, one still warm with a thin pool of melted pork fat on the bottom. The other contained an inch thick layer of congealed grease, studded with small black balls of dirt. Jimmy stood back and pointed at the cold pan. 'What do you think those are?'

Martin stared blankly into the pan.

'Mouse turds, man.' Jimmy clicked his tongue and sighed like an exasperated housewife.

'Ugh,' said Martin.

'You got it. "Ugh" is right.'

Jimmy returned to the table and began gnawing a pork chop. He glanced up at Martin, who suddenly imagined Jimmy eating him and everything else in the kitchen, organic and otherwise.

'That's not all, man,' Jimmy continued, masticating ferociously. 'Mutual of Omaha's Wild Kingdom has nothing on this place.' He pointed at the half-eaten pork bone on his plate. 'Man. This is really disgusting. I told her to get steak, but she gives me this crap.' Outraged, he raised his eyes heavenwards, waving the chop tantalizingly beneath Martin's nose. The smell fuelled the hunger in his belly.

'Steak's too expensive!' came a voice from the bedroom.

Jimmy stood up, strode to the bedroom door and nearly wrenched it from its hinges. 'You know what kind of diseases you get from pork!' He brandished the chop at his unseen wife. 'Not to mention parasites!' He looked back at Martin. 'They burrow their way into your flesh and breed in there, man. One day you have this kind of itching in your arm or somewhere. You give it a scratch and when the scab comes off it sticks its head out. A fucking worm head sticking out of your arm!'

'Yes,' replied Martin. 'That's horrible.'

'Hear that, Elaine?' Jimmy smiled lasciviously.

'I'm hungry,' Martin said. 'I'm going out.'

The sun had set and the air was cold. Leaves crunched beneath his feet. He walked briskly to the coffee shop. A middle-aged waitress appeared immediately at his table with a menu, a glass of water, a cup and saucer and a full coffee pot. 'Coffee?' she inquired, dispensing a cup before he had time to reply.

He reached in his pocket for his cigarettes and realised they were still in his room. He browsed the menu.

'You want to order now?'

'Yes. I'd like eggs.'

'Fried, poached, boiled, scrambled?'

'Fried.'

'How do you want them fried?'

'What?'

'Over easy, medium, hard, sunny side up?'

'Sunny side up, is that with the yolk on top?'

'Yep. You want them hard, soft, or what?'

'Medium,' he said. 'Not runny.'

'You want potatoes with that?'

'Yes …'

'French fries, home fries, mashed, boiled, baked?'

'French fries.'

'French fries,' repeated the waitress. 'And what about toast?'

'I'm afraid to ask.'

'What's that?'

'You have different kinds of toast?'

'White, wholewheat, light rye, dark rye … or there's sourdough, or you can have a toasted Kaiser, or an onion bun, or a bagel.'

'What's a Kaiser? Never mind. White toast, please.'

She wrote down the last detail. 'Is that it?'

'Do you sell cigarettes?'

'You'll get them at the counter.'

The ashtray on the table depicted a Scottish dancing girl in plaid, and the name MacDonald's. He strode confidently to the counter.

'Packet of MacDonald's, please.'

'Regular or plain?'

'What?'

'Filters?'

'Yes. Is that regular?'

'Yep. Large or small?'

'What, the cigarettes?'

'No, the packet. You want a small pack or a large pack?'

'A small pack.'

'Lights?'

'No thanks. The ordinary kind.'

'King size or regular?'

'I thought regular was filters.'

'It's also the size of the cigarettes.'

'Yes. Regular. Not king size,' he said, removing a two dollar bill from his pocket to make the purchase, 'it's like being a contestant in a quiz show.'

The waitress had turned to the cigarette shelf and reached up; her hand froze in mid-air, her fingers almost resting on a cigarette packet. 'What's that?' She half turned to face Martin and raised her eyebrows.

'Nothing,' Martin said, offering the money.

'You want plain or menthol?'

After he had eaten he paid the check and drank another coffee, smoking three cigarettes in rapid succession. He glanced up at a clock on the wall behind the cash register. It was nearly midnight. 'Well, I'm here now,' he muttered to himself.

'What's that?' the waitress said, passing his table.

'Just talking to myself.'

'Oh. Well. Sometimes it's the only way to have a decent conversation. Want some more coffee?'

He drank another coffee and smoked another cigarette, listening to the bass whine of the milkshake machine, the murmur of conversations from neighbouring tables in a multitude of accents and languages. He watched the slow flow of late night traffic and pedestrians. A car pulled up outside and the window rolled down. A burly girl in a T-shirt and white polyester shorts stepped from the doorway of a shop beside the restaurant and leaned through the open window. A moment later the passenger door swung open and she climbed inside. Suddenly he felt lonely and imagined himself playing host to Christine, on his return to Edinburgh; he would be worldly-wise, well-travelled, familiar with all the subtleties and idiosyncrasies of North American life. 'You've really changed, Martin,' she would say, to which he would respond with an impassive smile, 'but you seem … so much more …'

'So much more what?'

'I don't know.' He was unable to imagine how he would seem to Christine after having changed. Stronger? More solitary? Melancholy in an attractive way? His prolepsis failed him. He stubbed out the cigarette and left the restaurant. Rusty, city-illumined clouds obscured the night sky. He pulled his coat lapels over his chin. Cold air gnawed at his knuckles as he walked to Mrs Dombrowski's.

When he switched on the bathroom light, a cluster of cockroaches scattered across the opposite wall. He opened the bathroom cabinet and found two more nesting on the previous tenant's toothbrush. A gurgling sound came from the bathtub. Jimmy and Elaine seemed to be arguing in the kitchen, punctuating muffled speeches with slamming doors, crashing frying pans, sobbing and shouting.

He turned out the bedside light and went over to the open window, looked over the ledge through the maple tree into the street, and listened to the low hum of traffic and streetcars clanking along the nearby main street. Heat blasted from a vent beside his feet. From a branch overhead a bird nesting in the glare of a street-light chirped aggressively, thinking it was dawn. The extraterrestrial blue glare of a TV illuminated a room across the street and a tinny recording of an accordion polka came from the house next door.

He closed the window and returned to the bed, sat down and stared into the dark for a long time, thinking of girls in shorts, imagining Christine, and his family, long asleep in Scotland. Cool breeze whispered in the curtain. The sound of TV gunfire and sirens from the neighbour's house caught him on the verge of sleep. As his eyes closed the bird twittered again on the branch by the window. He wanted to write something about it, but instead repeated a few words several times in his head in the hope of remembering them in the morning, and slept quickly.

Chapter seventeen

He slept through the alarm and woke at six, tired and disoriented. Oleaginous heat embraced him like the smell of his own body. The stale odour of cooking, cigarettes and bad drains filled the unventilated room. He stared aimlessly into space for some minutes, recollecting the details of his arrival. A sense of solitude gathered about him. He muttered a few encouraging words to keep his spirits up, then got out of bed and removed his coat. His clothes adhered to him like old bandages. He peeled them off, opened the suitcase, removed a pair of jeans and a clean shirt, and went into the bathroom. Avoiding contact with the greasy plastic curtains he turned on the shower and stepped in. Murky water rose over his feet and lumps of matted black hair floated up on a whirlpool at the plug hole. He dried himself with his used shirt, shaved and brushed his teeth, deposited the razor, toothbrush and toothpaste in a glass on the shelf beneath the medicine cabinet. He could hear Mrs Dombrowski moving about two floors below. He put on his shoes and went downstairs.

'So you didn't wake up in time for the welfare office?'

'I'm sorry. I'm just going.'

'Maybe it's too late.'

'I was tired. I didn't hear my alarm.'

Mrs Dombrowski raised her hand and smiled coldly. 'I understand. You've had a long trip. You're in a strange place. You're not at home any more. At home maybe your mother doesn't need rent. She gives you a bed and a room for nothing. But here it is different. Here there is no mother. Just an old woman who cannot afford to accommodate a young man without money.'

'Yes.' He reached into his pocket as if searching for more money.

Mrs Dombrowki's expression became more sympathetic. She put her hand on his forearm. 'It's OK. You were tired. You look more rested now. I'm glad. Tomorrow you get me the money.

Maybe even today. Who knows? Believe me, I know what it's like to be in a strange country. Everything is new. Everything is different.'

She scribbled directions to the welfare office on a piece of paper and mumbled something about a pair of galoshes by the hall stand. As he walked towards the front door he found the view through the screen entirely obscured by snow. The temperature had fallen thirty degrees during the night.

To save money he retraced his journey of the previous day by foot and reached Seaton Street by seven. Snow had drifted up around the welfare office door where a hundred men waited for opening time. At seven thirty the doors opened and the crowd rushed in, elbowing and pushing. Martin strolled in casually; a number of latecomers pushed past him. In the reception area beside the glassed-in counter a small metal box dispensed tear-off strips like raffle tickets. He took a number and sat down at the back of the waiting room, next to an old man whose skin and clothing were all the same colour, a cinereous blue and grey plaid.

'What's your number?' the old man immediately inquired.

Martin examined his ticket. '76,' he replied.

The old man snorted angrily. 'Well, they won't see you today.' He turned away, laughing bitterly to himself.

Martin looked at the number in his hand, then up at the illuminated notice board above the reception area. Number fifteen was being served. 'It can't take that long to serve sixty people,' he said, to no one in particular.

'Eh? What's that?' the old man snapped.

'I said, 'It can't take that long to serve sixty people.''

The old man laughed again. 'It can't. But it does. It all depends how bad you need the money ... and if you need it today.'

'Oh,' Martin said.

'That's right.' The old man nodded. 'If you don't need it, you'll get it. And if you do ...' He raised his eyebrows in a pedagogical manner.

'You don't,' suggested Martin.

'Correct.'

'You're an expert then?'

'It's quite simple, sonny. Life conforms to a diabolical order, which is all that stands between us and total chaos. And the only consistent fact of life is that human needs are there to be frustrated.' He squinted sourly at the numbers board. 'Without this principle our lives would have no meaning at all.'

Martin considered his number disconsolately. The old man peered at him sideways, a cunning, feral look. 'Sell you mine for a fin,' he said suddenly.

'What?'

'Five bucks. I'll sell you mine. It's twenty-two. See?' He brandished the paper strip under Martin's nose. 'You'll be out of here by lunchtime.'

'No thanks.'

'OK. Two bucks, then.'

'No thanks.'

Martin slumped into his seat while the old man, muttering resentfully, stood up and wandered off through the rows of seats to find a buyer. He returned some minutes later. 'Two bucks and a fifty-six,' he said wearily. He sat down painfully in the next chair and coughed so thickly Martin expected him to vomit up lava. The old man noticed his alarmed expression. 'What do you expect after twenty-five years in a goddamned grinder?'

'Grinder?'

'At the steel mill. That was my job. Wading around in a fisherman's suit up to my ass in sludge.' He held out his hands for Martin to examine and gazed sadly at the subcutaneous grime. After a moment he reached into his coat pocket, glanced furtively around the room, unscrewed the top from a quarter bottle of whisky and took a long sip.

'It was a dirty job, then?'

'Shit, at least it was dirt you could see. Not like being a goddamned banker. Their hands may be clean, but their souls are as black as pitch.' He leaned over suddenly and muttered menacingly in Martin's ear. 'You're not a banking man yourself, are you?'

'Me?' said Martin. 'No, I'm not a banking man.'

The old man leaned back and surveyed him. 'No offence, if you are,' he said.

'I'm not a banking man,' Martin repeated.

The old man looked satisfied. 'I had my own truck and everything,' he continued. 'By the time I finished, myself and everything I touched was covered in crap.'

Martin could think of nothing to say. The old man screwed the top back on the bottle and slid it back into his pocket. 'Give you the fifty-six for a buck. Give you a shot from my mickey.'

A clerk was already locking the glass door as Martin's number appeared on the illuminated board.

'You'll have to come back tomorrow,' said a liverish woman in the booth as Martin approached.

'But I've been waiting all day.'

'You have to get here early. Seven o'clock.'

'I've been here since seven o'clock.'

'Earlier, then.' The clerk slid from her stool and walked over to the coat rack at the back of the office. Martin stared at her helplessly as she returned. 'Fill this in,' she said, reaching beneath the counter and producing a form. 'And be quick about it.'

He wrote as the clerk watched, tapping her fingers impatiently on the counter. 'Is that your address?' she asked, tugging the half-completed form from his hands.

Martin nodded.

'You're in the wrong office.' She wrote down the address on a piece of paper. 'And you got to go to Unemployment first anyway.'

Snow was falling again as he left the welfare office and walked to an intersection with the nearest main street. As he turned the corner a frigid wind gusted around the exposed building and a shower of freezing rain caught him full in the face. A streetcar appeared and he joined an unruly mob of people clambering on board. Melting slush washed back and forth along the streetcar floor. At each stop the car juddered, accelerating and braking unpredictably so that all the standing passengers, crammed together as more entered, skidded and lunged about wildly to keep their footing. It was soon impossible to see through the condensation-fogged windows. He tried to estimate by time and speed the distance they were travelling.

The streetcar came to a stop in the centre of town. Many of the passengers disembarked. He found a seat and immediately fell asleep. When he awoke he was once again back in the town centre, travelling in the opposite direction, having passed Mrs Dombrowski's street long before. He wiped the window with his coat sleeve and viewed the street. Rows of old stores were being torn down. A billboard by the window illustrated a futuristic office development towering into the sky. He dozed off again before the car had left the city centre and woke briefly to catch a glimpse of dull streets with paintworn shop fronts and malnourished pedestrians, then later, bigger houses with welcoming porch lights and wide lawns, behind them Lake Ontario slate grey in twilight vanishing at the horizon. An hour and a half later he woke again to find himself almost home. Condensation from the window ledge had soaked into his coat sleeve and his thin shoes were wet through, his feet already cold and numb. As he glanced through the window he noticed a sign above a shop advertising temporary unskilled work available. He left the streetcar at the next stop.

'Enjoy your sleep?' said the driver as the doors clattered open.

'Not much else to do on a day like this.' He scowled ahead at the snowbound street.

Martin made his way across the road, over a terrain of freezing slush to the shop, pushed open the door and entered. Three men huddled at a gas heater smoking cigarettes. One looked up as he entered. He seemed angry at Martin's intrusion but remained courteous. 'We're closed, sir.'

'I was looking for work.'

'Come back tomorrow at six.'

'In the morning.'

'Yup.'

'Do you have any work?'

'Won't know till tomorrow. You just take your chances with everyone else.'

One of the other men took a long drag from his cigarette and exhaled. Smoke seemed to belch from every orifice in his head as he spoke. 'It's been pretty good the last few days. Course now you got to work in this.' He nodded in the direction of the street.

Melting snow and salt had gathered in an unfordable lake at the intersection. Martin hopped up the street through ridges of thickening snow and pools of freezing slush to Mrs Dombrowski's, banged the snow off his shoes by the front door and made his way upstairs. The already familiar aroma of detergent and cooking fat permeated the stairway as he climbed to the kitchen. As he made his way towards the corridor leading to his room, a foot emerged from behind the half open door of Jimmy and Elaine's room, dragging it open. Inside a huge television flickered silently. He caught sight of an unmade bed piled high with laundry, a pair of woman's legs, and Jimmy sitting hunched in a low wicker chair clutching a beer bottle and staring up at him from beneath a Hitleresque fringe. Martin smiled uncertainly and walked by.

'Hello Martin.'

He heard the creak of wicker and the sound of a boot scraping on the floor. He turned and saw Jimmy making his way from the bedroom to the refrigerator.

'I got something for you,' Jimmy said, without looking at him. He opened the fridge door and pulled out a beer, knocked the top off against the rim of the sink and reached into his jeans' pocket.

'I won't, thanks,' Martin said.

'Won't what?' Jimmy turned towards him and took a long gulp of beer.

Martin coughed and rubbed his nose, trying not to look at Jimmy's beer.

'Oh? You want a beer? Oh yes, man, you can certainly have a beer, if that's what you want,' Jimmy said, leaning back against the fridge door, his hand still in his pocket. 'I don't usually share my beer with anybody man, but I'll make an exception in your case, if that's what you really want man.' He stared at Martin without moving.

'No, really,' Martin said, 'That's very kind, but ...' He half turned to the corridor but Jimmy stepped away from the fridge and crossing the kitchen interposed himself between Martin and his escape route.

'Don't you want to see what I got you?' he said, smiling coldly. Martin looked down at the rummaging movements in Jimmy's pocket. The hand suddenly appeared before his eyes, clutching a small tube of brightly coloured plastic counters. 'Here,' Jimmy said, still smiling.

Martin cautiously took the packet, looked at them and then at Jimmy.

'Bingo chips, man!' Jimmy said triumphantly.

'Ah,' Martin said.

'For the dryers, man.' Jimmy sighed and looked away as Martin tried unsuccessfully to feign delight and hide his incomprehension.

Jimmy patiently removed the packet from Martin's hand and tore off the Cellophane cover, spreading a few of the counters on his palm. 'You use them in the dryers ... instead of dimes ... At the laundromat!'

'Ah,' Martin said. 'That's great! Thanks very much!' He took the counters from Jimmy's hand and examined them with scrupulous enthusiasm as if they were Spanish doubloons. 'Wow. That's great.'

'Well. They'll save you some money anyhow,' Jimmy said, who appeared to have been seized by an attack of melancholy. He turned back to the bedroom, took another deep gulp of beer and kicked the door shut behind him.

The next morning Martin woke after seven, his chest heavy and his head thick with a cold. The house was silent, the air in the room warm and fresh, a cool draught sussurating over snow on the window ledge and through the half-open window moderating the heat from the vent. The silent house seemed to belong to him. He coughed: a lump of adhesive aquamarine phlegm shot inadvertently from his mouth and landed on his naked chest. He remembered the half-bottle of whisky in his case, climbed out of bed, dragged it from underneath and found the bottle, went to the bathroom, tore off a strip of toilet paper to wipe his chest, and returned to bed. He lay toasting himself complacently with sips from the bottle cap, savouring the pleasant, soporific effect of his illness. He lit a cigarette.

From the street he heard an engine revving and tyres revolving impotently on a patch of ice. The high-pitched whine of the car engine made him feel anxious, then hungry. He got out of bed again and went through the pockets of his trousers, coat and jacket, but found only two dollars. He returned to bed and drank another toast, but had to leap up abruptly when, taking a drag from the cigarette, the filter stuck to his lips, his fingers slipped along to the lit end and pulled off the glowing ember. The spark sizzled momentarily between his fingers and fell on to the blanket, burning a hole in it. Brushing the ember from the bed, he knocked over the whisky bottle. A sharp pain glowed in his two burned fingers. He went to the bathroom and angrily ran his hand under cold water. A cockroach peered back at him unperturbed from the rim of the tooth glass.

'You stupid fucking bastard,' he said to the mirror.

He arrived at the employment agency nearly two hours late. The majority of the day's workers were leaving or had already left. Two of the men he had met the day before worked the counter. Both were middle-aged, one genial, the other – who had done most of the talking – morose and vindictive. Harry the Genial handed Martin a form to fill in as the office emptied. Harry's partner, Bob, sat behind a desk chewing a cigar and drinking coffee, shuffling officiously through index cards and employment forms. 'They need a guy for the boxcars in Hamilton,' he muttered.

'You want to work today?' Harry looked up at Martin.

Martin nodded.

He had paused at the social insurance number box on the form. Harry noticed his hesitation. 'Don't have your number yet?'

Martin shook his head.

Harry lowered his voice. 'Just sign down there at the bottom. You'll be getting your card soon, right?'

'Yeah,' Martin said.

'There's just the one job left today. I should warn you it's not great.'

'Better than some,' Bob said.

Martin signed the form and Harry snatched it away, stuffing it into Bob's overflowing in-tray.

Bob rubbed his belly and grimaced.

'Any extra money for that Hamilton job, Bob?'

'You must be kidding. The guy's just starting.'

Harry handed Martin the work order. 'Like I say, the job's in Hamilton.'

'Hamilton? How do I get there?'

'Guy called Carson. He'll give you a ride,' Bob said.

'When do I get paid?'

'End of next week.'

'But I don't have any money.'

'Ain't life a bitch, eh?' Bob said, without looking up.

'When you come in tomorrow we can give you an advance,' Harry whispered.

'You guys should be in a cop movie,' said a voice. Martin turned to find a tall, bearded individual with hair tied in a ponytail, hovering at his shoulder. 'The nice cop and the nasty cop.'

'What do you want, Carson?' Bob said.

'I want my money hosebag,' Carson replied, in a jocular tone.

'Don't call me a hosebag, you son-of-a-bitch,' Bob said.

'Don't call me a son-of-a-bitch, you fucking doughbrain.'

Harry leaned over the counter and tugged at Carson's sleeve. 'How many times, Carson? Please. It's his stomach. It's ulcerated all to hell.'

'Not surprising, Harry. There's enough acid in his system to poison Lake Ontario. If he ever drowns in there the fish are done for.'

Carson looked at Martin.

'Hi.'

'Hi.'

'This is Carson,' Harry said. 'He'll be driving you to work.'

'Work.' Bob scowled. 'That's a laugh.'

'What's that supposed to mean?' Carson said.

'Hey, English,' Bob said, looking up from his desk. 'You want to know how this turkey got his start in Toronto?'

'Here we go,' sighed Carson.

'All he had when he first came here from Mange-La-Merde, Québec, or wherever it was, was an alarm clock. He sets it for five am, goes down early to the welfare office, sells his low number for a deuce, then goes and has the breakfast special at the coffee shop over the road.'

'I did that once, asshole. I should never have told you.'

'Come on, Bob,' Harry said. 'We thought it was pretty funny at the time.'

'That was before he got a real job and started acting like the Shah of Iran.'

'Someone wanted five dollars for a low number when I was there yesterday,' Martin said.

'Well, that's inflation for you,' Bob said, returning to his labours. Harry joined him at the desk and began shuffling through forms and papers.

'You been to Welfare?' Carson inquired. 'How did you make out?'

'They sent me to Unemployment, but I haven't been yet. I don't have a social insurance number.'

'Why not? You illegal?'

'No.'

Harry returned with a cheque. 'Here you are, Carson. Listen, go easy on Bob. He'll just stop finding you any work.'

Carson folded the cheque and put it in his back pocket. 'Where are you from, anyway?'

'Scotland.'

'Tough guys,' Bob said, smiling unpleasantly to himself.

'What's that, Bob?'

'Remember the Scottie Mods, Harry?'

'I don't believe so, Bob.'

'Those Scotch guys who came over here a few years back. Had a gang and all that up in Yorkville. Heh heh heh.'

'No,' said Harry, 'I never heard of them, Bob.'

'Anyway,' Bob continued, 'they made the mistake of going down to Detroit. Did they ever get their asses kicked! Spooks shot them full of holes!'

'That's amusing,' Carson said. 'I never realised you had such a sense of humour, Bob.' He turned to Martin. 'Hamilton, eh?'

'I think so.' Martin nodded.

'You poor son-of-a-bitch.' Carson reached into his pocket and handed Martin a five dollar bill. 'Here. You'll need to get something for lunch.'

'No, thanks,' Martin said.

Carson put the bill on the counter. 'OK. I'll just leave it there, and if you want these thieves to have it, that's up to you.' He turned and left the shop.

'Take it,' Harry whispered urgently, as Bob rose from his seat.

'Just don't try any of that hard man stuff over here, pal!' Bob said, glaring as Martin grabbed the bill and retreated to the door. 'And no fucking the dog!'

Martin followed Carson outside and down the snow-swept street to an old Ford sedan.

'It's not locked,' Carson said, climbing into the driver's seat. 'I hope you got your long johns on. The heater's fried.'

Martin opened the passenger and got in while Carson started up.

'Listen to that,' he said. 'Sounds like a Malmut with emphysema.'

They rocked back and forth as the engine reluctantly came to life.

'They don't usually hire here for jobs in Hamilton, but there's a bus strike and they can't get anyone.'

Martin nodded absentmindedly, and shivered. He tugged a piece of disintegrating toilet paper from his pocket and blew his nose loudly.

'There's some work gloves in the glove box,' Carson said, 'but it sounds to me like you should be in bed with a bottle of rye.'

'I need the money,' Martin said.

Driving west along the Lakeshore Carson asked Martin what he hoped to do in Canada.

'Just look around.' He peered through the window at the now impenetrable snowfall.

'How long have you worked for those guys?'

'A few weeks. I got some land in Quebec. Just came down here for the winter.'

'The money's pretty good compared to Scotland.'

'No wonder they live on porridge over there,' Carson murmured.

Chapter eighteen

The train pulled slowly into the siding and came to a halt by the loading dock. Carson opened the boxcar door and jumped back as several rolls of barbed wire bounced out and landed in the snow beside him. The other men approached the wagon cautiously, blowing on their hands and squinting into the snow-wet wind. A murmur of complaint dissolved in a gust as Martin stepped up to the door and grabbed the first roll. It was perversely entangled with others behind and above it, and it took several minutes to break it free. He turned round to find himself alone on the dock, the other men having wandered away to other boxcars in search of less onerous cargo. He was relieved, preferring to work alone. As he laboured he felt his feverish cold dissipating, the physical exertion raising his spirits.

At eleven o'clock the steam horn of a lunch wagon echoed from the front of the building, through the warehouse out to the loading dock. Martin dragged a roll of wire free from the boxcar as Carson appeared at the loading dock door.

'You want a coffee?' He helped Martin drag the roll into the warehouse.

Several haggard middle-aged men wandered among high steel shelves, carrying order papers and pushing carts loaded with boxes and rolls of wire. Illuminated by fluorescent lighting all materials – desk tops, human flesh, polyester shirts, tile flooring – had the same synthetic sheen. A high pitched whine from a boiler in an adjacent room pained Martin's ears. No one spoke, apart from the foreman, who shouted.

They walked through the warehouse and exited by a small door leading to a car park. A sharp wind blew around the warehouse wall scattering skeletal snow flakes against the cement. Above his head a pair of brown leaves fluttered from a moribund birch like dying insects. Between branches quiet cement buildings jutted against a grey, turbulent sky. The wind blew a sour paint smell across the lot from a body shop in the next unit. The cold ate into his bones. Carson and he strolled to the coffee wagon where men in plaid coats and working boots were lining up, rubbing hands together, counting change, or stamping their feet against the cold. Most were from the spray shop, the paint smell emanating from coveralls beneath their coats.

As they waited in the line up Martin coughed thickly and spat a heavy lump of yellow phlegm into the thin snow at his feet.

'Hmm,' Carson said. 'Looks like bronchitis to me.'

'It's changing colour. This morning it was green. I don't know if that's a good sign.'

'You ought to see somebody about that,' Carson said. He bought Martin a coffee and a cruller, and later a sandwich for lunch.

'It's very kind of you,' Martin said.

'What goes around comes around,' Carson replied, mechanically. He drew a pallet from a pile by the door and sat down. 'It's like Haiti in this place,' he said. 'I've never seen so many fucking zombies.' He indicated the foreman. 'Take that germ for example. He's an expert, just watch him.'

They watched the foreman carry a box from a pallet to a shelving unit, followed by a young acolyte.

'What he doesn't know about carrying boxes isn't worth knowing. Thirty years of experience goes into that technique.'

As they drove back to Toronto the snow had abated and watery moonlight glimmered on the lake. Martin reached in his pocket for cigarettes and found Carson's five dollar bill. 'I've still got your money,' he said, handing it over.

'Keep it,' Carson said. 'You can buy me a beer sometime.'

'You sure?'

'Sure.' He glanced cannily at Martin. 'Maybe you can do me a favour.'

Martin kept silent.

'You like to get high, don't you?'

'I suppose so.'

'With your bronchitis you could get me a prescription for Novahystex B.'

'Novahystex B?'

'I'll give you twenty bucks for a bottle. Give you some too.'

'What is it?'

'It's great. Makes you go all rubbery.'

'Makes you go all rubbery,' Martin repeated.

'Don't knock it.'

'Well, I don't know. I don't know my way around here.'

'You won't make any dough working in a job like this, Martin,' Carson said. 'You need a scam.'

'Oh?'

'Yeah. This here is the land of the middle-man. You use other people's money to get other people to work for you. For example: Last year my girlfriend and I went up into the woods north of Québec City. It's beautiful up there, man, you should go some time, and the people are great. Anyway … we took a tent and a canoe and a chainsaw. Found an acre of a woodland where nobody went, found out who owned it, and I asked him if I could buy it. The guy says, 'Sure', so I tell him we'll be back with the cash in the fall. Spent the summer camping out and cutting down the trees, sold most of the lumber to a dealer, took the cash to the owner and bought the land. We kept some of the lumber to build a cabin and some money to live on. So then we had a cottage on an acre of cleared land for nothing. Sally – my girlfriend – she's living up there now.'

'That's clever,' Martin said.

'So, you just apply the same principle to whatever it is you're good at, and there you are.'

'I'm not good at anything.'

'On the other hand,' Carson continued, 'there's always poverty to fall back on.'

They pulled up in front of the agency. Bob's gloomy silhouette loomed at the window. Carson left the engine running as they went inside to hand in their work receipts.

'You need an advance?' Bob said, sneering, particularly at Carson.

'Of course he needs an advance. Guy's got to have a brew after a hard day's work.'

'I think I'll just wander around tonight,' Martin said.

'Sure. Suit yourself.'

Bob handed Martin a ten dollar bill. 'I don't usually do that, but my mother's from the Old Country.'

'He's from Scotland, Bob. Not Transylvania, man,' Carson said.

Chapter nineteen

Martin caught a streetcar to the city centre. The snow was no longer falling and the wind seemed warmer when he disembarked in Chinatown. Street-lights illuminated sparse maples at the north end of a wide, cobbled avenue. The jagged sound of Scottish accordion music whined from cheap speakers in a bar across the street. Dodging traffic and pools of melting snow he made his way to the Arran Hotel, a low, whitewashed building with darkened eyehole windows set into the wall some feet above the pavement. He peered through the door and found a dimly lit room furnished with small tables and grey middle-aged men in workclothes, most sitting alone with two or three small glasses of beer in front of them. On the right hand side a barman wiped glasses and glanced up periodically at a TV on a shelf above the bar, where heavily padded men could be seen speeding over an ice rink, chasing a little black disc. A tinny strathspey blared from a speaker above his head.

Martin ordered a quart of beer and sat down at an unoccupied table. There was little conversation in the bar; each customer sat alone, a random, isolated particle floating in space. Now and then one of the men would turn to another and remark on the progress of the game; the other would respond with a kind of amicable dispassion, as if they had all been strangers together in the same bar for several lifetimes.

Martin finished his beer and, having nowhere else to go, ordered another. The bar door opened and the girl he had met at the candle stand came in, carrying a large beaded bag and a bunch of tiny red roses. She walked over to the bar.

'You ought to buy one of them, Karl,' one of the customers said. 'This place could do with a woman's touch.'

Martin heard the chime of the cash register. The girl chose a stem from the bunch and handed it to Karl. 'There's a nice one,' she said.

Karl polished a glass and set it on the counter with the rose inside it. The girl began moving among the tables, the hem of her long printed frock collecting a wake of cigarette butts and ash as she moved.

Martin looked up as she arrived at his table. 'I give them away on vibes, sometimes,' she said, holding out a stem.

'Oh. You should let me pay,' Martin said, taking the rose.

She folded her arms and surveyed him dispassionately.

'You want to sit down? You hungry?'

She considered him for a moment, then smiled.

'Right. The guy from the candle stand with the suitcase.'

'That's right.'

'OK,' she said, pulling back the chair. 'But they don't sell food in here.'

'Would you like a drink?'

'Could I just have some of your beer?'

Martin got up from the table and went to the bar for a glass. When he returned the girl was drinking from his own. He poured the remains of the bottle into the new glass.

'Did you find somewhere to live?' she asked.

He told her about Mrs Dombrowski's rooming house.

'Your neighbour sounds wild.'

'He's OK for a psychopath.'

'You got to know how to talk to them, eh? Typical Immigrantville,' she added.

'Did you sell any candles?'

'A couple. The Americans like the Mounties and the Indian chiefs. Though they look kind of weird when the heads have burned off.' She put down her glass and sighed.

'And you do this at night?' He indicated the roses. 'It's a long day.'

'It's not over yet,' she said, looking around the bar. 'Why did you come in here anyway? How come you don't go somewhere where there's music?'

'There's music in here. The Bluebell Polka, that's one of my favourites. And there's the organ music from the hockey game.'

She looked at him blankly. 'I suppose it is a little early for night life,' she said, glancing at her watch.

Martin could think of nothing more to say. As a diversion he picked up the rose from the table and sniffed it. 'It's paper,' he said.

She responded with the wan smile he'd seen at the candle stand.

'It looks real!' he reassured her, 'that's impressive.'

'Nothin' to it,' she said. 'It helps pay the rent. I do some dancing, too. Dancing makes the real money, but sometimes I'm not in the mood. Also, you meet a better class of people selling roses.'

'Dancing?'

'Stripping.'

'Stripping?'

'The money's good, man. You don't have to get involved. Fifteen bucks a show, five shows a day.'

'It's a shame you have to do that to make money.'

'I don't know. Bought myself a neat car. And I'm saving to buy more dolls. You could do some yourself.' She winked. 'You got a nice body, probably. And guys get more. Quite a bit more, actually.'

'I don't think so,' Martin said. 'On a cold day like this I don't think anyone would pay to see what I've got.'

'Wot aye-ve got!' she said, mimicking his pronunciation. 'I love your accent.'

'What about these dolls?'

'Rubber dolls. You know, sex dolls. For a piece I'm working on. I make sculptures. Well, they're sets actually, for my real dancing. I was trained in Dance theatre. I only do the candles and the roses for money, and when I get tired of those old drunks ogling my ass.'

'What kind of sculptures are they?'

'Rude sculptures!' she said. 'They're irreligious, you could say.'

'That sounds interesting.'

'Oh, it is interesting,' she said, coldly. 'Terribly interesting.'

Martin, embarrassed, brushed imaginary ash from his coat sleeve. 'What's your name?'

'Maggie.'

'That's a nice name.'

''That's a nice name',' she repeated. 'Boy, you're quite the silver tongued devil, aren't you?'

'You're pretty sarcastic for a hippie.'

'Who says I'm a hippie?'

'You look like a hippie.' He was surprised to see she looked hurt. Distracted by a shout from the neighbouring table, he glanced up at the TV.

'Someone's thrown an octopus on the ice,' a voice said.

'Damn Leafs getting shut out again,' bemoaned another voice. 'I keep watching this crap week after week. I don't know why. I guess it's a kind of sickness.'

'Where are you from?' Martin asked.

'I'm just a regular Canuck. White trash, you know.'

'What does your father do?'

'That's really funny, man. My Dad told me that's what people from Over 'Ome always ask you.'

'Yes. Sorry. I don't know why I asked that.'

'Because you couldn't think of anything to say.'

He laughed. 'That must be it.'

'He's a master finisher,' Maggie went on. 'Furniture. Pianos, antiques – stuff like that.'

'A craftsman?' Martin suggested.

'Yeah, a craftsman. But the chemicals are getting to him. He doesn't look so good these days.' She finished the last of the beer, and stood up. 'Listen, why don't I buy you a drink at my place?' She pushed her chair back under the table and collected the roses. 'It's either that or I spend the evening trying to sell these. And I'm tired.' She turned and walked to the door, trailing detritus from the bar floor in her skirt.

Martin got to his feet and followed. When he emerged from the bar, he found the air warm; an oily torrent of melted snow cascaded into a storm drain by his feet.

Maggie was climbing into a long black Plymouth, decorated with a *Viva La Raza!* bumper sticker, the body low over the wheels, only a few inches above the road. She released the lock on the passenger door, and he climbed in, pulling it shut behind him. Tiny lights flickered romantically on the dashboard.

'Some car.'

'It's a Mexican lowrider,' she said, turning the key in the ignition. 'Came all the way from Hawaiian Gardens, LA. Only problem is it's too close to the ground, and when it's like this outside, I have to drive everywhere at twenty miles an hour. It looks nice, but it's a wreck. It burns as much oil as gasoline.'

They arrived fifteen minutes later in a street of pre-war factory buildings, decrepit neighbourhood stores and flimsy grey apartment blocks. Paint peeled from balconies, young Oriental and black women, silhouetted in apartment lights and half hidden in the gathering darkness stared down mournfully into the street, bewildered children clustered about their knees. Maggie stopped outside an eight-storey office building. A solitary light shone from a window on the top floor. Across the street garish lights blazed from a submarine and sandwich bar where a solitary figure in a candystripe uniform leaned against the counter reading a paper. She turned off the engine. Cutters had been pruning the kerbside trees. She locked the car door and turned over a few of the smaller branches with her foot, revealing another lying beneath, the size of a small tree. 'Can you carry that?' she asked.

Martin spat ostentatiously on his hands, rubbed them together, and hoisted the branch on to his shoulder. As he paused to adjust the load, his foot slipped and he fell face down in the slush, the branch on his back. He stood up and made another attempt.

'Don't break any of the small branches,' Maggie said. 'I need them.'

She walked ahead of him to the office block and up half a dozen cement steps, pushed through stiff glass street doors and swept across a narrow, unlit lobby to a hand operated elevator. They dragged the branch inside. Maggie pulled the grille shut and they embarked on a languid ascent, Maggie driving. 'Your face has gone red,' she said, 'and you're all wet.'

The elevator came to a halt at the sixth floor. Maggie threw back the grille and led him to a door at the end of a dim hallway. An acrid smell of chemicals advanced to meet them. She unlocked the door and turned on a light switch. A red neon dancing girl buzzed to life on the wall to his right, illuminating one sector of an L-shaped pine floored loft. The only furnishings visible were a pair of directors' chairs and a chrome and glass table stacked with comic books, ornamental candles and an airbrush. On the floor beside the table sat a compressor, with a line leading to a socket at the wall. The loft floor was littered with bulging garbage bags, sheets of soiled coloured paper, paint cans, feathers, clothes, broken machinery – a car transmission, items of marine salvage, a commercial weighing machine with a smashed dial – more piles of comic books, bottles, dishes and ashtrays filled with dead butts. Two high windows faced the lake. Both were open. A cold breeze blowing directly from the lake prevailed over warm furnace air and made the loft chilly.

'Pardon the breeze, but I have to be careful I don't asphyxiate myself.'

Along a low stage at one side of the loft half a dozen mutilated life-sized rubber dolls leered from infernal shadows, the feet of one buried in a pile of stones, another melted around a wooden stake. Beside these the half-inflated arms of two more dolls reached out imploringly from beneath another pile of stones.

'Wow,' Martin said.

'That tree should fit along there,' she said, pointing to a space at the end of the stage. She shook out her wet skirt. 'I'll make some tea. And I got to change.'

She disappeared behind a wall into the concealed section of the L. He heard the scratch of a record needle, then a choir and the sound of a kettle being filled. She returned a few minutes later wearing jeans and a sweatshirt, carrying a long cardboard box, a surgical mask, and a short length of twine.

'You like the music?' she asked.

'I have a catholic taste in music.'

She glanced at him suspiciously. 'It's Palestrina,' she said. 'I've been using it for inspiration.'

'It was a joke,' he said.

She pulled the mask over her face and helped Martin to drag the branch up to the stage and arrange it against the wall. It stood upright without falling over. 'Perfect,' she said. 'Look at that.'

She plugged in the compressor, connected the airbrush and sprayed the wall and branch lurid red. Unwrapping the cardboard box, she took out an inflatable rubber doll and, using the twine, tied it to the tree. The doll, its neck slightly twisted, gazed senselessly into space. Its tiny, uninflated feet hovered sadly in mid-air.

'Sebastian,' she said, taking off the mask. 'Only thing I need now is some darts.'

'What is it?'

'I'm calling it The Soul Kitchen,' she said, 'due to the heat. Well, the spiritual heat. It's a kind of rogue's gallery. I love Christian martyrdom. It's like a snake eating its own tail. Any martyr is one less fanatic in my book.'

She threw the mask on to the floor, unplugged the compressor and disappeared into the alcove, returning with two mugs, a bottle of Calvados and an unlit joint, which she held between her teeth as she talked.

'The missionaries in South America used to baptise Indian babies and then smash their heads against rocks. They meant well, though. They wanted the little heathens to go straight to heaven.'

Martin nodded. 'I didn't know that.'

'You want to meet his friends?' She went to the stage and presented Sebastian's neighbour. 'Meet Ugilious,' she said. 'This reverend gentleman met his Maker in the fifth century AD, stoned to death for overturning a statue of Saturn.'

'Obviously a troublemaker,' Martin said.

'Next Eulacia,' Maggie continued, passing on to the melted doll. 'Keep your hands off Eulacia. A poor virgin. Burned at the stake at the age of thirteen.'

'What did she do?'

'Who knows? These days she would have got grounded, I guess ... And there are poor Candida and Paulina, buried in stones. It was their old man's fault. He was one of those principled guys everyone else suffers for. He converted to Christianity, so they took it out on his kids.'

'It's amazing,' Martin said.

'Things were different then.'

'No, the sculpture.'

'Well, thanks. But they don't understand it here. It's all macramé and beadwork. Nice, nice, nice.'

'It must be expensive.'

'I want more dolls. I want a hundred of them, a thousand. For my opening I'll fill them with helium and put little paper wings on their backs and put them out the window to float all over the city.'

She slumped down in one of the director's chairs and poured a shot of Calvados into her mug. Martin joined her. 'Should I close a window?' he asked.

'Only problem is the fumes,' she said.

'What is all this stuff, anyway?' Martin gazed around at the debris on the floor.

'I keep everything,' she said. 'It's supposed to be very anal, isn't it?' She leaned over, picked a garbage bag from the floor, and tore a piece from the top. 'This whole bag is nothing but tickets.' She pulled out a handful of papers. 'Can you believe it? Bus tickets, transfers, restaurant receipts. I keep all this stuff to remember where I've been. I can tell you who I was talking to, who I was going to see, exactly, by looking at this stuff. It's better than a diary.'

'You should bury money,' Martin said.

'Oh, well, I do that too.'

'There's Goeballs,' she said, stuffing the papers back into the bag and throwing it on to the floor.

A mutilated cat appeared from the alcove. Following the line of the wall it rubbed its way slowly around the room towards them. Its ear was missing, it limped, its coat bald along one side. As it left the safety of the wall and turned towards them Martin could see it also lacked an eye.

'Goeballs?'

'My dad called him that. It's from some old song. Something to do with him having no balls. 'Hitler has only got one ball ... Poor old Goeballs has no balls at all."

'Oh,' Martin laughed.

'The funny thing is he wasn't fixed. They were bitten off by a dog.'

'Oh, God.'

Goeballs limped over to Martin and twined himself affectionately between his legs.

'He just gets up to eat. So he won't starve to death while he's sleeping.'

Martin stroked the cat's battered head.

'So, what are you doing in Canada, anyway?'

'Odd jobs.'

'How odd?'

She lit the joint as Martin told her about the Hamilton warehouse.

'Sounds cold.'

'It is cold.'

She passed him the joint. He took a long drag.

'You don't have a boyfriend.'

'No way. Don't need some guy spoiling my fun.'

'Maybe you could have fun with a guy.'

'Maybe. But I'm happy already, so why spoil it? Besides, you know what they say. Behind every great man is some ambitious chick like me wishing he'd get out of the way.'

He took another drag from the joint, handed it back to her

and tried again. 'Your parents don't live together?'

'No, my mother lives in LA. I visit her sometimes. What about your folks? Are they here too?'

'No. My father died before I was born. My mother lives with my uncle in Scotland.'

'What's your uncle like?'

'He's a musician but he doesn't have fingers, and he's a sort of priest, only he doesn't have a god.'

'Sounds weird.'

'Yeah.'

'And your mother?'

'She's autistic. Shut down. After my father died, she sort of stopped. She's a bit like a prisoner doing life.'

'She sounds weird too.'

'Yeah. The whole family's weird.' He furrowed his eyebrows and stared at her weirdly.

Maggie giggled quietly, then slid from the chair and stretched out on the floor. As she exhaled; a blood-red trail of smoke gathered above her head. Martin watched her dumbly, bewitched by her languor. The air, the surfaces of objects, glistened like snow in firelight.

'So, what are you here to do?'

'I don't know … I just wanted a change.'

'You could have had a change where you were. God. There must be plenty of crappy jobs in Scotland.' She stubbed out the joint in one of the ashtrays.

'Everything in Scotland's been there for three hundred years.' Martin said. 'It seemed better to go somewhere else, do something new,' he said. As he spoke, for no reason he could fathom, he was gripped by an overwhelming desire to be on his own. He stood up. 'I should get going,' he said. 'I need to be outdoors now.'

'I didn't mean to depress you.'

'No,' he said. 'I'm just tired. I just need to be outdoors.'

Maggie rose to her feet slowly, stretched back in a graceful arc, touching the floor with her fingertips. 'Yes, well. I guess you've to be up early in the morning.' She straightened. 'I've got to get some sleep, too. '

They walked to the door and stood, almost touching, in the narrow space.

Martin sensed romance, and paused on the threshold. In case there was some chemistry between them that he could not feel himself, he leaned over and kissed her clumsily. Her lips were warm, but he felt nothing.

She stepped back and glared at him. 'What are you playing at?'

'I thought ...'

'Yes. I guess you did.' She laughed. 'Actually, now I come to think of it, there is something you can do for me.'

'Yes?'

'If you don't mind. It's a kind of unorthodox request.'

'Oh?'

'Well, you're not supposed to take everything off,' she said, 'when you're doing a show, that is, but the owners sort of expect it – not to mention the crowd. Trouble is, it's the dancers that get busted, not the club owners.' She reached up and patted his hair. 'Well, some of the girls make wigs. Merkins. That way, you can't get busted. And your hair, it would be ideal. Don't take offence, but it's like you've got this whole crop of pubic hair growing right there on top of your head.' She squinted into his face. 'You're not offended?'

'I don't think so.'

'It's beautiful,' she said. 'Like wool. No, it's much better than wool.'

'Like pubic hair.'

'Yes.'

'Well, I've always wanted to be in show business.'

'I've got some scissors.'

'In case you met a dickhead.'

'Right.'

She slipped across to the alcove and returned clutching a paper towel, snipping a pair of nail scissors. 'This won't hurt,' she said, 'they're real sharp.'

'We haven't talked about a price,' Martin said.

'You're adapting pretty quick, aren't you?' she said.

Martin leaned over as she harvested a handful of hair and held it up to the light. 'Perfect,' she said, wrapping the clippings in the towel. 'Thanks.'

'I've got more.'

'You want to go into business?'

They retraced their steps to the door.

'Shall I visit you again?' he asked.

'Sure,' she said, 'only I'm not always here. I'm moving, actually. Got a place near the Parkway.'

'Oh.'

'But I come by most days to feed Goeballs. So, yeah. Come by.'

Later that night he was lying on his bed, irritably awake, hypnotised by a snowfall of luminescent sparks rushing towards him through the darkness when he was disturbed by a rap at the door. 'Martin? You in there man? Come on, man, I know you're in there.'

Jimmy waited.

Martin waited.

'I got something for ya. Something real special.'

Martin glanced at his clock. It was one am. He abandoned the bed and went to the door. 'You'll wake Mrs Dombrowski,' he said, peering into the brightly lit hallway.

'Shit, man. Never mind.' Jimmy stared wildly into his eyes and grabbed his arm. 'Come with me, buddy. I got us a real treat.'

He led Martin along the hall, tiptoeing in an exaggerated fashion like a cartoon cat, periodically putting his finger to his lips and laughing through his nose. They continued through the dark kitchen to his room. Elaine was sprawled on the bed, watching television. She looked up and smiled sweetly. 'Hi.'

'Hi.'

'Elaine don't like the stuff and it sure ain't no fun partying on your own ...' Jimmy slumped down on the bed and gave his wife an affectionate squeeze '... so I thought, My good buddy Martin could probably do with a pick-me-up.'

'It makes my head hurt,' Elaine said. She smiled again and asked Martin precisely, as if addressing a foreign aristocrat, if he'd like a cup of tea.

'Tea would be great,' Martin said. 'Just milk, thanks.'

'Shit, Elaine,' Jimmy said. 'You don't want poor Martin here to think we woke him up just to come over and drink tea.'

Elaine got up from the bed and went to the kitchen. Jimmy leaned over to a shelf on the headboard and produced a small white packet which he brandished triumphantly at Martin. 'Now this is really something. Know what it is?'

'No.'

Jimmy leaped from the bed and excavated a small chair from a pile of laundry. 'Well, sit down here, my man,' he said, setting the chair down before the TV and dusting off the seat with his hand. 'Meth,' he said. 'Pure fucking meth. From Mexico. A friend brought it from Texas.'

'Meths?' Martin stared curiously at the packet.

'Methedrine. You never tried it?'

'No.'

'Well, you're in for a treat. You can keep all that fancy cocaine, buddy. This here is the real McCoy.'

He took a surgical scalpel, a two-dollar bill, a little mirror from his shirt pocket, and sliced open the packet. He set the mirror on the TV, chopped up two fat lines, rolled the bill and handed it to his visitor.

'Is it cut with anything?' Martin said, pretending to be knowledgeable.

'No, man,' Jimmy laughed. 'This is pure fucking poison.'

'Of course.' Martin laughed along, as if he had intended to make a joke. He took one of the lines. Jimmy removed the bill from his nose, leant over the TV and ostentatiously snorted the other. 'What do you think?'

'Great,' Martin said.

Elaine returned with a mug of tea which she handed deferentially to Martin. 'I'm afraid we don't have any cakes,' she said.

'No cakes,' Martin said, looking surprised. 'I don't usually drink tea without having a cake.'

'Really?'

'Shit,' Jimmy said. 'He's just putting you on. Aren't you, Martin?'

'Is it OK?' Elaine said.

Martin sipped the tea. 'It's the best tea I've ever drunk in my life,' he said.

After a moment's tense silence Jimmy said, 'You want me to show you how I killed that cop?'

Before Martin had time to reply, Jimmy had darted behind him and wrapped his arm around his throat. 'Now, don't move, Martin. That's the main thing to remember when a sixth-dan black belt has you by the throat.' He whispered softly in Martin's ear. 'All it took was just one shot in the liver, and he was gone.' His outstretched fingers prodded Martin softly below the armpit. 'You hear a lot of big fucking talk about the heart, man, but I tell you the liver is the king of the internal organs.'

'I've heard that,' Martin said, breathing evenly into his abdomen, trying to remain calm.

Jimmy released his grip and patted Martin heartily on the back. 'So you take care of your liver, you hear me, Martin?'

He smiled complacently at Elaine. 'See? He's OK.'

'Elaine was worried, I could tell,' he said to Martin, with mock confidentiality.

'No I wasn't,' Elaine said quietly. 'It's just sometimes you're so rough.'

'But I knew you wasn't a wimp, Martin.' Jimmy smiled again.

For half an hour they all sat together on the bed. Elaine ate a bag of potato chips and watched the silent TV. Jimmy or Martin would laugh from time to time, or nod to each other and smile tensely.

Martin retreated slowly through the open door. 'Thanks very much for the methedrine and the tea.'

'Just take care of your liver,' Jimmy said, 'and your liver will take care of you.'

'Thanks, Jimmy. I'll remember that.'

'Oh, and ... uh, Martin ...'

'Yes, Jimmy?'

Jimmy winked at him and smiled yet again. 'Don't laugh at my old lady, man.'

Chapter twenty

The bus strike and the job in Hamilton lasted two months. Carson traded a friend's social-insurance card for the Novahystex prescription, which Martin never obtained, and picked him up at Mrs Dombrowski's house each morning at seven thirty for the thirty mile drive to the warehouse, stopping for breakfast at a coffee shop by the lakeshore on the way. He took him to a bar in Chinatown and introduced him to half a dozen of his friends from Québec; two girls passing the summer in the city, selling flowers on the street for college money, and a group of folk musicians making their way west. The girls were the prettiest Martin had ever seen, but he felt dull and clumsy in their company, resenting his exclusion from the hearty Québecois conversation and unjustly suspecting that much of the laughter around the table was at his expense. After the bars shut he loitered at a donut store to avoid Jimmy and Elaine, returning to Mrs Dombrowski's in the early hours of the morning for four or five hours' sleep, waking restless and bilious in the hot room, the alarm exploding like a fire bell beside his head.

The early snow melted quickly and for a few days the temperature rose into the fifties. Sheets of melting snow slid from the roof, sunlight shone in through the vacant maple branches by his window and he woke at weekends with the sound of neighbourhood children playing street hockey. One morning on an impulse he bought a sketchbook in the local Dominion store, and in the afternoons sat at his window making rough caricatures of the neighbourhood: Portuguese women, dressed apparently for eternal mourning; veranda beer drinkers, Chinese street-hockey players in facsimile Maple Leaf suits, an itinerant knife sharpener who appeared weekly, dragging a grinder on a cart and ringing a bell, the chime echoing timelessly among the trees. As Martin watched, he metamorphosed into a mythic character named Saint Shabby, his machine became a banjo and the cart a dog, as woebegone as his owner. Saint Shabby, named in honour of Ray, wandered the streets of the world, a disconsolate eternal, bound to fulfil a hopeless vow, not to rest until he had composed a song for every human being on the face of the earth.

Occasionally Martin was surprised by a vivid recollection of Robertson or his mother. Even after a few weeks' separation, it was as if they had disappeared into a realm of memory where fictitious characters, inanimate objects, and real people co-existed insubstantially. He wrote no letters, almost believing that contact with his family and friends could be maintained simply by bringing them to mind.

The respite from bad weather was brief; autumn had passed away quickly and the fluctuating temperatures settled into a tireless cold. As the snow froze into a permanent icy skin on the pavements, he grew accustomed to falling several times a day until he learned to adopt a penguin-like gait, legs and arms rigid in preparation for an unexpected slip.

He passed Christmas alone at Mrs Dombrowski's, leaving the house for a few hours to eat the Special Dinner at the empty coffee shop, buy a roach motel from a variety store, and wander the Yonge Street record stores, and the downtown streets. In the late afternoon he joined a crowd at the Simpson's window to watch the robotic Santa Claus display, descending later into a labyrinth of underground malls to browse by acres of imported suits, white gold jewellery, Italian leather, shoes, illuminated like priceless museum exhibits in the windows.

As night fell he rode an elevator like a vortex to a thirtieth-floor piano bar stuffed with tropical plants. He sat by the window in a revolving leatherette armchair and admired the view. Below on all sides streamers of car lights slithered down grids of streets; illuminated, empty office buildings blazed in the dark, a surge of light and power in a magic city. He read the drinks card and daydreamed as he waited for the waitress, speculating on his as yet unknown vocation and looking about enviously at the other customers. All appeared to have attired themselves in the malls below. They seemed like another species, liberated from all unfavourable circumstances – bad weather, physical discomfort and ugliness, unpleasant emotional states, disease, even mortality itself.

He ordered a mint julep which he finished quickly, returned to ground level and rode the streetcar home, sat on the bed in the dark drinking whisky from the tooth glass, toasting his cockroaches as they ambled along the bedroom baseboards and over the bathroom walls. He unwrapped the roach motel and inserted it by the wall where the traffic was thickest. The house was empty. Even Jimmy and Elaine had gone away. He drew another cartoon in his sketchbook of Saint Shabby falling headlong down an elevator shaft, his banjo and dog tumbling along beside him. Above their heads a boot protruded from a doorway. After midnight he undressed and got into bed, wrote Christmas cards for Alberta and Robertson, Christine and Ray, his first communication, sending them a few days later. The phone rang in the downstairs hall. He wondered if it was Maggie, but realised she did not have his number. He was content to be alone.

One Saturday afternoon in early January he was walking home to Mrs Dombrowski's from Kensington Market. A few black patches of long-lying ice scarred the cracked Tarmac of the street, but the day was bright and fresh. A crowd had gathered on the pavement in front of a new supermarket to watch a gaudy paper dragon dancing in the doorway. Crashing cymbals, gongs and drums repelled the demons of insolvency. Stepping from the kerb he fell face forwards over the hood of Maggie's lowrider. A pair of sunglasses peered between the spokes of the steering wheel. The passenger door swung open. 'I've been looking for you all day,' she said. 'You want to work tonight? Good Money.'

'Doing what?' He climbed in beside her.

She laughed. 'You don't have to take off your clothes.'

'I don't know.'

'My dad's boss has had some break-ins at his warehouse. He needs someone for security for a few days. He'll probably pay fifty or sixty dollars a night for you to look after the place.'

'Fifty dollars a night?'

'Yeah. Maybe sixty.'

'That sounds unbelievable.'

'You can look after yourself, can't you? It is in a kind of colourful neighbourhood.'

'I can look after myself,' he replied, surprised at his own self-assurance.

'Well then. You'll probably make more in ten days at Bebe's than you do in a month now. Anyway, I got you something for self-defence.'

She dropped him outside a gloomy sandstone building surrounded by old warehousing and across River Street from a housing project. Before driving away she reached over into the back seat and handed him a carrier bag. 'Security,' she said.

Just inside the door Martin encountered a round, pruritic man in his forties, scratching the seat of his trousers. 'Bebe?'

'Mr Benzini to you, boy. Come on in.'

Bebe led him to the far end of the warehouse, where several skids of broken furniture lay overturned in a pile of splintered wood and torn upholstery.

'Look at this mess!' Bebe cried. 'Bastards. They broke in last night and hot-wired the Towmotor.'

'How many?'

'Who knows? A bunch of local kids.'

'Kids?'

'Yeah! Kids!'

'Oh.'

'Listen. Do you have a weapon? You might need something to scare them off.'

'A weapon.'

'If they know someone is here they won't bother you. Still, it might help you keep up your morale. It gets kind of spooky in here after dark.'

'I'll be OK.'

Bebe rummaged through a pile of rags and emerged with a thick steel pipe. 'Here. Use this.'

'Thanks.'

'It's OK.'

'So, I stay until six. Is that right?'

'At least until it's light.'

'And it's sixty dollars a night, right?'

'It's robbery. Jesus. Cheaper to let them break in.'

'Some of this stuff looks pretty valuable,' Martin said. 'This can't be a very secure place to keep it.'

'I told her to tell you fifty. You can't trust anyone, these days.'

Martin looked down at the floor and tapped his foot.

'Well, OK, sixty a night. But there's no insurance. If you get killed you'll have to bury yourself.'

'Fine.'

'And it's seven nights a week. It's only for a few days, till my regular guy gets back from Acapulco.'

'Fine.'

Bebe led him back to the warehouse entrance. He lifted a set of keys from a hook on the wall by the door. 'OK. This is for the door, and this is for the padlock on the gate. The cops come around about once an hour. If you need a phone there's one across the street outside the MiniMart. But don't use it. Someone could break in while you're away.'

'I see.'

'I hope you brought some coffee.'

Martin shook his head.

'Well, the MiniMart on the corner sells it. Go and get yourself one before I leave.'

Martin walked across the street to the tiny neighbourhood supermarket and looked in the window. Three-dimensional religious tea trays depicting the Nativity and the Crucifixion undulated in the late afternoon light. A row of brightly coloured plastic gravity birds bobbed up and down, dipping their beaks in glasses of water. At one corner of the window he noticed a dartboard and a set of darts. He went inside, bought two coffees, a packet of donuts, and the darts set, and returned to the warehouse.

Bebe left. There was the sound of a car on the gravel, and the steel gate closing. Left alone, Martin paced the length of the warehouse, brandishing the steel bar at imaginary intruders. He opened Maggie's supermarket bag and found a small axe, a black handled Mexican switchblade knife, another copy of *On The Road*, and a packet of Oreo cookies. He paused for a moment to wonder what he had done with Carole's stolen copy of the Kerouac book, and if there was a divine imperative that he read it, somewhere.

He pulled down a little wooden chair from a stack at the back of the warehouse, set it in the middle of the floor and rested the dartboard on it. As it grew dark he closed the door and turned on the light. A single bulb overhead gave off a dull beam that illuminated a few square feet of the warehouse and left the remainder in darkness. He paced back and forth into the shadows and out again, gripping the axe in his left hand, the steel pipe in his right.

Some hours passed. He finished another game of darts. Despite the steady activity he was cold. Strange noises came from inside and outside the warehouse. He became restless. Picking up the steel bar and the axe, he went outside into the yard and walked up the frozen driveway towards the high chain link fence which surrounded the yard and bordered the street. There were few lights in River Street. A clear full moon illuminated the yard and its environs. Martin shivered by the fence and looked across the housing project. He was standing in the shadow of a tree. Four punks were walking up the street towards him. The leader noticed him lurking behind the fence, nudging his friends, he nodded in Martin's direction. They strolled up to the fence. Martin took a firm grip of his weapons.

'Hi,' said the punk.

Martin nodded.

'You must be the night-watchman.'

Martin nodded again.

'What's the axe for?'

'To scare off anyone who might try to break in.'

The punk considered this. 'Shit, man. You won't scare nobody with that dinky little axe.'

Martin took a tighter grip of the steel pipe.

'I can get you a decent axe.'

'Oh?'

'A big sucker, man. Cut a fuckin' dude's head off with it, man.'

'Uh-huh.'

'Just wait here.'

The punk led his friends in the direction of the project. Martin paced nervously by the fence. Some minutes later they reappeared, the first carrying a long-handled woodcutter's axe.

'Here you go, man. You'll scare the shit out of people with this thing.'

'How much?'

'Two bucks,' the punk said.

'That's a fair price, dude,' his friend averred.

'That seems fair,' Martin said pompously.

'You drive a hard bargain, man.'

Martin reached in his pocket, took out a two-dollar bill and handed it through the fence. The punk threw the axe over.

'Thanks.'

'You need that little axe?'

'You want it?' He threw it over the fence.

'Let's see how you look,' the punk said.

Martin grasped the large axe in his right hand, the steel pipe in his left, and brandished them menacingly.

'My word,' the punk said, standing back and assessing Martin thoughtfully. 'Isn't that something?'

'That's heavy, man,' his friend agreed.

Martin straightened up and smiled complacently.

'Need any weed?'

'No thanks.'

'OK, buddy.'

The punks said goodnight and strolled away towards the project. Martin lowered his weapons and looked up at the moon. From the darkness he heard a solitary voice raised in song: *Shine on … Shine on, Harvest Moon …* and the sound of wild laughter.

During the night a light snow fell and the wind rose, rattling the corrugated roofs of the neighbouring warehouses. Martin climbed a drainpipe to the flat roof of the building next door, sat in the shade of a chimney and smoked a cigarette. Bright moonlight illuminated the lake; late traffic cruised on the Parkway. River Street was empty again, the project apartment lights went out. Back in the dark warehouse he played another game of darts, looked at some of the furniture, found an old wingback chair, took the Oreos from Maggie's bag and sat down to read *On the Road.*

Thin grey light hovered at the high warehouse windows when he awoke, queasy and chilled through. His knees had locked in the cold and it was several moments before he could move his legs. He packed his bag, stored the axe and the pipe in a mahogany wardrobe at the back of the building, locked the warehouse door and gate, and set off through the project.

The streets leading to the centre of town were still deserted, apart from an occasional drunk, or a passing taxicab. He walked up to the park where he had first met Maggie and bought a coffee from the delicatessen, huddling from the wind beneath the leafless birch, crouching in the snow to watch the early morning traffic circulate the park perimeter. Now awakened by the wind he decided not to return to the rooming house, but instead walked south, to the waterfront. The Centre Island ferry was about to leave. He paid his dollar and went on board, sat on a bench in the tiny cabin, and watched the city recede into wide, featureless lakeshore panorama.

When the ferry docked, having no alternative, he resumed walking, across the island, along the icy lakeshore boardwalk, smoked a cigarette, staring numbly over glaciers of heaped up ice at the lake's edge, and over the winter sea-grey lake to the horizon. Children from the island cottages played in a snow-covered park, wrapped in enviable winter clothes. He tried to light another cigarette, but a gust blew out the last low flame of his lighter. He ate an Oreo biscuit and returned to the ferry.

Stepping ashore in the city and walking north he felt himself submerged immediately in the density of buildings, and pictured himself from a peregrine's eye view of fortieth floor boardrooms, his anonymous cartoon character's trivial destiny unfolding far below the sealed windows and the hermetic, air-conditioned axes of power.

On the way home he passed Maggie's office building, stopped at the submarine joint to drink a coffee, returned to the building and rode the staggering elevator to her floor. There was no one in; as he knelt down to slip a card with his phone number beneath the door, a cat paw appeared, snatching at his fingers. He took the darts from his bag and stuck them into the door.

At home he found Jimmy stabbing a fork repeatedly into the kitchen table as if trying to impale an invisible cockroach. Behind him the bedroom door was ajar; Elaine sat crouched over the end of the unmade bed, head in hands.

Jimmy looked up as Martin passed. 'Hi, man,' he said, laying down the fork. 'What's happening?'

'Not much.'

'Would you like a beer? There's a 2-4 in the fridge. Help yourself.'

Something in his tone made Martin pause.

'Everything OK, Jimmy?'

'That cop, man.'

'What cop?'

'That cop I killed.'

'Yeah?'

'It was an accident. I thought he was going to kill me. He and his buddy drove me down to the beach. If I hadn't been a juvenile, I would have taken a slide for sure. Hard time in Kingston, maybe. But it was an accident. The judge believed me.'

'So. Is everything OK?' Martin asked again.

Jimmy smiled distractedly. 'Yeah. You can't expect miracles, eh?'

'I've been working all night,' Martin said. 'I've got to get some sleep.'

'Sure. We'll have a beer when you get up. There's a 2-4 in the fridge,' he said again.

'I will.'

'Sweet dreams!' Jimmy said, as Martin turned away down the hall.

'Hi, Martin,' said a muffled voice from the bedroom.

He opened his door and looked with a growing, habitual disappointment for a letter which was not there, lay down on the bed, talking and laughing silently with an imaginary Christine.

Chapter twenty-one

'You seem to be doing OK at this night-watchman job,' Bebe said, after a few days.

'I don't mind it. Nothing's happened.'

Bebe indicated the furniture. 'You like some of this stuff?'

'Yes, I do,' Martin said. 'I like wood.'

'Fred gets back from Acapulco soon, and he sleeps here, so I can't give you the night work any more. Besides I don't think those little pricks are going to break in here again for a while. But I could use someone at the auctions. You reckon you could fix some of that stuff they broke? I got the clamps and that shit. Maggie's old fella could show you. Also, I do pianos. He does all the finishes. Maybe he could use some help. You might learn something.'

'What would the money be like?'

'I can't pay you what I paid for the night work. Three bucks an hour for working in the day. Fifteen bucks for the auctions.'

Bebe gave him a day to think about the offer. Martin walked across town to the employment agency. Bob was at the counter, reading through a pile of order forms. At the desk behind him sat Harry, writing in a notebook, a cigar in his mouth, a long stick of ash balanced precariously over the pages.

'Where have you been?' Harry said.

'I've got a job,' Martin replied. Bob gazed at him sourly, then went to the desk and returned with an envelope. 'You have a job.'

'I got a better job.'

'He's learning,' Harry said.

'You can cash this at the kike's across the road,' Bob said, handing him the envelope.

'He was in Auschwitz, Bob,' Harry said.

'If you believe all that shit.'

'What the fuck do you mean by that?' Harry stood up and approached the counter.

'Nothing.'

Harry rolled up his shirtsleeve and laid his arm down on the counter.

'He's got a number on his arm, right here,' he said to Martin. 'A little blue tattoo.' He leaned across the counter as he rolled down his sleeve and smiled bitterly. 'Bob is one of those Nazi sympathisers. Toronto's full of them. Half the fucking cab drivers in this town are war criminals.'

'You're exaggerating,' Bob said. 'Besides, I'm not a Nazi sympathiser. I fought in the goddamned war against the Nazis.'

'Well, just watch what you're saying, Bob. You don't want the limey here to think we're all anti-Semites.'

'I am an anti-Semite, Harry,' Bob said.

'Well, keep just quiet about it. You push friendship too far sometimes.'

'You're not Jewish are you, Harry?'

'I couldn't have a friend who was an anti-Semite,' Martin said. 'And I couldn't work for an anti-Semite either. So you can keep your money.' He pushed the envelope back across the counter and went out into the street.

For a moment he stood by the door, blinking into the snow. 'That was really fucking smart,' he said into himself. 'That's really going to make a difference.'

He walked over to Spadina Avenue, bought a bottle of wine as the liquor store closed, and detoured through Kensington Market to drink coffee at a Jamaican café. A bitter wind blew unimpeded from the lake, scraping surgically at his fingers. A crowd had gathered around a mountain of salt-encrusted ice at the corner of Dundas Street, waiting for a streetcar, or for a light to change. A streetcar clanked up to the nearby stop; faces peered out at the street from a fog of condensation, like dead souls on a journey into the afterlife. Mouths opened and shut in soundless conversations.

Two cars contested the crossing as the light changed. Martin stared with fascination at the crowd on the sidewalk then back to the streetcar. Impersonal panic seemed to rise into his body from the dead ground. I could die here, he thought, if I had no shelter.

A group of jostling textile workers shivering inside cheap

coats and worn shoes, pushed past him as the lights changed. Swept along by the crowd, he crossed the street, hopping between pools of viscous, salty water, staring intently into the tide of bewildered eyes, angry foreheads, pinched mouths, sweeping past him. He felt a horrible affinity with the women: debilitated by cold and poverty, his shoes breaking at the heels, his shabby coat indistinguishable from a thousand others, the colour flushed out into a sea of monochrome, his identity disintegrating into a vast, volatile communality as impersonal and capricious as the weather.

'What the fuck am I doing here?' he muttered to himself, stopping in his tracks and squinting through cold, gusting snow at a street he no longer recognised.

He walked south for a block and caught the Queen streetcar home, cursing Bob as he stuffed his last dollar into the fare box.

The next morning Bebe met him at the warehouse door with a pair of overalls and introduced him to a short, dour man in late middle age. They shook hands. Two yellow, reptilian eyes, bulging behind thick glasses observed him curiously.

'Wesley.'

'Martin.'

'Maggie's buddy.'

'How do you do?' said Martin.

'I do terrible, thanks all the same,' Wesley said. He set off towards the yard, shuffling almost, as if in pain. Martin followed him to a shed beside the warehouse. A cold wind blew in at the open door. Two aluminium vats sat at the back of the shed in a haze of toxic air, stacks of polished, ebonised wood behind them against the rear wall.

Wesley peered into the vats. 'This is the stripper,' he said, nodding at the first, 'and this is the white spirit.' He bent down and removed a packet of steel wool from a shelf beneath the vat. 'Don't put the stripped wood into the spirit until you've cleaned all the finish off. Otherwise the thinner gets all fucked up with paint remover and the finish will just set back on it when it's dry.' He glowered at Martin, dubiously. 'Don't damage the fucking wood.

Not a scratch. Not a chip. And make sure there isn't a single spot of finish left on it. You can't sand finish off this kind of wood.'

Bebe appeared in the doorway, scratching his neck furiously. 'You'd better keep an eye on him for a few minutes, Wes,' he said, taking a half-smoked cigar from his pocket and striking a match on the wall as he left.

'You think he's got fleas?' Wesley said.

They lifted the soundboard of a piano and lowered it into the first vat.

'So,' he went on, 'handouts not big enough in Scotland, eh?'

Martin dipped a piece of steel wool in the stripper vat and began rubbing at the thick ebony finish. He heard Wesley chuckling behind him. 'Look at the crap they hide under these ebony finishes.' He leaned over Martin's shoulder and pointed at the sectioned varieties of wood in the soundboard. 'Don't ever buy one of these things if you can't see the grain, boy.'

After a few minutes of scrubbing, Martin withdrew his hands. 'They're stinging,' he said. 'Are there any rubber gloves?'

'Ain't no point in using rubber gloves,' Wesley said, 'they just melt.'

A few days later, to Martin's relief, a young boy appeared at the warehouse door, looking for work. Martin was promoted to sanding the stripped piano wood while the boy scalded his hands in the vats. Fred the helper did not reappear. Wesley showed Martin a card from Rosarita Beach. 'Fred's bought a condo in Baja. Bastard's retired. No more slave labour!' he announced, as Bebe walked by. 'If I had any sense I'd do the same thing.'

At weekends Bebe's truck would pull up outside Mrs Dombrowski's in the early morning, filled with consignment goods for auction out of town. Martin would watch with amazement Bebe's sleight-of-hand at the podium as he pulled imaginary bids from thin air for rubbish, bought the best pieces back and reloaded them on to another truck for quick transportation to a store in New York State where the purloined goods could be sold profitably.

After the auctions Bebe drove away in his Cadillac and

Wesley and Martin returned to the city in the empty truck, Wesley dropping him off at the end of his street. Wesley rarely spoke when he drove, and Martin soon gave up trying to engage him in conversation.

One evening the old man asked him to drive. Martin admitted he had never learned. Wesley stared at him in disbelief.

'How old are you? And you never learned to drive? Where do kids your age go to fuck in Scotland?'

'Same place as you did, probably.'

'I doubt that very much. When I was a kid in Glasgow I used to screw girls on top of the gasometer at Riddrie.'

Martin laughed.

'You ever screw Maggie?' Wesley said suddenly.

'No.'

'How come?'

'I don't really know her.'

Wesley laughed. 'Well, she wants to bring you down to visit me next weekend. It's not my idea, believe me. She thinks I don't get enough company. I told her I see all of you I want to during the week.'

Martin arrived back at the house as the phone rang. Mrs Dombrowski beckoned to him from the kitchen. 'You shouldn't give people this number,' she said. 'It's my private number. Don't be long.'

He took the receiver.

'Thank you for the darts,' Maggie said. 'I'll give you a credit in the programme.'

'You sold it?'

'I've been given fifteen minutes for a short piece. Getting paid three hundred dollars. A musician I know saw the sculptures and fixed it up. It's real handy. I've got to move out of here soon.'

'Wesley says you want us to visit him next weekend.'

'You don't mind? Only he's kind of lonely, these days. Fred was about his only friend, and he's moved to Mexico.'

'My uncle gave me a bottle of malt whisky before I left. Maybe he'd like it.'

Mrs Dombrowski hovered beside him throughout the call. He handed her the phone and went upstairs. Jimmy and Elaine's door was closed, the room silent. He opened the refrigerator, took a beer from Jimmy's case and returned to his room, lay down on the bed and read the last few pages of *On The Road* before falling asleep, fully clothed.

Chapter twenty-two

Wesley lived on a long tree-lined street in an apartment above a fur store. Maggie and Martin climbed the white wooden stair at the back of the red sandstone building. They paused for a moment on the threshold; chilled sweat slid from beneath Martin's hat into the corners of his eyes. The screen door was unlatched and the inner door open. He knocked but no one answered. Maggie pushed by him and walked in.

Polluted sunlight glowed in the small sitting-room window on to a Lay-Z-Boy armchair, where Wesley sat facing a soundless television as if posing for an oil painting. He turned slowly and looked up at them, reaching out his hand without smiling. 'Hi, baby.'

Maggie walked over to the chair and kissed him on the forehead.

He was wearing a worsted suit with wide lapels, silk tie, new loafers, smelt of pomade, and had the air of a dispossessed king. Photographs and ornaments surrounded him on cabinets and bookcases. He looked as if he had been left alone in the apartment as a child and had grown old waiting for someone to return.

'I don't have any booze to give you, Martin,' he said, glancing at them aggressively.

Maggie winked and Martin responded to his cue. 'I brought some Laphroaig for you.' He pulled it from his coat.

Wesley stood up and perused the label, carried the bottle off to the kitchen. Maggie and Martin removed their coats and sat down on a narrow settee opposite the window. They heard a cabinet door open. Wesley returned a few minutes later with two glasses; one half-full for himself, the other containing a two finger shot for Martin. 'I don't believe in women drinking Scotch,' he said, nodding at his daughter.

To Martin's surprise Maggie did not respond. The two men sipped their drinks.

'When did you come to Canada?' Martin asked, to break the silence.

'Before you were born. Ontario was Scottish country then. They were all masons at Queen's Park. It was before Saint Laurent let all the Papes in. And all the other minorities Liberals love.' He sipped his whisky and gazed stonily at the silent TV. 'Anyway. I was a booth boxer. You know what that is? Working class kids beating the crap out of each other for money. Everybody did it where I came from. And I wasn't much good. I didn't need too much encouragement to get the hell out of there.'

'Where was that?'

'Glasgow. Place called Dennistoun. Same street as Chief Sitting Bull stayed in when he was with the Wild West show.'

'You're kidding.'

'No, I'm not kidding. Before my time, of course. I'm not that old, for Christ's sake.'

'It must have been a hard life.'

'It's hard all over.'

Maggie had remained silent during this exchange.

'Worked on the trams for a while. The Mount Florida service, through Blackhill. You know Glasgow? That was a goddamned rough area, I'll tell you. The conductress was an old broad named Flo. It was funny sometimes. In those days the pubs shut at nine thirty, and that was the end of your night out, so by ten o'clock they were all on the tram home. Well, they wouldn't pay Flo the fare and I wouldn't help her either. Shit, I didn't want any trouble. I knew when I was out of my depth. Anyway, they'd offer you anything but money. Fish and chips, glass of wine, but never money.' Wesley's chuckle disintegrated into a hacking cough. He took a sip of whisky, which seemed to calm him, and winked at Maggie.

'So,' he said to Martin, 'How do you find working for Mr Benzini?' He pronounced the boss's name bitterly.

'It's OK.'

'Where did you find this guy, baby? Under a mushroom? Typical Scottish bullshit, of course. Never say what they mean. OK in Scotland can mean anything, lousy or wonderful.'

'I suppose that's why people get rich here,' Martin said, 'They don't mind working hard.'

Wesley leaned over in his chair and gasped a hoarse laugh.

'Fifteen-hour shifts for twenty-five bucks!' He turned to Maggie. 'We pick him up at seven in the morning and he gets home at ten at night, and in between he lifts about a ton and a half of furniture. Benzini's a fucking Philistine. Knows nothing about furniture. He took over my business. I'm a craftsman, goddammit. Now I'm just a fucking dogsbody. On top of which, he's a goddamned thief.'

'What do you mean?' Martin asked.

'He buys all those antiques cheap, so he has a receipt to show the owners, then sells them out of town at the real price and puts the dough in his pocket.' He looked imperiously at Martin. 'So anyway, where does getting rich come into your picture?'

'I don't mind. I'm not going to do it for the rest of my life.'

'Ah.' Wesley reclined his chair and closed his eyes. 'I'm not going to do it for the rest of my life. I'm not going to end my days like this dumb old fuck, is that what you mean?'

Martin gulped hurriedly from his glass.

'This is real good whisky, Martin,' Wesley said, opening his eyes. 'Not long ago you could get arrested for bringing that over here to me. Liquor laws dictated we all drink alone. The divide-and-rule principle, beloved by all rulers. You have to fill in a goddamned form to even buy the stuff. Which may explain the insular and inhospitable temperament that thrives in these parts.'

He finished his glass.

'And the weather. The winters don't make for much conviviality in the natives either.'

Martin looked to Maggie for inspiration.

'You see the Leafs the other night?'

'I think so. I think I saw them in a bar. Someone threw an octopus on the ice.'

Through the open window they could hear traffic idling at the stoplights below. A peal of laughter rose from the street.

'Five years I've been up here,' Wesley mumbled, 'and I don't know anyone.'

At five o'clock, after nearly an hour of silence, the old man struggled laboriously to his feet and turned up the sound on the TV. It was a game show. He picked up his empty glass from the arm of the chair and, without speaking shuffled out into the kitchen, stooping as he passed to collect Martin's glass. Maggie followed him. The laughter of the game show audience was deafening and hysterical. From the kitchen the sound of a whistling kettle insinuated itself into the bedlam in the living room. A few minutes later Wesley reappeared, carrying a tray of coffee mugs; Maggie followed with a plate of enormous donuts.

Wesley lifted his mug in a toast. 'One thing about this country,' he said, as if resuming an interrupted conversation, 'is good coffee.' He leaned back in his chair and stretched his legs over the foot-rest. 'Not like that shit they give you in the Old Country.' He slurped contentedly.

An hour later Maggie stood up. 'We better get going, Dad.'

Wesley walked with them to the veranda and leaned against the railing, chewing a wedge of imaginary tobacco, and staring over the neighbourhood yards towards the city. 'Well, he's a good worker,' he said to Maggie. 'Knows all the woods now, don't you boy? Knows how to make glue, how to mix finishes. And he's got good hands for wood, but his mind wanders.'

'You should get these compliments in writing,' Maggie said.

'Thanks for your hospitality.' Martin offered Wesley a handshake, which the old man ignored.

'Shit, it's cold,' he said, expelling a trail of saliva over the steps, watching it fall to the railing below, where it spun and gleamed in the crisp sunlight.

'Spring soon,' Martin said.

'One more snowfall at Easter and then maybe.'

The sun slipped behind a cloud. Martin pulled his coat around him as a gust of cool air blew across the veranda. 'Thanks for the coffee,' he said, commencing his descent of the stairs.

'An old guy's a boring companion for young people.'

Martin muttered a denial, but Wesley had opened the screen door and pulled Maggie back into the room. Martin turned the corner at the first floor and felt a sticky sensation on his palm as his hand brushed over Wesley's freezing expectoration.

'Listen, Maggie,' he heard Wesley say, 'if you want a child, have one of your own.'

'What do you mean?'

'He doesn't complain. That's a strength. He's a nice kid, but don't you think he's a little passive? All these kids are. Never stand up for themselves.'

'Really?'

'The new kid who took over from your buddy here. Getting his hands burned to hell in that stripper. Jesus.'

'You did the same thing yourself when you started.'

'That's different. I always figured that I was unusually dumb.'

Martin climbed back up the stairs and looked in through the screen door. Maggie and her father were standing together, their feet touching, their arms around each other.

'Shit, though,' Wesley said, 'if he was a man he'd tell Benzini to shove his job. Only a boy puts up with that crap.'

She rested her hand on his shoulder. 'Are you OK?'

He shrugged. 'I got a terrible Charley Horse in my leg. I got boils. My mouth tastes like a parrot cage. Otherwise I'm fine.'

'Your colour's bad. You don't look well.'

'It's old age, Maggie. It's got nothing to recommend it.'

'Apart from wisdom.'

'Oh yeah, right, apart from wisdom. I look at my body and it's someone else's. Still can't stop looking at all those cute young girls.'

She kissed him.

'It's unbelievable what you have to do to get by,' he said. 'You have a marriage which is nothing, and that makes you half of nothing. You prostitute yourself, lie, do whatever is necessary. In the beginning you think you have some kind of vitally important message to carry, which must get through, and that's how you live with all your betrayals, and how you can go on living with yourself when you despise yourself.'

Maggie reached up and stroked his arm, but Wesley only smiled, coughed, and finished his speech. 'One morning you wake up and you can't even remember the fucking message, and where does that leave you? All that debasement for nothing.'

He opened the screen door. 'Anyway, don't worry about me. Worry about you. The air here is bad, that's all. It gets me down. Too many chemicals. If I had the dough I'd move to Phoenix, or down to Baja with Fred.' He winked. 'Fred still gets plenty of action, you know. And he's older than me.'

'That was strange,' Martin said, as they returned to the car. 'And you didn't say much.'

'Well, he likes you. He's only polite to people he doesn't like.'

'He didn't even give me any Laphroaig. My whisky tasted as if it was made in a bathtub.'

'Wouldn't surprise me.'

Chapter twenty-three

Maggie drove him back to Mrs Dombrowski's. On the way home they stopped at the Chinatown bar and had a beer. As they returned to the car Maggie looked across the street. Through the tall windows of the community centre they could see a group of Chinese women and ungainly, self-conscious westerners practising t'ai chi, watched by a taciturn old man. Occasionally he grabbed a student's arm and muttered a brusque instruction.

'What's that?' Martin said. They crossed the road and stood in the hallway of the centre, watching the class. 'Yoga?'

'It's like yoga. I came to a class once. They believe you have this cosmic energy inside you, which is blocked up in most people. You do these exercises and it liberates all your energy. You don't get sick. It's a martial art too, you speed it up and it's like Kung Fu. They say you can't even touch a t'ai chi Master. They can disappear at will, and knock you down with pure energy.'

They waited for the group to finish.

'I don't have the patience,' she said, as they returned to the car. 'It takes six months to learn all the moves.'

She hardly spoke until she pulled up at the door of Mrs Dombrowski's. 'Life's short, isn't it?' she said. 'There's so much to know, and no time.'

'It seems endless to me,' Martin said.

They exchanged a long look and Martin felt his spirits sink. Maggie's expression seemed contradictory; the right eye, weak, afraid, the left, curious and alert. He knew she was searching him for something he lacked.

'You don't want to do anything tonight?' he asked.

'I'd love to, Martin, but I've got to work.'

The electric window hummed shut as he leaned over to kiss her.

It was only after the lowrider had skidded precariously away along the icy street to the main road that he realised this almost automatic kiss was their first.

He pushed through the screen door and came face to face with Mrs Dombrowski. Her expression was cold and distressed. 'Where have you been?'

'I was visiting a friend,' he said.

'How well you know that guy upstairs?'

'Who? Jimmy?'

'Yes.'

'Not very well. Why? What's wrong?'

'I never had any trouble here before.'

'Really. I don't know him at all. What happened?'

She turned her back and walked off down the hall. Martin stood uncertainly at the foot of the stairs. 'Come,' she said. He followed.

When they reached the dining-room she sat down heavily in the first available chair and sighed. 'There's coffee in the pot, if you like,' she said coldly, nodding at a percolator on the sideboard. 'There's a cup and saucer in the kitchen, in the cupboard over the sink.'

'What happened?' Martin asked again, returning from the kitchen, sitting down opposite her and pouring himself a cup. He replenished hers.

She nodded curtly. 'He try to kill his wife. I wake up at eight, hear her screaming, him screaming, all kinds of noise. Then nothing. You'd already gone, I guess.'

Martin nodded.

'Well, I'm an old woman. And he's a big man. Well, he's skinny but strong. I didn't want to go up there. It was so quiet suddenly. I couldn't hear anything. But anyway, I go upstairs. I get to the kitchen and I can hear someone sobbing now. Both of them. The door is open, so I go in. He's got her in one hand, and a knife in the other. Blood everywhere. He's crying. She's crying. What could I do? I came back downstairs and called the police. He didn't say anything. They take him away, and the ambulance takes her. They're waving at each other as the cruiser drives away.'

They sat in silence for several minutes. Children shouted in the next yard. A bird chirped on the phone wire by the upstairs window.

'Are you all right?'

'No, of course I'm not all right.' She glanced briefly at Martin. 'You're not taking drugs up there?'

'No,' Martin said.

'I don't want any of that here. We had plenty of bad times and we never took drugs. You people don't know what bad times are.' She stood up slowly, lifted Martin's half finished cup from the table, and carried it through to the kitchen.

Martin folded his hands on the table and ruminated aimlessly. When Mrs Dombrowski did not reappear, he rose to his feet and went back along the hallway and out on to the porch. He smoked a cigarette and returning indoors, went upstairs to the kitchen. As he entered he thought he could taste vomit, but the impression lasted only a moment. Afternoon sunlight shone in the window. The door to Jimmy and Elaine's room was ajar, but he did not enter. The house seemed deserted. The neighbourhood was quiet, unnaturally silent. He went to his room. On the floor inside he found a letter with an Edinburgh postmark, the address scrawled in Robertson's ornate copperplate.

Dear Martin, he read,

I'm in the study at the mahogany desk, where you often espied me in the evenings from your incommodious vantage point in the rose bush by the window. Before me is your charming Christmas card, depicting an unfamiliar hybrid conifer draped picturesquely in snow, and within your cryptic message conveying a desire that your mother and I enjoy a 'Merry Christmas'.

Merriment would be a somewhat hyperbolic description of our mood on that day. I assure you however, we did rise to occasional moments of Good Humour. Your mother prepared a delightful luncheon, consisting in the traditional fowl, seasonal vegetables, flaming pudding, mince pies, and so forth. "All the trimmings", is I believe, the expression. We were sadly conscious of your absence, and this impinged on what might have otherwise been a day of unbridled high spirits.

I trust you passed the Christmas period pleasantly. You provide no details of your accommodations and circumstances. It has been some time since your departure, however, and the confirmation that your card provided, that you do have an address, indicates your first contact with the New World has not been an unmitigated disaster. I have assured Alberta that we may safely assume you would have returned poste haste *to your native shores should your survival have been seriously at risk. It would be gratifying for both of us to receive further news – of your sources of income, new acquaintances, impressions of the amenities and modes of livelihood available to you in your new locality. I hope you will favour us in future with correspondence on these matters.*

As I write, I periodically lay down my pen to listen to a gramophone record which is currently playing. It contains a performance of a reel composed by the great Scott Skinner. I'm sure you would recall the piece. Perhaps you are unaware that the performer on the record is the extraordinary Jean Carignan, the musical prodigy from Québec. Despite the absence of any noteworthy culture in your new home, I wonder if you have had the good fortune to attend a performance by Monsieur Carignan? I have, of course, taken great delight in the performances of the Hot Club of Paris, *which you so kindly presented to me.*

Affairs at the Institute are proceeding as fruitlessly as usual. In recent weeks there have been very few inquiries from the general public regarding our work. Some of our friends have left us, one in particular explaining, in what I would describe as a tirade of quite intemperate vituperation, his disillusionment with the vision of life espoused by myself. I could not entirely fault his scepticism, assailed as I am by many doubts in the vision I wish to impart, and I realise it cannot be easy to sustain loyalty to the eccentric philosophy of an alternative evolution, after the initial enthusiasm has worn off. I believe this man's friends had begun to ridicule his spiritual interests, and it came as no surprise that he finally succumbed to the baleful influence of unenlightened public opinion.

Due to these setbacks, and much encouraged by your mother's abiding faith in the views I hold but express with such ineptitude, I am passing more of the time here in the study, committing my thoughts to paper, in the hope that they may prove instructive to whomever may read them in the future. I find the home environment – the ancient bookcases, the antique desk, oak panelling, the poorly executed, and probably specious family portraits in their ostentatious frames, conducive to a sense of comforting ephemerality. It is reassuring for me to contemplate, as I often do, the relative insignificance of one man's ecstasies and tribulations in this everlasting universe of things. How inconsequential one's mistakes seem in this larger context.

You are, I need hardly remind you, constantly in our thoughts. I hope your new life proves salutary. I wonder if you have made contact with your grandmother?

Your mother asks me to send her love. She intends to write you, but, as I recall from the period of her sojourn in England, she may well not. Do not think badly of her, or that your affairs are a matter of indifference to her. Nothing could be further from the truth. Some people merely find it difficult to express themselves by way of a letter. Perhaps you have inherited this reticence from her.

With affection, Melibee Robertson.

Martin lay back on the bed, clutching the letter. The echo of Robertson's obsessive, meandering burr filled the room, and the unnerving, empty, floating sensation he had sometimes experienced when listening to one of his uncle's talks. He fell asleep and woke in the evening to hear Mrs Dombrowski in the kitchen, running water into a bucket. He went out into the hall. The kitchen floor was covered with blood soaked linen and piles of clothes. Through the open doorway of Jimmy and Elaine's room he heard the old woman scrubbing at the floor. He pushed open the door and went in behind her, staring over her shoulder into the pink suds slopping queasily in her bucket.

'Can I help?'

She stood up stiffly, rubbing her knees. 'I been sick already.'

He took the brush from her hand. 'If you felt like making coffee, I'll finish this off.'

She looked up at the wall behind the bed. 'That's the worst. I'll have to get new wallpaper. That will all come off if you wash it, but I can't have a new tenant moving in with those stains. It's not sanitary.' She turned towards the door. 'You sure you don't mind?'

'I could do with some coffee in a while.'

'Sure. OK.'

He sat down on the stripped bed and listened to the linoleum clattering as she made her way downstairs. An insidious stink rose from the mattress. He stood up again, took the bucket to the kitchen, watched the pink froth swirl down the drain, threads of loosening blood spinning in a crimson arc before vanishing. He filled the bucket with soap, bleach and water and went back to scrub the walls. He worked enthusiastically, taking a perverse pleasure in the distraction of blood, the stink of the mattress, the odours of bleach and grease, and coffee floating up from the old woman's kitchen. He was glad also to dispel the uneasy aftermath of Robertson's letter in physical labour.

As Mrs Dombrowski had predicted, the wallpaper began to peel off as it became wet. He tore away the loose strips and smoothed down the wall, pulled the bed away from the wall and swept underneath, wiped the TV and the tiny window overlooking the backyard. He searched through a chest of drawers behind the door for Jimmy and Elaine's belongings. There were only a few clothes, a broken watch, the *nunchaku* sticks, but no letters, or other personal items.

Only their anonymity remained, as eloquent as a portrait. He returned to the kitchen as the old woman's head appeared at the top of the stairs. Street-light, brightened by snow on the sill shone in the kitchen window. 'Coffee,' she said.

He followed her downstairs to the dining-room, sat down and watched her pour the coffee. 'So,' she said, handing him his cup, 'did you ever bury money in the yard?'

'No, I forgot.'

'Well, I expect you'll remember this place anyway.'

He finished the coffee and went up to his room, shaved, put on his coat and hat and went out, walking back across town to the Chinatown bar.

Carson and one of the folk singers were leaning on the fence of a neighbouring house, smoking a joint. Inside, a reggae band played; a deafening, atonal bass rattled the bar windows.

'Cold, eh?' Carson said.

'Zero degrees Kelvin,' Martin said, 'at the most.'

He told them about Jimmy and Elaine.

'Jesus,' the folk singer said.

'I'd like to get drunk,' Martin said. 'You want something?'

'You're OK,' Carson said.

Martin went into the bar and returned a few minutes later with full glass of rye. 'Actually, I don't really want this.' He offered the glass to Carson, who passed it to the folk singer, who drank it immediately.

'This is Marc,' Carson said.

Martin and Marc shook hands.

'Want to leave town?' Carson said.

'Why?'

'I'm going back to Montreal. I miss Sally. And Marc here and his buddies are heading off West. We're all going to live on pogey for a while.'

'You could come with us, if you like,' Marc said. 'A tight squeeze, but we got a station wagon. And girls.'

'It'll be an exciting journey at this time of year,' Carson said. 'They don't even have chains.'

'It sounds great, Marc, but I'm going to stay for a while.'

'You won't find any girls in T.O. like Québec girls.'

'That's true,' Carson said.

'I know,' Martin said.

'You should go in and dance for a while,' Marc said, 'Warm up your bones. Talk to Joelle.' He pointed through the glass of the door at a Hispanic-looking girl at a table by the little dance floor.

'She likes blond guys.'

'I can't dance,' Martin said.

'Everybody can dance.'

'Not me. I think too much.'

'Hmmm. A good poke is what you need.'

'I know.' He shook hands with Carson. 'I've got to go. I'm tired. I don't feel like being here after all, but I'm glad I saw you. You really helped me out.'

'No problem.'

'Sorry about the Novahystex.'

'That's OK.' Carson took a pen from his inside pocket and wrote down two addresses on a grocery receipt he retrieved from his pocket. 'This one is my parents' place in Montreal,' he said, handing the receipt to Martin. 'And this is the cabin. If you're ever in Québec, come and see us.'

'I will. Good luck ... You're a folk singer, Marc,' Martin said, as he turned to leave.

'I play fiddle and boots.'

'Boots?'

'Yeah.'

'Have you ever heard of Jean Carignan? My uncle keeps asking me about him.'

'The taxi driver?'

'No. He's a fiddler.'

'No, he drives cab.'

'I heard he was one of the greatest violin players in the world.'

'Maybe in the world he's a great fiddler, but in Canada he drives cab.'

'Wow,' Martin said and, following Marc's cue, fell into a brief, respectful silence.

'I've got to be getting inside,' Carson said, walking to the bar door. 'Too cold out here for me.'

'Ya, me too,' Marc said, nodding at Martin, 'Take her easy, man,' he said, following Carson and closing the door behind him.

In the background Martin saw Joelle glance in his direction and smile. Turning for home he stepped off the kerb into a lake of freezing slush.

The house was in darkness. He removed his soaking shoes and left them at the door. As he turned on the kitchen light cockroaches scattered from the sink and the cooker, vanishing into a thousand crevices behind the cupboards and the furniture. In his room the congested floor of the roach motel fluttered with gesticulating insects. He peered at them pitifully, sympathetically, feeling immobilised himself by the adhesive surface of his own world. He sat down on the bed and lit a cigarette, then stood up and went to the window.

It was snowing again; big flakes melted on the hot window and he looked down into the dark street. A middle-aged black woman was making her way gingerly along the icy sidewalk, pulling a small trolley loaded with bags of groceries. She paused to lean against a street-light and looked up suddenly at his window, the only source of light on the building. They stared at each other, or so it seemed, although it was too dark and the woman too far away for Martin to see her eyes or even her face clearly. As he watched her he could feel a part of himself slipping away, and observed with relief an undefined but crucial change occur in him. He wanted to invite the woman up to his room but she had been accosted by a white-haired rubby who had staggered shouting from an alleyway behind the apartment building across the street, and was already moving on. Besides, he thought, she would never have come.

He thought about the people he had watched struggling through the saline mud on Spadina Avenue, and wondered why it had ever occurred to him that he was in any way noteworthy; or that from his infinitesimal point of observation he would ever begin to see the wider panorama, all the infinite kinds of happiness, confusion, sorrow – precise, durable emotions that would always remain private, or at least an enigma to him, because each life was an entire world, and how could he see it all, remember it, classify it, let alone understand it, all that energy, experience, all that knowledge?

He remained at the window and watched the wino, his shadow swaying in the street-light, watching the woman, raising his arm in an ironical farewell, and spitting a long drool into the gutter that froze on his lips. From a pocket in his jacket he pulled out a small bottle and took a swig, turning suddenly as if having heard someone behind him, and losing his footing, balanced for a moment on one foot like a tightrope walker, astonished by his own grace.

Chapter twenty-four

After numerous false alarms that lasted for several weeks, spring came. The storm drains in all the streets flooded with rivers of melting snow and the trees metamorphosed overnight from a state of petrifaction into a renaissant world of green. Martin remained at Mrs Dombrowski's and continued working periodically on the saga of Saint Shabby. Letters from Robertson arrived regularly, but he heard nothing from Ray or Christine, and eventually no longer noticed his disappointment at their silence.

A salesman moved into Jimmy and Elaine's room, his rare appearances in the apartment signalled by the playing of Frank Sinatra records and the soundtracks of musicals in his room late into the night. Martin wrote a letter to Alberta which was answered by Robertson with his usual prolixity. He still went to the bar on Friday night, but missed the company of Carson and the Québecois, watched the bands and sat alone, talking to no one in the friendly crowd. He continued working at Benzini's, and met Maggie occasionally. *The Soul Kitchen* had received a good review in a local paper. They visited Wesley, whose health seemed to be in progressive decline, his pallor yellowing as the weeks passed.

One afternoon the Plymouth drew up at the warehouse gate. Martin and Wesley were dragging a heavy loading plate from Bebe's truck into the loading dock at the rear of the warehouse. The car horn sounded and Martin looked up as Wesley dropped the plate on the cement door of the dock. A deafening metallic crash echoed through the building.

'Do you have to drop it like that?' Martin said.

Wesley ignored him.

'Can't we just lay it down, rather than dropping it?'

'Stop whining,' Wesley retorted. He looked up the driveway. 'You got a girlfriend in Scotland?'

'Sort of,' Martin said. 'I did have.'

'Well, you better go back there and find her. You won't get anywhere with Maggie.'

Martin looked at Wesley in surprise, then jumped from the dock, hurried up the drive and climbed into the passenger seat of the Plymouth.

'Hungry?' Maggie inquired.

'Fucking starving.'

She drove at her usual languid pace to Yonge Street and pulled up at a tiny wood fronted restaurant with blinds in the windows, sandwiched between two office buildings. They took a table by the window next to the cash register. Martin toyed with a spiral plastic honey server and stared out at the traffic. Exhaust fumes floated by the window; jewels of colour illuminated the dusty haze, the bright clothing of passers-by, regenerating trees, ornamental flowers in glass fronted offices. An old woman at a corner table picked at her meal like a praying mantis. A waitress in a shapeless, bleached-out dress, an expression of etiolated blankness on her face, wandered aimlessly from the cash register to the kitchen at the back, carrying a saucer, or a pot of honey, as if unaware of her actions.

'Did you ever see Marat Sade?' Martin asked.

'Come again?'

'Not much of an advertisement for the food.'

After some minutes he lit a cigarette. A waitress materialised at his elbow. 'There's no smoking in here.'

He returned her colourless stare. 'Then could I have a menu, please?'

He stepped to the door to discard the cigarette, and the woman wandered away to the kitchen, locating the door apparently by accident. She returned some minutes later with the menu. 'The special today is millet goulash. The soup is parsnip broth.'

'I'll have the zucchini and turnip breadcake,' Martin said morosely. 'And perhaps we could have a colonic while we're waiting?'

'You're a real fuddy-duddy, aren't you?' Maggie said. 'You're like those American tourists who stay at the Holiday Inn wherever they go because the bed and the closet are always in the same place.'

She ordered mushroom soup and an avocado sandwich. The waitress evaporated before they had time to ask for drinks.

'It's not the food that bothers me, it's the fact they make you feel like part of a conspiracy when you eat in these places.'

'Actually, they're not all like this.' She smiled patiently. 'So. You must be getting tired of your rooming house?'

'I wouldn't mind a change.' He told her about Jimmy and Elaine. 'And if I get woken up one more time by *The Surrey With The Fringe On Top*, I may get dragged out of there with blood on my hands.'

'Well, you can have my place, if you want it. The rent's controlled. The landlord doesn't declare it as income.'

'Have you found somewhere else?'

'I got another commission. It's out West. They saw the review. I had an idea for something I'm calling *The Cockroach Cathedral*. They're giving me the money for it. The stage will be the inside of a roach motel. All the dancers are stuck to the floor, like cockroaches, right? They can only move their arms, or at the most one foot. It's beautiful. I got some of the idea from those t'ai chi women. Remember? I started learning the set ...' She spoke in a rush, looking around him, rarely at him. Martin felt himself disappearing. '...and in the end ... this is great ... the Cockroach God appears, and he gives them this kind of burning-bush religious speech ... It's not very long ... about how they have to have faith in futility, and futility will set them free. And then, suddenly, they're no longer stuck to the floor, they're completely free.'

'It sounds like hell.'

'We may live like cockroaches,' she said, 'but we can dream like angels.'

Martin smiled to cover his embarrassment. 'I'd love to see it.'

'I didn't think you liked that kind of thing.'

'I thought *The Soul Kitchen* was great.'

'You only saw the set. You never saw the dance. Besides, you never say what you mean, Martin. It's your religion.'

'When are you going?'

'Hey, man, don't look so sad,' she said. 'You should be happy for me. I've been real lucky. It can take a long time to get a break. There are a whole lot of talented people growing old here waiting for a break like that. A real commission.'

'I am glad. But you're about the only person I know here.'

'So. Make some new friends.'

'I'm not interested in making new friends.'

'That's the spirit.' She laughed. 'It's T.O. No one wants to go out in the winter. Everybody's like that. But now it's spring, OK? Time for a change.' She reached over the table to him, rested her hands on his. 'Listen Martin. I do like you. But all things must pass, right? My time for being in T.O. is over now.'

'Sure,' he said. 'I'd do the same thing ...'

'You could do me a favour though,' she said.

'You want more hair?'

'No!' She laughed. 'But maybe you could look in on Dad sometimes. He doesn't look so hot. He is kind of boring, but he likes you.'

'I see him at work every day.'

'Yeah, but no one ever visits him at the apartment. And he'll be lonely when I go.'

Throughout lunch they amused each other with a running commentary on the idiosyncrasies of people in the crowd passing by the café window, chatting casually as if nothing momentous had happened, although Martin felt as if he'd been detached from an anchor and set adrift.

'So. Do you want to see the apartment?' Maggie said as she paid the bill. 'Really, I insist – I'm celebrating.'

As they entered the street Martin lit a cigarette. At the Bloor Street intersection a crowd had gathered at the crosswalk waiting for the light to change.

'I've seen them waiting at two in the morning when there's no traffic,' Martin said.

'If you carry on like this,' Maggie retorted, 'someone is going to say to you, "If you don't like it, why don't you leave?"'

'I mean, they're so bloody law-abiding, and then you get characters like that,' he continued, indicating a swarthy middle-aged man in a sandwich board, pacing back and forth on the opposite the corner.

COMMUNISTS STOLE My WIFE
Took Her AGAINST HER WILL To LATVIA
COMMUNIST SYMPATHISERS
In the LIBERAL GOVERNMENT
Helped TERRORISTS in the
ABDUCTION and FORCible DIVORCE
VICTIM OF THE CATHOLIC/COMMUNIST CONSPIRACY

Maggie's new apartment was on the first floor above a corner restaurant in a quiet working class stretch of Queen Street. There were four rooms. A bathroom and kitchen, each the size of a closet, a sunlit bedroom, and a newly painted room converted for living and working, with rush matting on the floors, lamps and paper blinds, paintings on the walls, the smell of turpentine.

She made coffee and they climbed through the kitchen window on to a flat roof. Below was a courtyard opening into a quiet, residential street, running north. City skyline looped the horizon like a row of broken teeth.

'It's a palace,' Martin said.

'I'm glad you like it. I did a big spring clean in your honour. Can you make the down payment?'

'The way I feel about it, I'd rob a bank.'

'Well, it's yours in a week. You can say goodbye to *Oklahoma*. I'm leaving Saturday.'

He looked across the city, encouraged by the elevated perspective. A cluster of sparrows flew by and settled like black leaves in the neighbouring trees. Maggie climbed back through the window and returned with two bottles of beer.

'You were telling me about a cartoon you were working on. How's it going?'

He shrugged. 'I do a bit every now and then. I can't imagine ever finishing it. Whenever something new happens, I just do another drawing.'

'Who is Saint Shabby, anyway?'

'Well, he started off as someone I knew once, then I saw your saints, but now I think he's becoming me.'

She reached up and rested her hand on his cheek. 'You've been on your own for a while.'

'Well, yes.'

'You bought me a coffee once. Remember that?'

He laughed. 'It seems a long time ago.'

'I was having a miserable day,' she said. 'I was standing there in the cold, with all those ridiculous candles. I felt ridiculous. It made my day when you bought me that coffee.'

Martin ran his fingers through her hair. Her eyes absorbed his attention and he escaped from himself briefly, watching her change second by second.

'There's something I want to give you,' she said.

Chapter twenty-five

She broke open the popper and held the pungent handkerchief over his nose. His heart raced, he felt his face burn, his blood rush out of control, and he wondered if he was about to die.

As they kissed he thought of Christine's light, mischievous body, comparing the women, laughing to himself, imagining Christine's likely rebuke: 'Two birds and you're a connoisseur already!'

Maggie's body felt weighty and powerful in his hands, as if every muscle was synchronised for maximum power. He clung to her like an acrobat on a whale, laughing silently from deep in his belly at his own lack of control. Their sweat ran together. He had never experienced so much heat. Every spark of energy in his body flowed into his penis, and his brain stopped working altogether. He was relieved, relaxed, filled with pain, longing, love, hunger, sorrow, loneliness.

When she fell asleep he watched her in the moonlight. She slept soundlessly. Her skin, bathed in silver light was immaculate, her face beautiful, ageless, humourless.

'I love you,' he said, aloud – at the same time thinking, I don't want to be with you.

He woke early, oppressed by an unremembered dream. Leaving the door on the latch he went downstairs and bought rolls and cakes from a bakery on the opposite corner.

Returning to the apartment, he made coffee and joined Maggie on the bed as she awoke. 'Where's Goeballs?' he said.

'I took him to the vet for a hot shot.'

'What?'

'Well, I couldn't take him with me, could I?'

'Why not?' he shouted, surprising them both. 'I could have taken him!'

He threw the cakes across the room. Maggie suppressed a smile.

'Shit, Maggie.'

'Jesus. If I'd thought you would have taken him I would have given him to you, for God's sake.'

'Of course I would have taken him.'

'Well, it's too late now.'

He stood up and stepped back a pace from the bed.

Suddenly she was crying. 'See?' she said. 'This is what happens when you're not ideal. When you're not fucking perfect. Like you could change shape to be whatever someone wanted.'

'What do you mean?' he said, hesitating between the bed and the door.

'What do you want, Martin?'

'What do I want? I don't know. I want everything. I want you and I don't want you.' He shrugged. 'I want two lives. Another life to do the things I decided not to do in this life.'

Maggie regarded him scornfully 'That's what you call greed, man. Having your cake and eating it. Never being committed. I'll tell you what's ironic, Martin. You'll spend all your time trying to have both lives and you'll end up with no life.' She jumped out of bed and put on a T-shirt. 'It's all yours,' she said. 'Come any time after Saturday.' She pulled on her jeans and stood for a moment, not looking at him, waving her arms slowly, back and forth, as if trying to discharge static from the air. 'I'm not taking anything else, so you can have whatever there is. The landlord runs the restaurant. I'll leave the keys with him.'

Martin paused at the door, looked helplessly around the room. Maggie came over to him. They kissed and he left.

Three days later, when he moved into the apartment, he found a pencil sketch of himself on the bed. Beneath the sketch, a title: *The Programmed Conversation, with Curls.* He would carry the picture with him for years and when he came across it would wonder what she had meant by it.

Chapter twenty-six

In late July the humidity intensified until the apartment perspired like a fevered body. Muscular bolts of lightning flashed over the city, deafening thunder followed. Returning from work Martin passed the afternoons at the aluminium table in the kitchen, watching baseball games on TV, or he would move his chair out on to the roof to drink beer in the long, sticky evenings. He passed this time reading or drawing, rising from time to time to stretch his legs and look down over the roof into the courtyard where the apartment janitor swept dust back and forth across the Tarmac, like a Japanese monk in a temple garden. A pair of cockroaches, stowaways from his suitcase, were busily bringing forth a dynasty behind the baseboards.

As darkness fell he wandered across the city to Chinatown, or up Yonge Street to sit in bars and listen to rock music, succumbing in the early hours to loneliness and fatigue, returning to the apartment as tired neighbourhood drunks staggered home from the local tavern. One evening he fell asleep on the streetcar and woke as it reached the beach. He walked down a warm street that smelt of honeysuckle and barbecued steak. Voices murmured from the shade of porches. He continued on to the boardwalk and gazed contemptuously at the placid lake. Lifeless waves splashed on the shore. Not even a real sea, he thought. Torches flashed along the gravel; children ran by brandishing grunion nets. The smell of mussels on his fingers came into his mind, and a fleeting smile he could hardly recollect. A woman with a curious dog passed him. He smoked as he walked, tossing the butt into the black water and watching it float to shore.

'I hate this fucking job,' he said one afternoon as Wesley dropped him off at the apartment. 'Bebe is ripping people off all the time.'

'Every job's like that,' Wesley said. 'It's the nature of the beast.'

'I thought I'd be getting away from all that.'

'From work?' Wesley raised an eyebrow. 'Fat chance.' He turned off the ignition. 'What's the matter with you? Homesick?'

'I don't know. To be honest, I'm half terrified most of the time. I don't have anything to go back to, and I can't think what kind of future I've got, unless I just keep travelling and hope for something better later on. I didn't even know my father. And my uncle tries to understand things, but he can't make sense of anything. And my mother hardly speaks. What am I supposed to do? I shouldn't be laying all this on you, you've got troubles of your own.'

Wesley took a hip flask from the pocket of his coveralls and unscrewed the cap.

'Sorry,' Martin said. 'I didn't even know I was feeling like that.'

Wesley took a swig and handed Martin the flask. He breathed in a sea wind, salty, peaty, sunlit. 'Laphroaig?'

'Don't tell Bebe I drink and drive,' Wesley said. 'He'd probably like to get rid of me. Can't do much lifting, these days. Some days I feel rough.'

'And I miss Maggie,' Martin said, following his own train of thought. 'Other people too, but mostly Maggie, even though we're not that close.'

'So. What are your plans?'

'I don't know. It's time I went home, I suppose.'

'How long since you came?'

'About a year, a bit less.'

'That's not so long.'

'I only expected to be here for a few weeks.'

'The first seven years are the worst,' Wesley said, taking back the flask. 'And what about Scotland? You really anxious to go back? Think you'll feel more at home there now?'

'My family is there.'

Wesley nodded.

'Don't you ever miss it?' Martin asked.

'Scotland? Shit, yes. Of course I miss it sometimes. I'll hear some music or something. Or I'll think about someone.' He leaned back in his seat, took a sip from the flask. 'I was going back with all the money I was going to make in Canada. Buy the folks a new car. My mother new clothes. A stove. But it never happened. I sent them money, that was all. I guess I never wanted to go back. And they never wanted to come here. Then they died, and that, as they say, is all she wrote.' He drained the flask and pushed it back into his pocket. 'I better get going.'

'Me too,' Martin said. He opened the passenger door. 'I know I'm wasting my breath, but I think you should see a doctor.'

Wesley's glance revealed desperation.

'I just mean, maybe a doctor could give you a line ... you could take a few days off.'

'Oh, don't worry about me,' Wesley said. He changed the subject. 'I can appreciate it's not that simple,' he said. 'Your family being in Scotland and all that. But you've stuck it out for a year.'

Martin let the door fall shut and leaned back in his seat.

'Limey cultural snobbery,' Wesley said. 'Everyone has it. They think people here are too materialistic, that all anyone thinks about is money. That's America. Not Canada. You've made friends here. You have a job. You're learning a skill. You're beginning to put together a life that you made for yourself, not one that was given to you by your father, or your social standing, or the way you talk. It's your own. You may not like it, but it's yours.'

'I don't feel like a Canadian.'

Wesley leaned over and pushed open the door, laughing weakly.

'That's what it feels like to be Canadian, Martin. Believe me, it's a change from the Yanks and the Brits, or the Scots, who are always so damn sure who they are.'

He started the engine. Martin climbed out, slammed the door, and leaned through the open window. 'Thanks, Wesley.'

'Thanks for what?'

'The whisky.'

'Maybe it's time you had a vacation. You must be due a week or two. I'll talk to Benzini.'

'Oh, I don't know.'

'I'll give you some dough for the rent. Why not take a month off? See the country or something. Get a driveaway to Florida, or something.'

'I don't know …'

'You don't know how to drive. Right. How old are you?'

The next morning Martin arrived at the warehouse to find Wesley and Bebe deep in conversation. He began working at his bench, filling the scratches on a newly-stripped piano soundboard with plastic wood. A few minutes later, Bebe appeared at his shoulder, waving a brown envelope in his face. 'The old fellow reckons you need a vacation.'

Martin opened the envelope and found two one hundred-dollar bills.

'I can't spare you for long,' Bebe said. 'Three weeks at the most. Wes is finding it hard enough to keep up.' He nodded towards the door. 'You may as well get going now.'

Martin laid down the pallet knife and collected his coat.

'Don't forget to come back,' Bebe said. 'Half of that is an advance.'

Wesley looked up from his work. 'Got a plan?'

'Maybe I'll start my own business,' Martin said.

Wesley took out his wallet. 'Listen. You can't get far when you got rent to pay. I told you I'd help with the rent.'

Martin held up his hand in refusal, and Wesley shoved a hundred-dollar bill into his palm. 'A promise is a promise. I don't have anything to spend it on anyway.'

Martin walked home across the Don Valley Bridge, ate a late breakfast in the restaurant downstairs from the apartment, crossed the road to the sporting goods store and bought a sleeping bag, a canvas travelling bag with a Montreal Canadiens logo, and a pair of cheap sunglasses. He returned to the apartment and packed a few clothes, the switchblade, the copy of *On The Road*, his notebook of Saint Shabby sketches, and the remains of a mickey of whisky.

He rode the subway to the north end of the city and caught

a bus to Highway Ten. It was already four o'clock when he walked down the on-ramp and stuck out his thumb. A steady stream of traffic spun past him like racing cars from a starting grid, tyres screeching and exhaust belching, demented, wild-eyed drivers fleeing the city. After a few minutes a horn sounded from the jam of waiting cars. A middle-aged man with two children beckoned him through the windshield of a new Buick. He opened the passenger door and Martin climbed in, as the children, a boy of about eight and a girl a year or two older, clambered over into the back seat. He smiled at the man and the children and reached for his cigarettes, but noticed a heavy smell of pine deodorant and a green cardboard fir tree hanging from the driver's mirror. A transfer on the glove compartment read, 'Thank you for not smoking.'

'Sorry,' the man said, 'but Rupert has asthma.' He jerked his thumb towards the back seat where the small boy peered back at Martin. The car drove north at a steady sixty. No one spoke. Vapour trails evaporated in the high summer sky. Martin removed his coat and reached into his bag for the sunglasses, leaned his head on the seatback and watched the white lines vanish beneath the car's hood.

The man drew off the road outside a country town a dozen miles north of the city. As Martin opened the door a fresh breeze brushed against his face.

'This is as far as I go,' the man said. 'At least you're out of the city.'

The traffic was thinner now. As Martin put his bag down by the road and folded his coat he became aware of an unnerving silence descending around him after the passage of each car. As the minutes passed, shadows from a silver birch and pine wood on the opposite side of the road edged towards him over the hot tar, an encroaching coolness shivering from space. He felt the world assume a tangible massiveness now that he was out of the city. Momentarily disconcerted, he waited until a car had passed and tried to sing to himself, but his voice came out threadbare and weak, soaked up in the silence of wind and trees like the ineffectual buzz of an insect.

He felt suddenly inconsequential, as if he could disappear easily, entirely, even a few feet from the road. Beyond the range of those who carried him in their thoughts his immunity to anonymous death, or even an anonymous life, had vanished. He was now face to face with the world's immense unfamiliarity. He wondered if he should turn back, but the challenge of the journey rekindled briefly in his mind.

He stood vacillating by the road, his mood swinging between exhilaration and panic, until another car picked him up and drove him a further thirty miles, depositing him among low, haunted hills as night fell, where another appeared almost immediately like a providential baton carrier, to transport him into the north country. Darkness had fallen when the last ride pulled off the road. He stood by the turn-off and watched the tail-lights disappear, a low, moonless sky sinking in a shroud over black country. He walked a few yards off the road into the matted dark, stamped down a low bush into a thorny mattress and laid out his sleeping bag, took Maggie's switchblade from his travelling bag and slipped it into his sleeping bag, for protection against human or animal predators. The night was silent, and he slept quickly.

Chapter twenty-seven

Steve picked him up in the cold dawn, driving a ten-year-old Dodge Charger with a broken bucket seat and a thick smell of oil. He looked to Martin as if he had been living in the sump for ten years. He drove at eighty and recounted the plots of horror movies in graphic detail. He was heading west to start a new life in the prairies. 'Never been there. You ever been there Martin? It's booming, and it's either that or I'm gonna kill myself. I made up my mind. I'm wasted. I got nothing left of my life. Used it all up. And I got nothing back in Toronto.'

In North Bay, huge, predatory insects clung to the walls of buildings like alien invaders. In Sault Sainte Marie they stopped to buy gas. They took a walk by the ship canal and Steve bought him a beer in an empty tavern. When they returned to the garage the car was surrounded by a group of young boys selling THC. Martin declined. Is this it? he wondered, glancing at Steve as he opened the car door. Is this the Mad Axeman?

He dozed as the sun set and his anxiety receded into a malaise of fatigue and boredom, waking occasionally when Steve turned on the radio for a five minute blast of heavy metal, or burst suddenly into enthusiastic conversation after fifty miles of silence.

'This is Wawa, Martin,' Steve waved at a sign by the road. 'If I was to drop you by the road in Wawa, you'd probably never leave.'

'It doesn't look like much,' Martin observed.

'Shit no. It's the asshole of Ontario. But you'll never get a ride out of here. Half the population of Wawa are hitchhikers who never got a ride. All the fruitcakes who escaped from Penetang used to hide out in the woods here. They'd catch rides with people and drag them into the fucking woods and eat them. Hitchhikers always disappearing round here. And nobody'll give you a ride.'

He stared intensely at the road ahead like a chicken mesmerised by a chalk line. 'Fifteen hundred miles at a steady eighty. We should be there in a day, Martin. You were lucky I picked you up. Maybe when we get to Winnipeg we could get a place together. I don't know what I'm going to do in Winnipeg. I don't know anyone in Winnipeg. And I'm spending all my money on gas to get us there. I sure as hell could use some good luck right now. Have a smoke, Martin.'

Night fell as they came down a hill over Lake Superior. Haunted pine forests gathered around the car, sucking in the headlights to an obsessive beam on the lonely road. Somewhere in the woods lay the bodies of dozens of missing hitchhikers, buried in shallow graves or decomposing in leaf mould, a skeletal arm or a grinning skull shining among wet pine needles.

Through the trees great moonlit breakers crashed on the grey rock-strewn shoreline. Martin looked over nervously at Steve. The driver stared unblinking at the road ahead, tapping his fingers restlessly on the steering wheel. The colour had vanished from his eyes. Only the whites were visible; two infernal headlights glowing in his skull. Martin shivered. High pine branches danced overhead in a black sky thick with rushing clouds and a thin, glittering moon.

'You must be tired,' Martin said.

Steve turned slowly and contemplated Martin for a long time, still maintaining his speed.

'Everything's fine, Martin. Everything will be fine when we get to Winnipeg.'

They drove in silence through the night, passing deserted gas stations and tiny, dead towns, down over the hills towards the prairies. It began to rain heavily and Martin pulled his hat down over his eyes and slept for a while, his head bumping softly on the cold, wet window, waking up hungry and lost as the sun rose behind them. Along the straight stretch of road he saw a neon restaurant sign revolving in the morning mist, and looked over at Steve who seemed to have grown a beard during the night. Two red eyes glared at him from a shapeless face.

'You ever see *Texas Chainsaw Massacre*, Martin?'

'You can just let me off at this restaurant, Steve,' Martin replied, reaching over into the back seat for his bag. 'I feel like looking around at the country for a while.'

Steve turned towards him and Martin watched the infernal light in the driver's eyes evaporate, the desperate determination of flight transformed into a childlike fearfulness of being alone on an empty road. 'What's the matter, Martin? Is it too cold? I can turn up the heater if you like, man.' He switched on the heater fan.

'No. It's not too cold, man.'

Steve slowed down and pulled off the road into the forecourt of the Husky restaurant. Martin opened his door and breathed in fresh morning air and the smell of resinous pines. Fallen rain dripped from gloomy trees towering above them. Above, clouds swept over a cold, silent sky.

'Can I buy you some breakfast before you move on?'

'No, that's OK, Martin.' Steve looked at his watch. 'I can get to Winnipeg in time for lunch.'

Martin climbed out and looked back into the car. 'Need some money for gas?'

'No thanks, Martin.'

'Thanks for the ride. It was a long way.'

'That's OK, Martin.'

Steve gathered his years together and the boy's face vanished.

'Good luck, Steve.'

'Happy hunting, Martin.'

He reached over and slammed the door shut, then squealed off the gravel and away, a cloud of black smoke hanging in the crisp air.

No T-Shirts, No Jeans, No Bare Feet, No Tennis Shoes, No Rucksacks, No Bags, No Leather Jackets, No Dogs. Martin read the sign in the vestibule, checked himself, walked in confidently and took a seat in a booth by the window. Two truckers were eating breakfast at the counter; another customer sat in a corner booth concealed behind a newspaper.

'You'll have to remove your hat.'

He looked up. The waitress gazed out at the highway, chewing on her pencil, flapping her pad aggressively against her thigh.

'I beg your pardon?'

'The hat. You'll have to take it off,' she said, without taking her eyes from the window.

'Why's that?'

'You want to make trouble, you can eat somewhere else. There's another Husky station about eighty miles down the road.'

'It didn't say anything on the door about hats.'

She turned towards the counter, a martial gleam in her eyes, slipped her pencil seductively between pursed lips, tapped the wet end against the order pad, swaying her behind gracefully a foot from Martin's upturned face. 'Charlie!'

A hiatus followed. The two truckers paused in mid-conversation. In the corner booth a hairless cranium rose up from behind the newspaper like a full moon from the sea. A burly chef squinted from a cloud of percussive fat smoking on the grill.

'What is it, Laura? I'm busy.'

'Guy here won't take off his hat!'

'So. Ain't nothing on the sign about hats.'

Laura sighed theatrically and clattered across to the counter. 'Mister Osbaldeston said, "No Hats." He said he's bringing in a new sign on Tuesday.'

Charlie glanced up, turning a blazing burger on the grill and shaking the french fries basket in the deep fry.

'I think this is what you call an amnesty period, Laura. You know, so all the guys can get good haircuts for the day when they can't wear their cat hats in here any more.' He winked at the two truckers and guffawed.

'It's OK,' Martin said, strolling up behind the waitress. 'I'm just passing through. I'll take off my hat. I can understand how important this is to you. What would happen if everyone came in dressed as they pleased? The floodgates would open. Every possible excess would occur. You'd see people wearing things you couldn't even describe. Things you couldn't put down on the sign. Besides, I've heard of this regulation before, in Toronto.'

He smiled conspiratorially at Charlie, but was surprised to find the chef's expression hostile.

'Take off the hat and sit down, sir,' Charlie said, turning back to the grill.

As Martin returned to his seat he glanced over at the corner booth. The newspaper had come to rest flat on the table. The face behind it glanced back at him blankly, a bald, middle-aged man with soft, pink skin, wearing frameless glasses, with bushy black eyebrows that looked false. His head wobbled precariously, like a turnip on a windblown scarecrow. Beneath the head, a shapeless, neckless body bulged inside a tight pinstriped cotton shirt tied with an Arran tie and wrapped in a tweed jacket. Two pudgy hands folded together bounced thoughtfully against thick lips.

Martin looked away and sat down. A few moments later, Laura returned indolently, and he ordered a cheeseburger and coffee. The bald man slipped into the booth without speaking, sliding his empty coffee cup along the table. There was a pungent, odour of old milk. He leaned back in his seat as Laura returned, banging the burger plate and coffee cup and saucer down on the table.

'You want anything?' she said to the bald man, wrinkling her nose.

'Coffee,' he replied, in a smooth, high pitched purr.

Martin looked up uncertainly as the waitress filled the bald man's cup.

'You need a ride?' the bald man said. 'I don't usually give rides to people, but I have to get to Duluth today and I'm falling asleep. I need someone to talk to me, and keep me awake.'

'Great,' said Martin. 'Thanks.'

'I'll get that,' the bald man said as Laura tore off the bill and handed it to Martin. Squeezing short, round fingers into his jacket he pulled out a wallet. Laura eyed Martin suspiciously.

'Martin,' Martin said politely.

'Yeah. Jerry,' the bald man replied.

The sun had risen over the encircling pines as they crunched across the gravel to a dilapidated cube van in the car park. Jerry walked ahead, rolling gracelessly like an old man with sore feet. Sparse, pale clouds migrated in the high blue sky.

'Buzzard,' he observed.

Martin looked up. Wings like shards of black glass hovered briefly high above the forest, then vanished behind the trees.

'Got to watch them buzzards,' Jerry continued, chuckling mirthlessly. 'They'll eat anything. Long as they don't have to kill it themselves.'

He unlocked the passenger door and Martin climbed in. He lay back in his seat as the engine started up and gazed happily towards the road.

'You made a big mistake with Charlie back there,' Jerry said, as they pulled out on to the highway. 'People are touchy in this neck of the woods about strangers using three syllable words. Walk into a Husky station with a big vocabulary and you might as well be toting a .303. It's looked on as an act of aggression.' He squeezed his neck around and stared blandly in Martin's direction, neck veins pounding inside his shirt garrotte. 'Besides, it's domestic. He isn't going to take your side against a girl who went to school with his daughter, even if she is a doughhead.'

They sat in silence; the van bumping uncomfortably roofwards at each irregularity in the road.

'So ... Talk!' Jerry said, impatiently.

Martin, slouched in his seat and nearly asleep struggled to an upright position. 'It's a bit warm. Do you mind if I open a window?'

'That's the idea,' Jerry said. He beamed encouragingly. 'Why don't you go right ahead and open the window, if that would make you more comfortable?'

'What do you do?' Martin asked, rolling down the window.

'Wouldn't you like to know?' Jerry said, with a secretive smile. 'People always want to know, don't they? What do you do? I bet I can guess what you do,' he continued. 'First, I'll guess what you do, and then you can guess what I do.'

'OK,' Martin said.

'You're ... a film star!' Jerry tittered, little bubbles of mucus bursting in his nostrils.

'No ... seriously ... Let me think ...' He examined Martin

thoroughly from head to toe, wiping his nose on his jacket sleeve. 'Let me see your hands.'

Martin held them out and Jerry bent forward to scrutinise them. The van veered dangerously towards the ditch. Martin lurched forward and grabbed the steering wheel.

'Oh, you don't need to worry about my driving,' Jerry said. 'Well, there are calluses on your hands, so I guess you do work,' he smirked. 'They don't look to me like the hands of a clever young man, so I would say that you are an itinerant worker, unskilled.' He smiled complacently. 'How did I do?'

Martin said nothing, disappointed by the candid accuracy of the bald man's analysis.

'At least you're not a writer. And at least you don't play the bongos,' he muttered coldly, his smile vanishing. 'You don't play the bongos, do you?'

'Well, no,' Martin said. He slumped back into his seat. At least he was keeping the bald man awake, he thought.

'These days everyone you meet is either a writer or they play the bongos. You go to parties and everyone who can't do anything with their hands is a writer, and everyone who can't do anything with their brains plays the bongos. Only trouble is it seems to work out the other way around. You spend all evening listening to the inane plots of meaningless novels, and in the background someone who can play a musical instrument is being set upon by arrhythmic amateur bongo players pounding on Tupperware boxes and shaking rice jars.' He regarded Martin for a moment. 'See what I mean?'

'No,' Martin said.

'If you don't do anything, it's best just to say so.'

'So you don't do anything?'

Without warning Jerry pulled the van abruptly over to the soft shoulder and stopped. 'You think so, eh?'

'Oh. You're a salesman?'

'A salesman! That may be what I do, but it's not what I *do*!'

He threw open his door and jumped out on to the verge. Martin heard the back door open and the sound of violent rummaging behind him. Then the door slammed and Jerry reappeared, perspiring heavily, his tie askew, brandishing a leather attaché case with a combination lock. He threw it down on the seat between them and glared at Martin with intense annoyance. 'So you think I don't do anything, do you?' He fumbled excitedly with the lock and threw open the case, glanced at Martin suspiciously and closed it again, grinding the van into first gear and pulling back on to the highway. A vortex of sound and dust dragged the van across the road as a speeding tractor-trailer accelerated past, horn blaring. Jerry looked askance at the trail of tumbling leaves and grit in the big truck's wake. 'Asshole!'

As they bumped off along the highway he continued muttering under his breath, wiping the sweat from his pink forehead. The forest had fallen away from the roadside and the sun rising into the open sky beat down on the dashboard, throwing a brash glare into their eyes as they continued west. Gradually Jerry regained his composure. 'What do you know about rediffusion cables?'

'Not much,' Martin said.

'You know what I'm talking about? TV cables?'

'Yes.'

'Did you know they take a two-way signal? You can transmit on a rediffusion cable as well as receive?'

'Oh?'

'This is how the governments of the future intend to keep tabs on the population. See, the transmission facility in the home is simply dormant. It can be activated by a signal from Washington, or Ottawa in your case. Eventually everyone will have cable. They'll have the whole country wired up.' He turned to face Martin, a fanatical magnesium spark in his eyes.

'Oh?'

'Jesus. You're a passive son-of-a-bitch, aren't you? Doesn't anything excite you?'

Martin nodded frantically, fatigue transforming his attempted enthusiastic smile into a manic grimace.

'OK, OK, don't overdo it,' the bald man said. 'I realise you

Canadians are a phlegmatic race. Anyhow, you know what I have in here?' He patted the attaché case. 'A complete home cable transmitter. What's sauce for the goose, mister. Instant access for every American to the rich and powerful. All I need is an investor and every home in the country could have one of these babies.' He glanced slyly at Martin. 'That's after I've had my little say so, of course.'

Martin stared back blankly, struggling to think of a response. His eyes closed. 'How long have you been driving for?'

'Twenty hours. Came from New Brunswick yesterday.'

'Wow.'

'Wow is right. I don't know how I do it. I must be unusually gifted.' He beamed at Martin with a mad, self-satisfied smile.

'I can I trust you, can I?'

'Yes, of course.'

'I've got a gun in here,' he said, patting the attaché case. 'I'd shoot your ass, if I thought I couldn't trust you.'

An hour later Martin jerked awake as the van slewed off the road towards the ditch, the driver slumped over the wheel.

'Wake up!' he shouted, grabbing at the steering wheel.

'Jesus!' said Jerry, dragging the wayward vehicle back on to the road.

Ten minutes later a similar sequence of events occurred.

The third time it happened Jerry braked and turned off the road on to a mild incline above a field. 'This is no good. It isn't working.'

'No,' Martin said, his face falling forward on to his chest.

He woke once and heard the bald man snoring softly, a high pitched cat purr punctuated by occasional troubled squeaking noises.

The night had passed, and the sun had risen overhead when Martin surfaced, his eyes sore, a tense feeling in his sinuses. He looked over to see the driver gazing at him sweetly. 'You look nice sleeping.'

'Oh,' Martin said.

'Like a little child and a very old man.'

'Thanks,' Martin said.

Jerry leaned back in his seat and stretched out his arms. 'It gets real lonely on the road. I spend most of my time driving,' he said.

'It must do.'

'This is a wonderful invention,' he said, picking up the attaché case from the floor where it had fallen during the night. 'Even if it doesn't impress you. If everyone had one of these in their homes, we'd have a real democracy. Access to the media is one of the major attributes of power, you know. Everyone would be as important as everyone else. Everyone could tell everyone about their lives. No one would need to feel lonely or anonymous any more.'

'Wouldn't that be boring?' Martin said. 'Most people's lives wouldn't be as interesting as the programmes they already have on TV.'

'Are you kidding me? Don't you know how eager people are to meet other people? Jesus Christ, don't you ever read the papers? The classified section? The personal column?'

Martin looked out of the window at the cool fields, corn swaying in the haze. He rolled down the window and heard a crow shriek. There was a smell of spruce and fragrant grass on the breeze.

'I wonder what time it is?' he said, recalling the pawnshop where Robertson's forgotten watch probably no longer resided. 'Shit,' he muttered under his breath, recalling the outstretched hand at the bus station, Robertson's parting speech, and a gift gone for ever, absorbed into a continent of things, reposing in the pocket of some anonymous Canadian.

'I'll give you ten bucks for a blow-job,' Jerry said.

'What's that?' Martin said absently.

'What do you mean, "What's that?" '

'Oh,' Martin said. He opened the passenger door, picked up his bag from the floor and straightened his hat.

'You must need the money.'

Martin jumped down to the road. 'Thanks very much for the

lift. You're awake now, you'll be OK,' he said. He walked a few steps up the incline of the road into the breeze, then turned back for a moment. 'Good luck with the invention. It's a good idea. You're right. Too many people are lonely.'

He took off his hat and tossed it through the open passenger window on to the seat. 'Have a hat,' he said. 'I'm sick of wearing it.'

Chapter twenty-eight

He walked away from the van and up a slow incline between aromatic spruce trees. Hot sun beat down on the road. Tar oozed from the road like lava. He could smell sweetgrass in the fields, the cool shade of pine woods and hot wild flowers. Grasshoppers and bees sang thickly all around him. From the tree line at the summit of the hill, long fields dropped away from the road in bands of yellow and green towards a river hidden in trees. At the crest of the road a gravel track led away to the right, through an open gate up to a white A-frame bungalow, with steps on to a shaded porch, and an open front door.

He walked slowly by, looking up at the house, then stopped to adjust the shoulder strap on his bag and rested for a moment on the melting tar. It clung to his shoes as he continued walking. Looking down he saw a sleeping rattlesnake curled up on the road ahead of him, its chin resting on the rattle like a cat's tail. The snake smiled peacefully.

'Hello,' Martin said, without approaching.

He stood and observed the snake. His tongue was dry. Looking up at the house, he imagined the shady interior and cool water flowing from a tap into an icy glass.

An old woman appeared through the screen door. She leaned against the porch frame and scanned the fields and the road in each direction as far as the horizon, then squinted up into the sunlight and the huge, aimless, birdless sky. Her glance fell on Martin, as if picking out a target from a radio bearing. 'Hello there.'

They looked at each other for several moments without speaking.

'Thirsty?'

'Yes,' Martin said.

He picked up his bag and walked up the gravel drive.

'Ain't you hot in that big coat?'

'I've got nowhere else to put it,' he said.

She took him inside and poured him a glass of milk. The breeze from the fields blew through the open front door. Grasshoppers hummed in the silence. She pointed to the dining-table and told him to sit down, brought him cold chicken and salad from a tall fifties refrigerator and watched him eat, her elbows resting on the table. A fly buzzed at the door, collided with a window and fell silent.

As he came out on to the porch the cube van rumbled by on the road below, the bald man at the wheel, face pressed up close to the windshield, Martin's hat pulled down over his eyes.

'Thanks for your hospitality.'

'I have a son of my own,' she said. 'Always hope strangers will do the same for him.'

He picked up his bag and set off down the track to the road. As he reached the gate a Whiteliner trailer careened round the corner, dust and gravel skidding into the air. He waved a thumb up at the driver, caught a glimpse of the driver's head snap round, and a moment later heard the airbrakes engage and saw the truck slow down. He ran along the soft shoulder and turned momentarily to wave up at the old woman. She was leaning on the porch rail gazing in his direction but at some point far beyond him. Her fingers lifted slightly from the rail in a preoccupied farewell.

An ornate logo of midnight blue-flamed lettering along the side of the truck proclaimed the name *Manifest Destiny*. The passenger door opened and Martin threw his bag up on to the seat. As he climbed into the cabin he rested his hand for a moment on the muffler. A searing pain shot from his palm directly into his brain and he paused on the step, briefly immobilised like someone paralysed on a live cable. Settling into the seat he nodded at the driver and opened his hand. A thick red bubble of skin rose up from his palm as he watched. He leaned forward, clasping the hand into his belly to stifle impending nausea. The driver glanced at him curiously, then put the truck in gear and pulled back out on to the road.

They made good time. Martin dozed or half-fainted, the burning in his hand intruding into his consciousness like a bad memory. He became aware of a city rising from the flat country, a long, wide avenue bordered by steel grey office blocks, the faces of pretty girls in late sunlight. He dozed. The driver shook him awake on the west side of the city.

As he watched the truck turn off the road a few hundred yards past him a farmer in a hand-painted pickup pulled in beside him and drove him a few miles west, leaving him at the summit of an embankment. A small town lay below on one side, and on the other a Husky restaurant and gas station. 'Hard place to get a ride,' the farmer muttered, as Martin climbed out. 'There's been murders. People say hitchhikers did them. Still,' he smiled, 'good luck to you.'

Martin watched the pickup turn off on to a farm track and followed its dusty progress to a vanishing point in a sea of yellow grain. An occasional car appeared over the hill on the horizon, widening slowly as it approached, passing in a blur and converging into a point at the crest of another hill a mile or two west. Dust drifted down among the wheat, and the warm breeze of the car's passing faded. A bird cried sadly from the fields. He sat down on his bag and scanned the huge sky, sharp points of light dancing in his eyes, a buzz of dying city noise in his ears clouding the cool, prairie silence. Ten or fifteen minutes passed between cars. A fresh wind blew through the wheat, mile upon mile of stems and heads rising and falling like the undulations of an enormous sea creature, the modulating hiss of the wind indistinguishable from the wash of surf on a shoreline. He wished he could believe there was a message in all this movement, something aimed directly at him, that he was capable of understanding, that would clarify all the befuddlement in his mind. He felt like a man in love with an imperious woman, craving her attention as she passes by, oblivious to his presence. The wind swept back and forth in ignorant splendour over the prairie, the wheat reflecting the gold of the sun, superficially luminous and animated, but still at heart, while he, agitated and alone, sought a point of entry.

A tractor-trailer slammed by, the airstream nearly sucking him into the road. He lit a cigarette and watched a high cirrus cloud slip off the sky in the north. He walked across to the Husky station to ask for rides. A burly attendant told him to leave. The sun moved west, gathering mist as it dropped toward the horizon. Martin heard a bicycle bell and looked down the embankment. Two young boys waved up at him from a track leading to the town. He waved back.

'You'll never get out of Brandon!' they shouted, pedalling off along the track in a cloud of dust, shrieking with laughter.

Chapter twenty-nine

The boys' prognosis nearly proved correct. In two days no one stopped. Sometimes a car would pull over to the side of the road fifty or a hundred feet beyond him; he would pick up his bag, elated and grateful, run up the road, only to see the car accelerate away as he reached for the passenger door, a chorus of oaths and laughter hurled at him through the driver's window. On the first night he walked a few hundred yards beyond the gas station lights, laid out his sleeping bag in a field, in the shadow of an abandoned army fort, and slept. Woken in the middle of the night by the intensifying pain in his hand he looked up to find a curious barn owl hovering over him in the silent, star-filled sky.

He awoke at dawn and walked back to the Husky station for breakfast. A blonde waitress with pale eyes scanned the horizon as he read the menu. 'You'll never get out of Brandon,' she said sadly, as he paid the bill.

On the second night he returned to his camping place. As he prepared to retire for the night a gangling shadow surmounted by a ten-gallon hat appeared over a hump in the road. He waited as the figure approached and nodded in response to a non-committal grunt as the cowboy reached him. 'Where ya headed?' the cowboy asked, dropping a canvas bag at his feet and surveying Martin from a superior altitude of several inches.

'Vancouver,' Martin replied tersely.

The cowboy grunted again and peered back along the highway as if staring into the sun. 'You a hippie?' he asked suddenly.

'No.' Martin looked along the highway in the opposite direction. Deserted prairie road enveloped by vast twilight exacerbated his sense of solitude and vulnerability.

'Shit, man, thass just as well,' continued the cowboy. 'I been up in Alaska a few weeks ago. Should see what they do to hippies up there.'

'Oh,' said Martin.

'Yeah, man. There was this one hippie up there was a cook or somethin'. Nobody liked him tha fuckin' gearbox. He went out with this chick in his van one night. Someone stuck a .356 through the window and blew his fuckin' brains out.' He jammed his thumbs into his belt and swayed slowly back and forth on the heels of his ornately tooled boots.

'Really?'

'No shit,' the cowboy said.

'That's nothing,' Martin said. 'You should see the things hippies do to cowboys back where I come from.'

The cowboy paused midway through his rocking motion and balanced on his heels, his brow furrowed.

'Yeah?'

'Yeah.'

'What sorts of things?'

'Oh, I don't know,' Martin said. 'You can probably imagine the kinds of things they do.'

'Yeah,' the cowboy said, laughing carelessly.

'Faggots with psychedelic drugs, you know,' Martin continued.

'Yeah,' the cowboy said, 'I can imagine.'

'Knives, too. They go more for knives than guns.'

'I get the picture.'

The moon appeared on the horizon, nearly full, sliding into eerie cumulus over a shivering ocean of fields.

The cowboy shuddered. 'Shit.' He rubbed his hands together and spat on the road. 'I better be movin along,' he said. 'There's a truckstop twenty miles down the road. You can usually catch a ride from there.' He smiled at Martin, an uncertain amalgam of friendliness and suspicion. 'That's if you're a cowboy, though. I tell you man, you should cut your hair when you get the opportunity. More chance of getting a ride. '

'Maybe I will,' Martin said. 'Thanks for the tip.'

'No problem.'

'OK.' The cowboy picked up his bag and walked away,

glancing back from time to time until his shadow evaporated into the descending dark.

As he awoke Martin felt a shadow flicker across the sun and knew immediately that someone was watching him. He kept his eyes shut and listened, turning over in his sleeping bag and reaching for the knife in his boot.

'Heh heh heh …' A voice laughed softly overhead.

Footsteps receded over dry grass and Martin heard the sound of someone urinating a few feet away. He stretched again and half opened his eyes, reaching down with his free hand to open the knife. He raised his head above the barrier of grass and looked towards the road. A fifteen-year-old Mercedes sedan was parked on the gravel shoulder a few feet from his head. He heard footsteps again crackling over the dry grass; a pair of tooled cowboy boots planted themselves between him and the road. Not you again, he thought.

'You got any more people in there? I need a push.'

Martin looked up. A forty-year-old Indian, wearing jeans and a pinstripe jacket, nodded down at the sleeping bag.

'I'm afraid not.' He pulled on his boots inside the sleeping bag, folded the knife shut, and crawled out. 'What time is it?'

'Nine, maybe.' The Indian walked back to the car and opened the rear door. 'You want a beer?'

'A beer would be great.'

The Indian returned as Martin folded his sleeping bag and stuffed it into his bag.

'What's wrong with the car?'

The Indian looked at the Mercedes and frowned. 'That's a hard one.' He reached into his pocket and produced a handful of nuts, bolts, and pieces of metal.

'What's that?'

'I was just driving along about fifty miles out of Winnipeg when the gearshift started flopping around in my hand. When I stopped the car I found all this stuff on the road. I called a towtruck and took her to a gas station. I had to choose a gear to drive in. I can only have one gear. The guy recommended third.'

'Oh.'

'Yeah. But I stalled on that hill. Lookin' over at you, as a matter of fact. See if you was dead.' He chuckled. 'Gone over a hundred miles, too.'

'It looks like a heavy car.'

'She's a beauty. European.'

'I mean heavy to push.'

'Oh, shit, yes.'

He sat down on the grass. The sun lazed overhead, a knife of light in the skin of the sky. 'Where you from?'

'Scotland.'

'Long way from home.'

'Yes.'

'I know all about Scotland.'

'Oh?'

'Sure. Same kind of thing happened there as happened here. The Highland Clearances. I know all about that. People got thrown off their land.' He took a swig of beer. 'John Spittal,' he said, extending his hand. Martin looked at his own hand, the scar now turning green at the edges.

'Martin Murdoch. I won't shake hands, if you don't mind.'

'How did you do that?'

Martin told him.

'Well, we better put something on that.' Spittal nodded towards the car and winked. 'I got special native remedies in there,' he said, 'hy-dro-gen pe-rox-ide, and Vit-a-min E.'

They stood up and walked to the car.

There was no traffic. From a thousand feet overhead a bird cry echoed over empty land.

'Ain't nothing stinks like an untreated wound,' Spittal said, sniffing Martin's hand. He unscrewed the cap from the peroxide bottle and poured half the contents over it. Martin gritted his teeth. They watched the scar frothing.

'What did you say?' Martin said, grimacing.

'I said, nothing stinks like an untreated wound. Take your

arm off in the end, a mess like that.' He looked back at his car.

'Well, I got to get going. I got no gears, but I do have an accelerator. You going west? I'll give you a ride if you help me get her started.'

Martin collected his bag.

'You can drive?'

'No.'

'Well, you can steer. I'll push and you steer until we get to the top. Stop when we get there.'

Half an hour later they were cruising west at a steady fifty, Martin stretching his legs out in the roomy interior, and conversing with Spittal.

'Are you a Sioux?'

'I'm not from round here. I'm half Iroquois, but I live in Calgary. I've been visiting my wife's family in Brantford.'

'Where is that?'

'Near Toronto. Six Nations reserve.'

'Oh.'

'So what are you doing on the road?'

'I'm going to visit a girl.'

Spittal nodded.

'You're married?'

'I was. She was an Ojibway girl. She burned to death down on the Reserve. They get short of water there. The river gets low. One day our house went on fire, and there was no water. I was away. So anyway, that was that.'

'That's terrible. It would be terrible burning to death,' Martin said, before he could stop himself.

'Yep. I guess so.'

Some miles further down the highway a gas station sign popped above the horizon, at the top of the next hill. In fields behind, oil wells pumped rhythmically like the gravity birds in the River Street variety store. Spittal depressed the clutch, braked slowly and drew up at the pumps. He kept the engine running while Martin filled the tank. As he was replacing the fuel cap a hand containing a twenty-dollar bill reached out of the driver's window. 'Better get us something to eat,' Spittal said.

They sat in the car, eating hotdogs and drinking beer. Martin turned his gaze away from the road and found the Indian staring at him inquisitively. He glanced away quickly.

'Don't like being looked at?'

'Not really,' Martin said.

'You got something to hide?'

'I feel as if I do, even though I don't.'

Spittal raised his foot from the clutch and accelerated out on to the highway.

'*Everybody got something to hide,*' he sang, '*except me and my monkey.*'

Martin dozed as they crossed the prairies, hundreds of miles of wheat and moonlight, and another day of conversation, long, agreeable silences, white skies, grain silos, immense lonely farms, oil wells, flat towns where tumbleweed floated over dusty roads, or thick clouds of insecticidal kerosene hovered in dim street-lights. On a long stretch of straight Saskatchewan road he glanced up and saw a young farm girl by the side of the road watching them pass. He imagined himself standing in the chest high wheat, his arm around a slender, long-sighted girl, time stopped in eternity, thinking to himself how easy it would be to ask Spittal to stop the car, get out and take that particular life, as if it were on offer like an item in a shop window.

In the late afternoon they came into Calgary. Flames of late sunlight ignited among forested Rocky Mountain foothills and distant snow peaks. Spittal pulled off the road at a truck stop, and switched off the engine. 'The beast made it,' he said, patting the dashboard, 'I can phone my buddies from here. They'll pick me up.'

Martin looked out of the window. Indolent pedestrians browsed in store windows and cars cruised home along a dusty street leading to the mountains.

'I'd invite you over, but – don't be offended – they're crazy,' Spittal said. 'You wouldn't get any sleep.' He smiled in the direction of the hills. 'It's a beautiful ride from here up into the Rockies, but don't hitchhike in town. It's illegal, and there are some real rednecks here. If you can't get a ride with one of these truckers, just walk down there a couple of blocks. And remember, there are wild animals up there who really do eat people, so I wouldn't advise sleeping by the road.'

Martin opened the door.

'How's the hand?'

The skin on Martin's palm had deflated into an ugly crimson scar.

Spittal opened the glove compartment and took out a small bottle of pills. 'Vitamin E,' he said. 'Just bite a hole in one of these every day and squeeze the stuff out on your hand. Get rid of that scar in no time.'

He handed Martin the bottle.

'I enjoyed talking to you,' Martin said.

'Well, when you get back to Scotland, you'll be able to sit there at your window in the evening, smoke some weed and remember the redskin who gave you a ride over the Great Plains.'

'I will,' Martin said.

'I better get going.' Spittal pointed over at the trucks.

'One of these guys will maybe give you a ride. Make sure they see you. Some of them are Americans and if you sneak up behind them they're liable to blow your head off.'

They shook hands. Spittal opened his door as Martin shut his, got out of the car and walked away to a phone booth without looking back. Martin watched him briefly then wandered away among the trucks to look for a ride.

Chapter thirty

As he walked across the forecourt of the truckstop a Shelby Cobra passed him and pulled over by the exit. The door opened and he gazed into a womblike interior illuminated by dashboard lights. A row of unnaturally white teeth and a pair of reflector sunglasses gleamed back at him. 'Get in,' the driver said, through an immobile smile.

Martin lowered himself into the seat and peered over the dashboard through a tinted windshield.

The driver reached over the back of his seat and produced two bottles of beer, opened them with his teeth and passed one to Martin. 'There's some weed in the glove compartment,' he said. 'Party down.'

'Where are you headed?' Martin said, his vocabulary changing to fit the atmosphere.

'I let my dick do the driving.'

A row of teeth flashed in Martin's direction.

'Your dick?'

'Yah, man. My dick. It's a fucking heatseeker, man. It could find poontang in the Arctic. It's like infra-red.'

'Oh,' Martin said.

'This is my poontang vacation. You know how it is ... Monogamy! It's a strain on the gonads. Am I right, or am I right? I mean, shit. You got all this testosterone pulsating through your system all the time. What are you going to do with it? Be reasonable. This is why wars start. Too much testosterone and not enough chicks. You follow me?'

Martin nodded.

'I got a wife in Portland, and I'm a happy man. She's a wonderful chick. But every year about this time I take to the open road in search of pussy. She's happy that I'm not pissing on our doorstep. Everybody's happy. And there are some damn fine women up here in Canada.'

'Sounds like fun,' Martin suggested.

'I have to admit. It is fun. Goddamnit, it is fun.'

He turned the blazing smile in Martin's direction. 'You're English, right? What are the chicks like in England?'

'Scottish.'

'From Scotland. Is that near Ireland?'

'Yes, near Ireland.'

'So. Those Scottish girls, they like to party down?'

'You'd do OK with a car like this.'

'No kidding?'

'Actually I've no idea,' Martin said. 'I don't know much about what Scottish girls like. I had a girlfriend there, and I didn't know what she wanted.'

'A good fuck, man. Everybody likes a good fuck.'

'Yes, I suppose.'

'There's no suppose about it.'

A Jimi Hendrix tape was playing on the eight-track. The driver turned up the volume as the road climbed into darkness. Dense pine forest gathered by the road as they passed through Banff. Electricity howled from the speakers. Martin peered up through the window and followed the blink of a satellite through the stars.

The eight-track tape ran out and the driver turned down the volume as the radio came on, playing country music. The empty road led them on, winding through canyons of black trees, moonlight illuminating glaciers and mountains. Jagged tips and precipices sailed, stars darted in the tide of night. Martin gazed from his window into the remote Arctic world overhead and imagined an abode of noble, ethereal beings, able to travel at will between earth and universe, free from ties of materiality and experience. His thoughts gradually became dreams and he slept peacefully as the miles unrolled, waking every now and then to listen to the road purring by below, the friendly glow of a lighted cigarette, the dashboard lights, the quiet radio lulling him again into oblivion.

He dreamed he had been appointed governor of a desolate

and beautiful country. He had arrived at the border, an unmanned gate, on his journey to take up the post. Before him a straight dust track led to the horizon, dividing low, flat fields on one side, and a swamp filled with broken pine trees on the other. He walked through the gate and along the track. In the swamp, two men were working, up to their knees in thick, black mud, dragging a fallen cedar from a tangle of waterlogged underbrush, towards the road. As he passed they looked up and waved.

The governor followed the track for miles. He arrived at a bay. Empty, sunlit sea rolled ashore on a wide strand of stones and sand. A dozen derelict timber mansions followed the curve of the track, facing the sea. Paint peeled from the clapboard walls, sand whirled over broken verandas. A shutter at an upstairs window banged in the breeze. Insects and wind buzzed through open windows and in empty rooms. Dust devils danced by his feet, and the air smelt of pinewood and the sea.

This is obviously not a prestigious post, the governor thought, as he strolled by a cluster of cedars towards the beach, and he asked himself, What are my duties?

He wondered what would happen were a passing stranger to inquire about the country. What could he tell them?

I could tell them something about nothing, perhaps.

Late the following afternoon the driver dropped Martin at the end of Granville Bridge in Vancouver. He walked over the road to a tavern and, with his bag, pushed through the door into a cool interior. A junkie was shooting up at a table near the bar. Martin sat down with his back to the junkie and ordered a beer. The sounds of pool balls knocking together came from a room behind the bar. He finished the beer and went back outside. A cool, salty breeze blew from the ocean, tempering the heat of the sun. Clear blue sky stretched from hills north of the city to the whitecapped water. He walked through the city and down to Stanley Park. He ceremoniously removed his shoes and socks and dipped his feet into the Pacific, feeling a strange thrill that resembled homecoming, and a rush of contented anonymity, as if his life force was being united with the immense, welcoming current of the Georgia Strait. He thought briefly of his mother, Robertson, Christine, Ray, but their images faded almost immediately.

He sat by the beach for an hour, deep in philosophical reflection, then growing hungry, picked up his bag and wandered back into town as night fell.

In a hotel on Water Street, filled with students and tourists from the Maritimes, Québec, Europe and America, he inquired pointlessly if anyone had heard of or knew Maggie. As night came on he asked the barman about accommodation; a group of Québecois students overheard and directed him to a luxurious hostel on the far side of Granville Bridge. He caught a taxi to the address and was given a bed in a long, convivial dormitory, where he fell asleep to a chorus of students singing Crosby Stills and Nash ballads in nasal New England accents.

He stayed in Vancouver for a week, passing the afternoons with his feet in the Pacific, attempting to rekindle his initial religious oneness with the ocean. He decided to return home through the States. He hitchhiked to the border and was refused entry by a barrel-chested border guard wearing a monumental masonic ring. He wondered if Robertson had ever been a mason, and what the secret masonic signs might be to facilitate entry into foreign countries. Returning to the hostel in Vancouver he was assailed by offers to guide him through clandestine entry points along the border, but instead caught a ferry next morning to Vancouver Island, where the immigration guards were reputedly friendlier. From Victoria he boarded an elegant ferryboat to Seattle. Viennese waltz music from the saloon greeted him as he went aboard. He stood on the deck and watched snow-covered Mount Baker glide by, exposed on the horizon among the pine green foothills like a great pearl breast.

He made his way east from Seattle, through the John Birch country of Eastern Washington, into Idaho and Utah to Interstate 70, along the Green river valley to Denver, across the flatlands of eastern Colorado, through Kansas and Missouri, where he observed with a kind of pity the isolated natives in tiny highway towns, marooned amid oceanic fields like victims of a divine practical joke. Crossing a narrow abutment in East St Louis he was nearly killed by a speeding tractor trailers sucking him into the road. He hitchhiked onwards into Illinois, Ohio, Pennsylvania. On a stretch of deserted road outside Columbus he saw a cloud of dust rising from the horizon and a few moments later heard the roar of motorbikes. As the gang came into view he looked around for a hiding place, but the flat country fell away from the road, leaving him exposed. He put his hands into his pockets and assumed as confident an expression as possible. I hope they've eaten, he thought, laughing to himself.

The leader raised his fist in a salute as the gang passed, none smiled, some saluted. The dust cloud followed them into the distance. Watching them, he felt as if there were no longer any centre to the world, only a nation permanently on the move, or a scattered city where he would wander for the rest of his life, looking for work, a room, drinking companions, a woman, wondering from time to time why he should feel so at home there.

He was finally arrested for hitchhiking on a toll road outside Buffalo.

'Boy, you sure are lucky to be leaving Buffalo,' the immigration officer said as he drove Martin to the border. 'I wish someone would deport me from Buffalo.'

As the outline of Toronto approached he realised he no longer knew where his home was. He only wanted to keep moving like this, aimlessly, always.

Chapter thirty-one

He arrived at the apartment as night fell, threw his bag on the floor, and went back out immediately, walked downtown to the Chinatown bar where he had last seem Carson and the Québecois women. It was Saturday night. A nervous blues band played in the corner. He took a vacant seat beside a speaker, ordered a beer and gritted his teeth as a harmonica solo pierced his skull. He turned his head and stared into the vibrating speaker to still the irritating flapping of his eardrum. Someone passed him an oily joint and he took a long puff. His neighbour said something, but when Martin replied his voice disappeared into a spongy abyss inside his head. He handed back the joint and returned outdoors. T'ai chi ladies were emerging from the community centre, barking irascibly to each other in Cantonese. Across the street, the Arran Tavern had disappeared and a restaurant complex with an ornate oriental gate was under construction.

He walked south for a block, bought a newspaper from a box at the corner, peered into the darkened windows of the Oriental food stores, entered a delicatessen, ordered a pastrami sandwich and a coffee, read the paper, paid the bill and left. He crossed the street again and made his way through a maze of back streets towards Yonge Street. At the corners streetlights illuminated blood-red houses hidden among maple trees. Voices murmured in the dark from warm tree-shaded verandas. Snatches of Cantonese, Portuguese and English drifted from open windows. An old duplex, gutted by fire, lay empty, surrounded by plywood and a hoarding advertising a new office block. A car cruised by, the window down, paused at a stop sign and wheels skidding on the broken Tarmac, slipped into the dark.

On Yonge Street the huge neon signs revolved, flashed and glowed overhead like a city floating in space; below, muscle cars, convertibles, nocturnal sedans cruised, music pounding dully from stereos. The bag lady known as the Queen of Sweden was huddled in a doorway, muttering angrily. He crossed the road to avoid a crowd of leather boys loitering outside the Charles Tavern, went into the donut store on the corner near the student hostel. The black bag-lady from the park was perched on a stool, drinking coffee and whispering to herself intensely. She looked up as he passed her and half-smiled. He ordered a cruller and coffee, gave the woman a dollar without looking at her and returned outside, sat on the steps of a nearby bank and watched the slow parade of night life. He passed an hour in the Yonge Station bar, drank a beer and watched a band of middle-aged men play rock and roll with weary expertise.

Returning home he paused on the Don Valley bridge, peered down into the narrow thread of river, followed its course until it oozed into invisibility among black factories and granaries by the lakeshore. A lightless ship was in the dock. He considered going down to investigate it, but lit a cigarette instead and stood for a while watching the tiny launch lights drifting over the black abyss of the harbour to Centre Island. Threads of car lights spun down the parkway and along the lakeshore. He turned and looked north at the huge city, stretched out like a prairie of light to the edge of the dark.

The flashing lights of a jet descended behind buildings to the west in a bland flame-red sky empty of stars. A streetcar rumbled by, its bell jangling, the overhead wires whirring eerily as it rose over the brow of the hill and vanished.

Chapter thirty-two

He opened the apartment door and went in, switched on the light and stooped to pick up a letter which he had missed on his return. After several moments he recognised the writing on the envelope as his mother's. A sense of alarm penetrated his fatigue. He tore it open.

Dear Martin,

I am very sorry that the first letter I should write to you in Canada should contain bad news. I now feel very guilty about not having written you before, but so little happens here as a rule, and I've always thought the last thing you probably want to hear about is anything ordinary. Especially as I do find myself complaining a lot to myself about how dull things are here, and this does not make for very interesting reading.

Anyway, I'm sorry to tell you that your uncle has been taken quite ill. He was arrested a week ago for assaulting a pedestrian on the street outside the house, while trying to talk to him about his beliefs. He seems to have had a kind of nervous breakdown and has been put in hospital for safety's sake. He has had a brief spell of treatment and I think he will be released soon, and fortunately the charges have been dropped because of this. I did not want to sign at first, but the lawyer suggested it would be the best in the long run, and our doctor thought so too.

I have been to see him and he seems in better spirits, although he gets very agitated at times as he says he cannot remember some things now, and this seems to frighten him. However, the Institute is going to stay closed for a while, and when he gets home he will recuperate and take some time off from working on his journal.

I think he will be home by the time you get this, and I know he would like to have some word from you. He will probably not be able to write for a little while, so any kind of communication would be very welcome for him.

I hope everything is going well for you, and that you have found a way of life where you feel more comfortable. It would be nice to hear about Toronto. I know how relieved I was once upon a time to get away from here myself, and it was only force of circumstances that brought me back to Scotland.

Your loving Mother.

He sat down on the bed and crumpled up the letter. In the month of his absence the cockroach population had proliferated. A dozen strolled nonchalantly over the far wall of the room; another scuttled from beneath the bed. He crushed it beneath the heel of his boot and watched disgustedly as the detached front half slipped down into a crack between the floorboards and continued doggedly on its course. He leaned over and removed his sleeping bag from his travelling bag and laid it over the stale bedcover. The smell of sweetgrass still clung to the material. Closing his eyes as he lay down, a recollection of long prairie road appeared in his mind, the percussive hum of grasshoppers, the dull pounding of Albertan oil wells.

He slept until late afternoon, waking from a dream in which he had been standing at the window of a vacant office, looking down on an empty city where an unnamed catastrophe was about to occur.

Sunlight poured into his bedroom over the neighbourhood rooftops, a shower of sparrows gusted by the open window. He heard traffic sounds and snatches of cheerful, neighbourly conversations drifting up from the street below. He got up, undressed, found a clean shirt and jeans in a pile by the bed, took a shower, dressed, went downstairs and along the street to a coffee shop, ate a long, late breakfast at a table by the window, watching the traffic and the passers by. He paid the bill and walked back over the bridge to River Street.

Bebe was leaning by the warehouse door, reading a paper. He looked up. 'Hello, English,' he said. 'Got back in one piece?'

Martin smiled. 'Do I still have my job?'

Bebe laughed. 'We've been taking a couple of days off. The

old guy is sick.'

'Sick?'

'He's in hospital. Just collapsed. Luckily I was there. Gave me a real bad feeling.'

'Which hospital?'

Bebe told him. 'He doesn't look so hot to me. I reckon he's ready to check out. Tell him I wrote Fred and told him.' He reached into his pocket, pulled out his wallet and removed two twenty-dollar bills. 'He's kind of pissed off at me. He's reverting to his roots, you know. You Scotchmen always blame the boss for everything.' He smiled glumly. 'I don't know what he could use in there, but get him something for me, would you?'

'Why don't you go yourself?'

'Shit, no thank you. Those places give me the creeps.'

Martin took the money.

'You can start again tomorrow?' Bebe shouted, as Martin reached the gate. 'We got stuff to move. We got a sale on the weekend.'

Martin waved without looking back.

Wesley's room was bright and clean. The patients themselves seemed incongruous, like a clerical oversight, unsightly rubbish left over from a renovation. On either side of the room two beds faced each other across an aisle of polished linoleum. Hepatic faces peered from immaculate white sheets, glowing brightly in sunlight. Beside each bed stood a cabinet with a jug of ice water, a glass, a stack of urine bottles. On some cabinets visitors had left bottles of soda and fruit, on one a portable television. The smell in the ward was corrupt and culinary, a warm odour of cooking oil, formalin and excrement.

The old man was immobilised, propped up on pillows, pinioned to his bed by tubes and wires, his hands folded peacefully on the blanket in front of him. It seemed to Martin that all Wesley's dignity had come to rest in his hands. A catheter chafed bitterly inside the old man's urethra and tears waited at the corners of his eyes. Femoral blood pumped from a shunt through a churning machine by the bed, a drip fed glucose into his forearm, a bandage covered a fistula scar on his left wrist.

'Not a pretty sight,' Wesley said, as Martin pulled up a chair. 'I tell you, Martin, if anyone ever offers you a free cystoscopy, tell 'em to go fuck themselves.' He cleared his throat and nodded at the bed opposite. 'Could be worse though.' He lowered his voice and beckoned Martin to come closer. 'Look at that poor bastard over there.'

Across the aisle an emaciated youth lay sprawled and half-conscious, his pyjama jacket and trousers open. Catheters extended from his chest and abdomen to plastic bags draped around the bed. The contents of the bags were of various colours, bile black, blood red, mucus green, urea yellow, and in one bag a pure virgin white fluid which looked to Martin like a distillation of the boy's departing soul. 'He's a brave young fellow,' Wesley said. 'You wouldn't think so to look at him. Not like some of these tough guys. Had one in today, you never heard such a goddamned fuss. They had to take him away to another room.' He motioned to the water jug.

Martin filled a plastic cup and handed it to him.

He sipped slowly. 'Shit, that's cold. Makes my teeth hurt. Take the ice out, will you, Martin?' He handed back the cup. Martin fished out the ice cubes. 'Of course, the goddamned ice is compulsory. I told them a dozen times, but they just smile at me. 'Poor demented old bastard. Doesn't he know it's nice to have ice? It's modern, and it makes the water taste clean.'' He blew into the cup, and looked up again at Martin. 'Still ...' he began, but lapsed into silence.

Martin's attention wandered to the window. Workmen on an adjacent roof strolled casually back and forth along a parapet, carrying lengths of duct and bags of tools. They were singing snatches of hit songs, or whistling tunelessly. He glanced back at Wesley in time to catch an averted, frightened glance.

'Did you find Maggie?' the old man asked.

'No. I don't even know her number, or I'd phone her.'

'Nothing doing, eh?'

'She won't know you're sick.'

'Maggie is practical,' Wesley said. 'She's got better things to do. I ain't bitter.'

'You shouldn't talk now,' Martin said, leaning over the bed and patting Wesley's pillow ineffectually.

'I better talk now, Martin. I may not be able to tomorrow.' He glanced sadly towards the window. Darkness was falling and he gazed for several moments along a ghostly corridor, where random car and streetlights, and the dull crimson pulse of an airplane rising into the night sky slipped across the reflection of the ward in the glass.

Both men fell asleep. Some time later Martin was woken by someone tapping his knee. He opened his eyes. Wesley, almost half out of the bed, was staring at him desperately. 'Bebe will take care of everything, you know. I have a policy, and I want to be created.'

'Created?'

'Cremated. But I want you to tidy up the apartment. Don't let Bebe in there. The keys are in my pants. Check everything. And whatever you find, send half to Fred in Baja. He was a good buddy to me when I first came here. I'm trusting you, Martin.'

Martin helped Wesley straighten up in the bed. 'He gave me forty bucks to buy you something,' he said, 'but I didn't know what you'd want.' He reached into his pocket and pulled out the money. 'He said he'd written Fred as well, to let him know about you being sick.' He opened the cabinet door and put the money on the shelf inside. Wesley smiled, but seemed unable to speak now. He closed his eyes and his breath grew quiet. He made a fruitless attempt to kick away the bedclothes, then became still. As Martin watched he seemed to grow thinner, his skin greyer. He muttered inaudibly. A patient across the aisle snored. The machine by the bed pumped rhythmically.

Martin watched him doze.

About two in the morning the colour rushed back into Wesley's face. For a moment he looked completely well again. Then his breathing became so shallow it was impossible to tell when it had stopped completely, and for several minutes Martin watched a dull pallor regain possession of the dead man's skin before he called a nurse.

He was taken to a room along the corridor. The nurse brought him a coffee, asked him a few questions about Wesley, inquired about the funeral arrangements. Martin told her his boss would take care of the funeral, that he would notify the old man's daughter. She left him alone, then returned with a plastic bag containing Wesley's clothes. A taxi pulled up at the hospital door as he walked out. He got into the back seat and rummaged through the bag for Bebe's twenty-dollar bills. He found them in one of Wesley's trouser pockets, along with a set of keys, which he kept. After he paid the fare, he returned the change and the spare twenty to the pocket.

Chapter thirty-three

He woke early the next morning and took the streetcar downtown, walked up Yonge Street to Sam the Record Man's and bought two Jean Carignan LPs. He asked the assistant for some cardboard to send them through the post. The assistant went away and returned with the records wrapped. Martin walked down a side street to the main post office and addressed the parcel to Robertson, then caught a bus to Wesley's apartment. It occurred to him to try to locate his grandmother in the phonebook, but his mind wandered as he gazed out of the window, and the idea went out of his head.

The day was humid. He craned his neck towards the open bus window, breathed in exhaust fumes and simmering heat. Passengers mopped their faces with sleeves or handkerchiefs, or fanned themselves with newspaper pages. He disembarked, walked round to the rear of the fur store and climbed the rickety staircase to the top floor. He took the keys from his pocket. The only Yale on the ring fitted the lock. He entered and went first to the kitchen, opened the cabinet above the sink and took down the nearly full bottle of Laphroaig. He poured himself a shot, went to the sitting-room and sat down in Wesley's Lay-Z-Boy.

After some minutes of prostrate semi-asphyxiation in the sticky, dead air of the apartment he stood up and began to investigate the rooms. The bedroom lay on the far side of the kitchen, sharing a wall with the sitting-room. The bed was half made, otherwise the small room seemed well cared for. A narrow dormer window overlooked the street. Beside the window, to the right, the roof sloped towards the floor, leaving a large area of useless floor space.

Most of the furniture was on the left side of the room; the bed, with its headboard beside the window, a closet, a chest of drawers with a mirror, its back to the wall behind the door, clustered with dehydrated cactus plants. To the right of the door stood a low bookcase. He knelt down and examined the books:

Robert Louis Stevenson, Burns, Hogge, Grassic Gibbon, James Joyce, Yeats, many of them old editions. He removed one or two of the older books and flipped through damp, copper-stained pages, paused to listen as a cicada whined electronically in the phone wires outside. The heat in the room was stultifying. The air sparked with static. He went to the window, opened it, leaned out over the red roof and breathed in the occasional cool gust rising from the traffic below.

He turned his attention to the closet. It was locked. He tried the keys and the second turned. A row of suits, jackets, trousers, shirts and coats hung like dead men in a hybrid vapour of mothballs and solvent. Martin chose a long black cashmere coat, took it from its hanger and tried it on. It was a good fit. He admired his reflection in the dressing table mirror. He exchanged the coat for a jacket from one of the suits, a wide-lapelled, double-breasted pinstripe, which gave him a gangsterish appearance. He put his hands in the pockets, leaned back on his heels and half closed his eyes, smiling coldly at an imaginary adversary. He removed his boots and jeans, took the matching trousers from the closet and tried them on. They were loose at the waist. He put his hands in his pockets to hold them up, and felt something in his hand. He pulled out a roll of money and tore off the elastic band. His hands trembled as he counted the notes, once, twice. Forty-three one hundred-dollar bills. The trousers slipped down around his knees. He kicked them free, nearly falling as he stumbled to the closet. He ransacked all the pockets in all the clothes, tossing the rolls on to the bed as he found them, double-checked, then sat down and counted the money. Eighty-three hundreds, a hundred and forty twenties, a dozen tens, over twelve thousand dollars altogether.

'Jesus,' he said. He stared at the money, repeating the word over and over to himself like a mantra. 'Jesus … Jesus …'

He stood at the window and held the bills up to the light to confirm their authenticity; stepped back in panic as he imagined felonious passers-by observing him; folded the money and distributed it in various permutations through the pockets of his jeans, jacket, shirt. He went to the kitchen and poured himself another whisky, stopping to fill a jug of water for the cacti. Back in the bedroom he rifled through the clothes again, searched the closet, the chest, looked beneath the drawers, pulled up the carpet and moved the furniture to search beneath, continued through the remainder of the apartment but found nothing more. As darkness fell he abandoned the hunt for more money, fell exhausted in the Lay-Z-Boy and drank another whisky.

He awoke in an unsettled mood. The night had advanced. There was little traffic in the street outside. He tidied the ransacked bedroom and went out on to the staircase. A few stars glimmered dully in red haze. He wondered if Wesley were nearby, watching him, and felt ashamed of his cupidity.

'What should I spend it on then, Wesley?' he said to himself as he locked the door.

In the yard he paused behind a tree to confirm that no one was watching him. He patted his fat pockets for reassurance and stepped out on to the sidewalk. A taxi cruised by. He put his fingers between his teeth and whistled. The taxi stopped.

Martin shivered as he pulled the door shut on an air-conditioned interior. He opened the window to admit the dusty heat. The driver said nothing, and drove at a leisurely pace through the somnolent traffic.

'See the Jays won again?' the driver said, after a time. 'I tell you, one day they'll win the Series.'

'You must be kidding.'

'Nope.'

'Wanna bet?' Martin said, in a generic American voice that seemed to belong to an alternative identity. 'I've got ten grand in my pocket that says you're full of shit.'

The driver lapsed into silence. Neither spoke until the car drew up outside Martin's apartment. 'Six eighty,' the driver said, turning off the meter.

Martin leaned over behind the driver's seat to obscure the man's view, and removed a wad of money from the inside pocket of his jacket.

'I can't change a hundred,' the driver said, glaring at the note.

'Who said anything about change?' Martin said, pushing it into his hand. 'Just do me a favour.'

'What?'

'Say the name "Wesley".'

'Wesley.'

'Say it again.'

'Wesley. What is this?'

'Promise me you'll remember that name.'

'For a hundred bucks I'll remember anything you like.'

'Just the name is fine.'

'Wesley,' the driver repeated. 'For five hundred I'll say it on my deathbed.'

'That's OK.'

'You robbed somebody, right.'

'No. I didn't rob anyone.'

'Diamond Cabs does not provide getaway vehicles for miscreants engaged in criminal activities.'

'I understand that,' Martin said, opening the passenger door.

'Got everything?' the driver said, glancing back over the seat.

'Yes, thanks.'

'You're sure? I'd sure feel bad if you left some dough in my cab.'

'Yes, I'm sure.'

'Wesley,' the driver said.

'That's it,' Martin said, pushing the door shut behind him and waving as the cab pulled into the road. 'That's the guy.'

Chapter thirty-four

The next morning he visited half a dozen banks and bought six one thousand dollar money orders, wrapped them in a sheet of writing paper and posted them to Fred's address in Baja. The phone rang when he returned. It was Bebe, informing him of the funeral arrangements.

A hot wind gusted over the cemetery as Bebe's Cadillac pulled into the car park. Ahead, the Lincoln hearse with Wesley's casket inside drew up on a grass verge and stopped. The doors opened simultaneously. Two burly undertakers' assistants emerged from the hearse and lit cigarettes as Martin and Bebe stepped out on to the narrow Tarmac lane that curled through the cemetery. Along the lane, rows of nearly leafless maples tossed violently in the hot breeze. On a knoll a hundred feet from the car, a hole in the ground and a mound of earth marked the grave.

Three more cars pulled up behind them. The minister from the funeral parlour where the ceremony had taken place hopped briskly from one and strode over the dry grass to the plot. Five women, none of whom Martin had seen before, appeared from the other cars and stood together talking quietly.

One of the undertaker's men strolled over to Bebe's car. 'We're going to need a hand,' he said, tossing his cigarette onto the grass and crushing it beneath his patent leather shoe.

Martin and Bebe stood by the hearse as the men slid the casket through the rear door. Martin stooped to slide his shoulder under it.

'Just lift it with the handles,' one of the men said. 'It's too goddamned heavy to carry on your shoulders.'

Martin and Bebe took hold of the two front handles and pulled. The assistants took the rear and together they carried the casket rapidly across the grass and laid it down unceremoniously by the plot, Martin apologising mentally to Wesley for the indignity of their performance. The women followed.

The minister presided at the head of the grave, his legs akimbo like a spiritual athlete waiting for the beginning of a race. He read salutary passages for the benefit of the deceased and the comfort of the living. Martin and Bebe stood side by side looking solemn. From time to time Bebe scratched his neck or his leg, mumbling apologetically. The assistants, a discreet pace behind, hands folded in front of them, stared at the ground. Behind him, Martin heard one of the women weeping. Heat poured blindingly from the ground and hung in the still, relentless air.

At last the minister closed his book and nodded to the two assistants who stepped forward, grasped the cords on each side of the grave, lowered the box into the ground and stood back. The minister concluded the ceremony, scattered a handful of earth into the grave, smiled vaguely in Martin and Bebe's direction, and began to walk in a dignified, pensive fashion to his car. The mourners waited for a few moments, as if expecting something more, then turned and followed uncertainly.

'So long, Wesley,' Bebe said.

The women were waiting by the Cadillac. One a fatigued, well-dressed woman of fifty held out a gloved hand to Martin. 'Are you a relative?' she said.

'No.'

'His daughter's not here?' said another.

'No. She's out West. I don't know her address.'

Bebe and Martin drove to a downtown bar and drank a silent toast to Wesley.

'So,' Bebe said, 'you wanna start again Monday?'

Martin leaned back in his chair and looked through the open door at the street. Passers by fluttered through the sunlight like figures in a nickelodeon, a leg, a body, two men in brief conversation, frozen for an instant on the threshold, shadows swaying on the bar floor. 'No. I'm going home for a while. Maybe I'll come back. I like it here.'

Bebe nodded. 'So. What did you find in the old fella's apartment?'

'Not much. Some books, clothes. Cactus plants. Should I call someone about the apartment?'

'I'll take care of all that,' Bebe said. 'Give the clothes to Goodwill. Maybe keep the cactus plants.' He knocked back his glass of rye and rubbed the rim with his thumb. 'What else?'

'Nothing else, really,' Martin said.

'No bank books? No cash?'

'No. Nothing like that.'

'That's strange, eh?' Bebe said. 'He never spent any money, far as I know.'

'Yes,' Martin said. 'I suppose so.'

'His family will be disappointed.'

'His family don't give a fuck,' Martin said.

Bebe looked at Martin for a long time, nodded, and laid his glass down on the table. 'That's right,' he said. 'They didn't.'

They stood up and walked to the door.

'Well, I got to be getting back to work,' Bebe said as they emerged, scratching his nose and squinting into the sunlight. 'You need a ride?'

'No, thanks. I'll walk back, get my bag, and take the bus to the airport.'

'You're going today?'

'Might as well.'

Martin walked with Bebe to the car. They shook hands.

'Shit,' Martin said.

'What is it?'

'He wanted to be cremated. I just remembered.'

There was a short silence as both men considered this.

'Thanks for the job,' Martin said, finally.

'You owe me a week's holiday pay,' Bebe said.

Martin instinctively reached into his pocket for his wallet, but Bebe rested his pudgy hand on Martin's and chuckled. 'Now where's a poor unemployed immigrant going to get a week's pay from just like that?' He opened the car door, climbed into a haze of hot leather and wound down the window. 'Nice day for a plane ride,' he said, starting the car, lifting his hand in a cursory wave and pulling out into the traffic.

Martin returned to the apartment, packed his bag, watered the plants and went downstairs to eat lunch in the restaurant. Finishing his meal he left the apartment keys by the plate and caught the streetcar to the Royal York Hotel. When the airport bus came he climbed on board, sat back and watched the city pass as the sun set. The bus cruised west along the lakeshore. Buildings declined in height, the road widened. He caught a glimpse of a cemetery and thought of solitary Wesley, lying elsewhere, unmarked beneath new earth, the worms tapping at his casket.

He was given a seat at the rear of the plane beside a middle-aged Scotsman, returning to Glasgow after years in exile. 'I'm a real Canadian success story,' he said, 'I arrived in Toronto twenty-seven years ago with nothing, and now I owe half a million dollars.'

During the flight alternating moods swept about the cabin like weather fronts. Martin sensed collective anxiety, naive optimism, impatience, excitement. An Australian in the next row demanded glass after glass of whisky with increasing querulousness. Across the aisle a group of Singhalese students shouted with delight during spells of turbulence. Martin, enervated by fatigue and discomfort, succumbed to spells of anxiety, but drew comfort from the other passengers' fear, the companionship of their powerlessness.

In the early dawn, waiting in the queue for the toilet he looked from the bulkhead window to the atavistic wasteland of the Atlantic, scarred with surf. He considered the impossibility of surviving for even a moment in its blind frigidity. The thought of such massive indifference gave him a childish thrill.

After a restless sleep he awoke as the plane descended over Ayrshire fields. On the northern horizon highland peaks gleamed like arrowheads in morning sunlight. The scattered debris of small towns extended eastward. Gradually, as the ground approached, he could identify models of cars, signposts, the colours of clothing, the shadow of the aircraft racing over the ground.

Suddenly the runway was beneath them, the plane bumped down, the airbrakes shrieked and shook the plane, the passengers laughed with relief as the Sri Lankans burst into spontaneous applause.

Chapter thirty-five

He crunched down the driveway and into the porch. The house was silent. Cold clouds drifted over a sky littered with flying leaves. The front door was unlocked. He walked along the hall to the kitchen, through half-familiar odours of pollen and coal. Approaching the kitchen door he heard the clatter of dishes. Alberta was at the sink, her back to the door. She had paused in her work and was staring absent-mindedly out of the window, a dripping dish scrubber in her hand.

'I'm back.'

She turned and dropped the scrubber into the sink, patting her breast theatrically. 'You gave me a fright,' she said.

'I thought I'd surprise you.'

'Well, you did.' She smiled.

He set down his suitcase and crossed the room, put his arm around her shoulder, kissed her cheek.

'You're looking well,' he said.

'Oh, yes.'

He sat down at the table.

'You'll be hungry,' she said. 'I'll make some tea. And some breakfast.'

'How is he?' Martin asked, as Alberta scurried about.

'He's sleeping now.'

'Sleeping? It's nearly twelve. It's late for him to be sleeping.'

'He sleeps a lot, these days. Quite unlike his old self. But it seems to agree with him. He doesn't seem to like his old records any more, so he sleeps instead.'

Martin puzzled over this observation. 'He's given up the Institute, then?'

'Oh, yes. One or two of the old people drop by now and then. He seems to like seeing them, but after they've gone he gets terribly depressed. And I'm not much company for him, I'm afraid.'

After a breakfast punctuated by diffident inquiries about his journey Martin carried his bag up to his old room and lay down on the bed. He fell asleep almost immediately and woke as rays of dying sunlight converged on the ceiling. He stopped at the bathroom for a quick wash, then went downstairs. Robertson and Alberta were in the drawing room, Alberta reading the paper and Robertson staring blankly at the coal fire. Robertson looked up and rose a little unsteadily to his feet as Martin entered. He took a pace forward, one hand resting on the chair arm, the other outstretched. 'Martin,' he said, his voice rising, as if uncertain of his nephew's identity.

Martin shook his hand warmly. It felt weak in his own. 'How are you?' Martin asked. 'Your hair's gone grey.'

'Ah yes,' Robertson replied, sliding back into his chair. 'It happened rather suddenly. Inertia and entropy. Colour slips away from things.'

Disconcerted by this reply, Martin stepped around the chair and stood smiling inanely at his uncle, his back to the fire.

'Would you like some tea, dear?' Alberta asked, letting the paper slide to the carpet.

Martin turned his smile in his mother's direction and nodded. Alberta stood up. 'Sit down here,' she said. 'It's warm.'

He drew his chair closer to Robertson's as she left the room. His uncle observed him with a vague, benevolent smile, then turned his attention back to the fire. A gust blowing across the chimney dislodged an avalanche of soot, which puffed out into the room. The coals flamed.

'Well, well,' Robertson said, turning again to look at Martin.

'You're having a miserable autumn,' Martin said. 'It's quite cold compared to Toronto.'

Robertson acknowledged this with a murmur.

'I was sorry to hear you hadn't been well. I was sorry to hear about the Institute.'

Robertson placed his hands carefully over his knees and rocked back and forth once or twice. Martin watched, uncertain whether or not to continue.

'One keeps expecting oneself to say something,' Robertson

said after a pause. 'One always has. One has always had things to say. And indeed I approve of language.' He nodded to himself for several moments. 'But what defies understanding is that sensation of not having anything to say about anything. The inexorable weight of the self-evident.' He looked Martin candidly in the eye. 'Do you ever find this?'

Martin's glance wandered nervously to the fire.

'You will,' Robertson said. 'And then what an ethical dilemma you'll be in!'

'I don't really understand,' Martin said.

Robertson exhaled heavily and sat back in his chair, lifting his hands from his knees and resting them on the arms of his chair as if preparing for flight.

'No,' he looked up again. 'Thank you for the gramophone records. I have to admit I found the sensation of actually listening to them unbearable. I believe prisoners in those German camps experienced something similar after the liberation, when given wholesome food after years of privation. Their metabolisms were no longer able to process proper food, you see. They had grown accustomed to surviving on dust and vermin.'

The door opened and Alberta entered, bearing a tea tray stacked with cups, a teapot and hot water jug, plates of sandwiches and cakes.

'Nevertheless,' Robertson added confidentially, 'I do enjoy the smell of gramophone records. And perusing the labels, too, brings back happy memories.'

Alberta knelt down between them and set the tray on the hearth.

'Ah,' Robertson said, rubbing his hands appreciatively.

'That looks great,' Martin said.

Alberta poured the tea as Martin fetched a chair from beside the window. 'The garden's looking nice,' he said, pausing to glance at the lawn, the breeze-swept flower-beds.

'That's more or less how we spend our time these days,' Alberta said. 'Melibee is quite a dab hand now, especially in the greenhouse. He restored it completely. Put in plumbing, everything. He does the carnations and tomatoes. These are his tomatoes.' She waved her sandwich at him.

They sat together by the fire, eating the sandwiches, drinking tea.

Robertson broke the silence. 'Do you recall that game "musical chairs" ?' he enquired suddenly.

Martin and Alberta stared at him.

'Perhaps we could institute a new game. A development, you might say.'

'Do stop, dear,' Alberta said.

'We could call it "musical smiles",' Robertson continued, chuckling to himself. 'Had you observed this strange phenomenon, Martin?' He turned to Martin as if expecting a reply. 'It's as if there is a constant moral obligation for one of us to smile. There may be nothing to smile about, yet there is undoubtedly a smile in the room here. Just a sufficient degree of happiness among the three of us for a smile to occupy one face.'

Alberta reached over and took Robertson's teacup. For a moment all three smiled.

The grandfather clock in the shadows by the door struck five.

'Well,' Robertson said, licking his fingers and taking back his refilled teacup. 'Tell us your adventures. Did you make any friends in Canada? What kind of work did you do? You did work, I presume?'

Martin began hesitantly. He recounted his search for work, his time at Mrs Dombrowski's, the journey west, pausing periodically for interruptions as Robertson laughed, or cried, 'Good heavens!' raising his feet from the rug and banging them down again in childish enthusiasm at some event that amused him.

'You sound dreadfully American, dear,' Alberta remarked, frowning mournfully as Martin paused, irritated and confused by their inappropriate reactions, and the anti-climax of his return.

'And you actually met a Red Indian?' Robertson asked at one point, with great animation.

'Your neighbours sound like very colourful people,' Alberta

added, when Martin described his rooming house.

Twilight dimmed the room. She stood up to switch on a lamp and put more coal on the fire. 'I didn't realise you were coming,' she said, 'or I would have made something special for dinner.'

Martin shrugged. The grandfather clocked chimed again.

'It was the money as much as anything,' Robertson said suddenly.

'Sorry?' Martin looked over at his uncle.

'The money drained away,' Robertson said. 'I'm not made of money, after all.'

'Well, you kept giving them money,' Alberta muttered. She turned to Martin. 'They all seemed to have such pathetic stories. He couldn't resist.'

Robertson gazed blankly at the fire. He seemed oblivious to their presence.

'New people came,' he said. 'Not dilettantish people, not curious people either. Not affluent, not youthful. They were older people; preoccupied and serious. People who were falling behind, who were unable to *catch up*.' He looked up briefly at Martin and Alberta. 'It suddenly seemed to me as if the world had been gripped by a kind of blind panic; the panic of refugees. It was as if the house was suddenly full of refugees, wasn't it, dear?'

Alberta seemed about to speak, but Robertson continued his monologue, his thick burr weak and barely audible, so that Martin had to lean forward to catch what he was saying.

'All of them were in flight from something. It was impossible. I gave one or two of them money, but that didn't help really. They were clinging on desperately to things I know nothing about. They talked all the time about their children, their families. They all seemed terrified of being separated.'

He stopped suddenly and spat into the fire. Martin stared in surprise at the expectoration sizzling on the coals.

At seven Alberta departed for the kitchen. Left alone, Martin and his uncle hovered in the silence like beetles in aspic. Martin picked up the paper and began to read. Robertson resumed his vigil of the hearth. Half an hour later the gong rumbled in the hall.

The silence continued at dinner. After they had finished, Martin helped his mother clear the plates.

'You see what he's like,' she said, as they stood at the kitchen sink, washing and drying. 'He's like a ghost.'

Martin put his arm around her shoulder but the gesture seemed contrived, uncomfortable. He took it away and they continued washing the dishes.

After they had finished, he opened the door to the garden and went outside. The night had grown warmer. A sprinkling of stars blinked low in the west; overhead, rural twilight blended into the rusty glare of the city. He walked into a square of kitchen light on the lawn and watched Alberta through the window as she wiped the table and poured herself a drink. He thought of taking a walk into the city, but decided instead to count his money and sleep.

The light switch clicked in the kitchen and he gazed up at the sky as his eyes grew accustomed to the new dark. He went back indoors. The light was on in the hall, and another shone from beneath the door of Robertson's study. He passed by without knocking, pushed through the tapestry at the end of the hall and went upstairs to his room.

He sat on the bed, aimlessly counting Wesley's money, refolding it into one thousand dollar wads and concealing it among the clothes in his bag, then undressed and climbed into bed, surprised to find it warm, a hot water bottle at his feet.

'Money for space,' he said to himself. 'Money for space and distance – thanks, Wesley.'

Chapter thirty-six

He woke early and dressed at the window. Sunlight crept across the lawn, refracting in dew. Birds pecked at worms. A milk float hummed somewhere. He finished dressing and went downstairs, out through the kitchen door and around the house to the drive. At a stop on the main road a bus waited fortuitously, the only vehicle in the street. He climbed on board, went upstairs, lit a cigarette.

The traffic in the city was still thin. He disembarked by the art gallery, walked up the steps into cold, deserted shade and crouched on his haunches for a moment, smoking and watching the few passers-by. His calves grew stiff and he returned to the almost empty street, walking west in search of a coffee bar. Nothing was open. A bus passed, a newspaper van dropped a bundle of papers at the news-stand beside the statue of Wellington's horse. He continued down Leith Street, along London Road, and before long found himself outside Ray's tenement building. He entered the cold close and climbed to the first floor. The name on the lintel had been changed, the door recently painted in glossy maroon. He listened at the door for several minutes but heard nothing.

Retracing his steps he chose a different route, by Holyrood and up the High Street. As he climbed the cobbled hill he smelled fresh baking and traced the source to a half-hinged door at the end of a close. Inside, a dozen workers sweated in the intense heat, surrounded by mountains of newly made bread and rolls. He bought half a dozen rolls and continued up the hill, walked down Lothian Road and climbed over a church wall into Princes Street Gardens, sat on the bandstand and fed the rolls to a gathering of pigeons.

She was among the first small crowd waiting at the Princes Street gate when the park attendant unlocked the chains and let them in. Martin recognised her immediately, although she wore no make-up and was dressed in a dull navy raincoat. She pushed a child's buggy and stopped periodically to murmur a few words to a concealed occupant. A shower of unmistakable sunset-red hair fell across her face as she leaned down to the child.

She came slowly along the path towards the bandstand, pausing to breathe in the scent of the gardens' floral displays, and chattering quietly, laughing from time to time as if the child had made a joke. She stopped to look up at the sky, where a wet line of cloud from the east was obscuring the sun. Turning her attention to the gardens she gazed around her and finally noticed Martin, watching her from the steps of the bandstand. 'Martin?'

'Hello, Carole.'

'When did you get back? It's been ages.'

Her voice had lost its abrasive edge. The light breeze almost carried her words away.

'Yesterday.'

She pushed the pushchair to the bandstand and sat down beside him. The scent of patchouli settled in the air around them. 'You look knackered,' she said.

'I was all right yesterday. But today I'm wasted.' He nodded at the pushchair. 'This your baby?'

'Little Ray,' she said. 'Not really a baby now. Almost sixteen months.'

The red-faced child regarded him suspiciously.

They sat in silence for a while, shivering.

'You want some tea,' Carole said at last. 'I don't live far from here.'

He sat in the only armchair and waited while Carole made tea in the kitchenette. The flat was quiet. A single bar electric fire buzzed in the empty grate. Cold autumnal light flooded the room.

'I'd forgotten no one switches lights on here unless it's dark,' he called to her.

'Switch on a light if you like,' she said, as she came in with two mugs of tea in one hand, and a kitchen chair.

Little Ray marched naked about the room like an emperor,

barking meaningless commands to invisible underlings. Martin pictured the child's imaginary uniform, heavy with braid and decorations. Suddenly the boy began urinating aggressively, revolving on his heels and watching the arc of his piss rising and falling on the carpet, a divine fertilising rain.

'Babies!' Carole said.

Martin stared at her.

She seemed stunned, her eyes clouded, all the brightness he remembered neutralised. 'Of course, their insides are so clean,' she went on, 'it doesn't really matter.'

'Ray is away, is he?' was all he could think of saying.

'He just went off.' Her smile disintegrated into vagueness.

'Went off?'

'Aye. He went back to his village in Fife. Last winter. I went to look for him, but he'd gone. No one knew where.'

'His village?'

'Aye. All that about being in London was crap. He was just a village boy. You ever meet that dealer Moscow?'

He nodded.

'Aye, well, Ray was hypnotised by him. A dealer's groupie, Moscow said. Those were all Moscow's stories. All that stuff about London was stories Moscow had told him.'

'Oh.'

'Aye. He hated his village. He used to say they were all paranoid of anything they didn't understand, and they didn't understand much up there.'

'What about Danny?'

'He went to London. Never heard about him since then. Christine wrote me once. She was in Manchester.'

'Is she a nurse?'

'Nearly. I think so. I don't see her.'

They drank their tea and watched Ray being bored.

'You'll be going back? You like it there?'

'I don't know. I wouldn't mind. I had a pretty good time. It's more fun there.'

'That wouldn't be hard.'

'But there was something missing.'

'What's that?'

Martin laughed. 'I don't know.'

'Well, you sound a bit like a Yank,' she said.

A clock from somewhere chimed noon. She disappeared to the kitchen for a few minutes then returned with a plate of sandwiches. 'Fishpaste,' she said, laughing. 'I always wondered what it was, so I bought some. It comes in a nice wee pot.'

Martin took a bite from his sandwich and said, 'When Christine was in that alleyway, I was hiding behind a wall.'

'What alleyway?'

'The night we were chased down Easter Road by that gang.'

'Hardly a gang.' She laughed. 'Just a few wee boys.'

'But I was there. I was hiding.'

'Good thing. They'd have given you a good doing.'

'They could have killed her.'

'Aye. But they didn't.'

'I never thought I was like that. I never thought I would let anyone down like that.'

'Aye, well.' She looked over at Ray who was standing at the low window waving his penis at passers by in the street below. 'It's best not to expect too much. Look at that wee man. What can you expect from him? He likes to eat and play with his willy, and he sleeps fine.'

'Do you think she knew?'

'About what?'

'About me being in the alleyway.'

'It's a long time ago. I don't know. I had other things to worry about.' She stood up and went to the window, lifted the child into her arms and returned to her chair. Ray lay back with his head resting on her shoulder, his thumb in his mouth, observing Martin. 'Christine thought my life was a dead loss,' Carole said. 'She thought I was wasting myself.' She let the boy slip from her lap, and stood up. 'Not that I can't see what she was on about. But things look different from the outside. Ray might have been useless, but he had his points. I told her I was happy, but she didn't believe me. Christine always thought she knew better.' She walked over to the window and sat on the ledge, facing him. 'I went back up to Ray's village. The first time I met one of his old pals from school. He took me up there for a picnic. It was nice. I grew up in the countryside, near Kirkintilloch. We only moved here when I was ten. Even now I feel cooped up here sometimes. You get to the point where there doesn't seem to be a single street you haven't walked down a hundred times before.' She smiled absently. 'So, anyway, I went up again last winter. I left the bairn with a neighbour. Caught a bus at the bus station. The wind was bitter. I had on almost all the clothes I owned, two T-shirts, my Afghan dress, two pullovers, a big woolly scarf wrapped inside my coat, a big stupid looking woollen hat my gran made me. I was hoping the bus would go along Princes Street. I'd take one last look at the art gallery and imagine I was never coming back. But, anyway, it went the other way to Queensferry. The wind nearly knocked the bus over when we went over the bridge.'

A car horn blasted from the street outside. Distracted by the noise she turned and peered out of the window. Clouds swept over the sky behind her, her profile shadowed in gloomy light.

'Through the front window it was all grey. Typical, you know. Rain lashing. I thought, Christ. What am I doing? The hills were all miserable grey, the sky was grey, grey clouds rolling about. As we got into the country there were the skins of dead foxes hanging on the fences. They had wires around their necks, and their coats were rotting in the rain. And there were crows hooked over barbed wire, wings flapping about, and I minded that one thing I hated about the country when I was wee was farmers.

'On the horizon there was a stand of pine trees. Some had been cut down to take away the grouse cover. For when they're shooting, ken. It looked like the place where we'd gone for the picnic, so I stood up and went to the front of the bus. "This'll do me," I said to the driver. "Are you sure?" he said. He must have thought I was radge.

'I got off, stood there in the rain and watched the bus disappear. Then I jumped over a ditch, got through a fence and walked across the field to the trees. The earth had just been ploughed. The wind was really cold and the rain was turning to snow. And then suddenly it was like I was sure of my ground, like I had these instincts I'd totally forgotten. I knew exactly where I was. I felt like an animal almost, all those forgotten smells in the air reminded me of so much I'd missed and didn't even know I'd missed. The wind in the wheat, the sound of streams in the spring, the feeling you get when you go outside after a storm. As the snow fell harder I stopped above a field leading down to Ray's village. No one was around, but there was coal smoke in the air, and the snow on the roofs, and the lights in the windows, looked guy welcoming and pretty. I squinted my eyes and searched for Ray's house. It was on the far side of the village, almost at the river. I didn't even know if his mum and dad were still alive, but I expect they are – they're not that old. They were probably having their tea. Anyway, I went on walking towards the pine trees and found some shelter at the foot of one. I was pretty tired by then. Starving, too.'

She shivered, tugged her pullover around her shoulders and returned to her chair. Little Ray climbed into her lap and fell asleep.

'Through the trees I could see the snow sweeping over the fields. It was so beautiful. I stuffed some dead bracken into my coat to keep warm. It was getting quite dark, but still you could see these huge black clouds whirling through the sky. Everything went quiet, the birds had gone, and nothing was moving inside the woods where I was. A branch creaked and dumped a whole lot of snow on me. Everything was shrinking, darkness and light coming across the field to where I was. At first I could see past the summit of the hill, to some elms on the next crest of hills. They were as black as a skeleton, like the claws of a bird. Then the wind went to the west and this whiteness came in layers over the hills, through the elm trees, the hedgerows, along the furrows in the field, over the wee stream by the fence, which was almost frozen, through the weeds and the wire of the fence, then around me at the foot of the tree, and into my coat and my eyes, and I could hear the bracken rustle and I lay back into the hollow of the tree and it was like nothing but whiteness around me, pulling me up into the air, and I felt weightless, like I had no body, and I was floating and flying, past the trees and through the wires, flying in the wind over the grass like snow, melting and mixing up with everything else and I felt really happy, and alive, and I said to myself, "I could live here," and then I realised I was flaking out so I got up and walked back to the road. I got a lift with this lorry driver who kept trying to feel me up.' She laid the sleeping child on the floor and stood up to switch on a light.

'That's a good story, Carole,' Martin said. 'You should write it down.'

'Oh yes. Very literary, me.'

The boy groaned, woke up, then fell asleep again.

'Are you cold?' she said. 'That fire's no much use.'

'It is a bit parky.'

She sat down on the floor and stroked the boy's stomach softly. 'I don't know why he left. He didn't have to on my account.'

'He'll be back.'

'Naw. I knew that right away. For a moment, anyway, I was brave. I felt so free to be rid of him.' Her lustre faded. She shrank into the present again.

'I'd better be going,' Martin said.

She picked up the child and walked with Martin to the door. 'It was nice talking to you, Martin. It was nice remembering that.'

He wandered back to Princes Street, stopped at the Café Royale, sat at the bar and drank a pint of heavy for old times' sake. He looked around the pub but saw no familiar faces. He felt invisible. He closed his eyes and tried to picture the field Carole had described, himself crossing it beside her like a revenant. He opened his eyes. The pub crowd resembled fish in a tank, drifting languidly, gesturing, mouths gaping. He felt as if he was observing another medium altogether, an opaque world in which he had no function. He put down his half-finished drink and slid through restless bodies to the door.

A cold wind blew along Princes Street, scattering the year's last leaves. A crowd of drinkers passed, little tourist families clustered at shop windows, a newspaper vendor stood at the corner handing out copies of the *Evening News*. 'Hello Harry,' he said, and crossed the street to the art gallery.

He sat on the cold steps and watched the beginning of the night's procession. An early crowd of youths and young girls passed. One of the girls stumbled in feigned drunkenness and her friends laughed. He stood up again after a few minutes as if having made a decision, and walked back the way he had come.

'I hope I'm not bothering you,' he said, as soon as Carole opened the door. He handed her a brown bag. 'It's quite early still, and I thought you might like some wine.'

She looked pleased to see him.

'I won't stay.'

Martin returned to his seat. Little Ray was still asleep beside the fire.

Carole went to the kitchen and returned with the two washed tea mugs and a corkscrew. 'No glasses,' she said, taking a seat on the carpet, beside the child, next to the buzzing fire.

'Your nails aren't so long these days,' he said, extracting the cork.

She stretched out her hand and considered it.

'You have beautiful hands, Carole,' Martin said, as he filled her mug. 'You can tell a lot about people by their hands.'

'Oh yes? And what can you tell about me, Martin?'

'I don't know,' he said, 'but I was with this guy who was dying a little while ago, and I noticed his hands,' he concluded, lamely.

She shrugged and stared at the fire.

'You look better without all that makeup.'

'Aye.' She laughed. 'Any more personal comments you'd like to make?'

'Yes, there are, actually.'

'I've lost weight since I saw you.' She put down her mug, stood up and turned gracefully on her toes. 'Don't you think so?'

'Yes.'

She sat down again and folded her legs beneath her. 'So where did you go?'

'Princes Street. Went to the Café Royale, the art gallery.'

'All your old haunts. See anyone?'

'No one I knew.'

'I never see anyone these days. Since I had the bairn. Can't afford a babysitter, so we just stay in mainly.'

'I thought it would be a mistake to get stuck here again.'

'Too small for you now, eh?'

They lapsed into silence. Martin replenished their mugs.

'Want to hear a record?' she said, after a few moments. She stood up and walked around behind his chair. He heard the crackling of the record, then a piano. 'It's not really hi-fi,' she said, sniggering.

'What is it?'

'Bruce Springsteen. *New York City Serenade.*'

'Carole,' Martin said, 'I came into some money.'

She looked at him quickly, suspiciously.

'Would you like to have a different life? I mean, I don't know if it would be better, but it would be different.'

'What do you mean?'

'We could go to America. If you didn't like it you could come back. I'd give you a ticket, so you could always use it.'

'What about Ray?'

'He doesn't need a ticket.'

'I don't really fancy America.'

'No.'

A vanishing raincoated figure came into his mind.

I won't make the same mistake again.

'Think about it, then. Like I say, you could try it and if you didn't like it you could come back.'

They finished the wine and talked for a while. At times Martin had the impression of looking back at the room from somewhere in the future. Carole aged before his eyes. The child was gone, embarked on its own life, and Martin had become an old man recollecting his youth with dismay, knowing he had missed something important.

He stood up to leave. Carole stood also, and they walked to the door.

'Something tells me I shouldn't ask you to stay,' she said. 'Though I'm tempted.' She smiled.

Martin nodded. 'No. Well. I should get home. My uncle's not well. I'll phone tomorrow about the other thing. Think about it, you'd like it there. Great music. Great dope!'

'I don't do that much now. I'm awfully dull, aren't I?'

After she closed the door, he lingered in the close for several minutes studying every detail of scratched paintwork, chipped plaster, the lines of light thrown by the dim close lamp on the landing above, inscribing the scene on his memory, anticipating that at some time in the future he might want to bring it to mind.

As he walked back to Taigh nan Òran he thought about how he had lost something, some kind of acuity in his senses, as if he had been invaded by dullness and now every moment that passed was slightly wasted; not that the world's magic had vanished completely, but that because of laziness, or some sort of affliction, everything had become a little too rapid for his sluggish senses to grasp. He stopped abruptly outside a hotel on Princes Street, causing a pedestrian collision behind him, struck by a terrible sense of dismay.

Chapter thirty-seven

Once upon a time, beloved reader, from the weighty darkness which precedes us and to which we return, I, Robertson appeared, a flash of flame, to dance over the floating world, a star born of love.

I had the piper's fingers and the tinker's eyes, so my parents were told, and I grew to adolescence among the great brotherhood of sea, sky and land; my kin were the bridge dancing people, the village killers and the holy men of the iron kirk, howling their great sorrows over the windy sea wracks at their implacable god.

As a boy I was instructed by Mr McRitchie, the nimble fingered one, in the operation of the two rowed button accordion, whence I graduated to the piano accordion. I showed dexterity and aptitude, and a prodigious memory for the repertoire of that noble instrument, and while still a youth I was frequently called upon to display my prowess at feichs *and village functions from one side of our island to the other. I will tell you that my spirit would dance within me with the thrill of the little music. And my sportive heart was much lifted by the sight of my meteoric sister Alberta dancing to my tunes, and the sound of her sweet soprano casting its spell upon these assemblies.*

I was in my thirteenth year when, much to my father's chagrin, we decamped to the torpid metropolis of Edinburgh. I well remember our long journey south. It was winter time, the hills barricades of ice. Ruddy clouds swirled through restless, grey skies. The lochs were frozen, gathering tribes of sleeping birds in a grip of ice; death cries echoed like hammers on a steel drumskin as they awoke, their helpless wings flapping in the empty air. My sister turned to me and said: 'Scotland is a Sunday', and we played a game of which day of the week was the best, and which countries most resembled them.

Once settled in the capital I was commanded to learn the pianoforte, and proved myself more than equal to the works composed for that instrument by the Romantics, the Pedantics, the

Baroquians and others besides. Despite this, and to my father's sorrow, I was drawn always to the frivolous and unimportant musics of the so-called Ordinary People.

I was not in my maturity before a baleful hatred crept to life in my brain, like a worm emerging from a sleep, and the fires of divers passions blazed at the windows of my soul's house. I looked upon the world with the eyes of an interloper, a constant bidding of farewell at my lips. A humourless rigidity took possession of my faculties, and within a few short years I emerged from youth as a man I did not know.

I attended the university without enthusiasm, and embarked on a Bohemian career performing the compositions of American Negroes for the begrudging applause of the student population in a small hotel. During the course of my clandestine activities I encountered a purveyor of anodynes, and within a short period of time had becomes one of his 'most trusted customers'. Thanks to the consumption of prodigious quantities of his goods, the malicious voice of the worm was subdued, the conflagration in my heart appeased, and I became briefly happy, gregarious, optimistic.

Unfortunately, my complacency was of brief duration. A fellow student, known to my father, brought my activities to his attention. As a consequence, my academic career was abruptly terminated and through the good offices of a business acquaintance, my father secured me a position on a ship of the Donaldson line, bound for Halifax, Nova Scotia. At the age of twenty on a clear day in late April, I watched from a ship's deck the shores of Scotland slip beneath the waves. I recall my sister standing on the jetty, her dark eyes as imperturbable as a compass hand piercing the long sky between us.

The years passed. Despite my unsuitability for the physical work I was employed to do, I was treated with kindness and consideration. In truth, I believe my role on the ships on which I served resembled that of a household deity such as Orientals employ to ward away evil, or of an object of charity whose presence brings divine benediction to his patrons. I was rarely the object of ridicule, and whenever I did succeed in performing some task satisfactorily *was heaped with a disproportionate amount of praise, so remarkable and uncharacteristic was my acumen deemed to be.*

One evening we were lying off Grand Bank awaiting entry to the St Lawrence Waterway. I had been passing an hour on deck discussing culinary matters with the ship's cook. In the distance, becalmed icebergs shone like great sailing ships in the merciless moonlit sea, and far below us placid waves lapped at the ship's side. At last, tiring of our pleasantries, the cook returned below and I was left alone. I pulled my heavy jacket around me and my scarf up over my face, and leaning against the rail peered through frost encrusted eyelids up into a vast black night, illuminated by the suns of worlds beyond numbering.

I was relatively undismayed when I heard a woman's voice rising from the waves below, somewhere at the ship's side. At first I believed that the apparition was an hallucination. However, the coherence of the creature's utterances soon aroused my suspicions. Whereas all my previous communications with phantasmal beings had swiftly degenerated into meaningless fatuities, in this case there seemed to be a definite cogency in the creature's words.

'Oh Man,' she declaimed, 'Poor exile from the world of marvellous Waters. We, your kinfolk still await your return. Do you not hear our song in your body, the cry of life swirling in your bones? Do you not dream of abandoning your habitats of stone and dancing with us again in the deep waters?'

I leaned over the rail and scanned the darkness and the quicksilver water for the author of this strange oration.

'On this star of waters, why be estranged? Your blood, your body, your mind, your thoughts and dreams, are they not those of a watery creature? Is it not curious that you search always for the fixed, the solid, the unchanging, when our world is a flux, a tide, an ocean, a drop of rain, gathering itself together, disintegrating, insinuating itself into form, abandoning form, freezing to ice or vanishing into air in the sun's embrace?'

At last, beneath me I located a pair of glittering, prescient eyes staring up at me from a rippling circle of reflected moonlight. As our eyes met, the creature, a halicore I believe it was, concluded its discourse with the following words:

'You are not alone. You will unite with us again, live again as rain, as ocean, as a creature of land, of sea, of air, unlocked forever from the cage of life. We are your memory, as you are ours.'

'Don't go!' I shouted, as a swell rose beside the ship and dark water closed in around the animal's head.

'Do not forget ...' the animal replied.

I stared into the widening ripple left by her departure, then looked about me to see if any other member of the crew had witnessed this strange event. The deck, however, was empty. Above my head I heard the tapping of a rope against the mast as a light breeze wafted from the night, but there was no one to be seen.

As I reflected on the creature's observations, my entire being swarmed with such tumultuous thoughts and emotions that I succumbed to unconsciousness. Several hours passed before my absence was noticed. When I was discovered I was carried to the sick bay. I had been badly frostbitten. My heavy scarf had protected most of my face, but my hands were naked. Two left fingers were amputated below the last knuckle, and the entirety of the right index finger. As I came to I wept helplessly and heard as if from a great distance the sound of a button accordion and my sister's feet tapping out the rhythm of a ghostly slip jig on the bare floor of an empty house.

Our ship continued its voyage to Montreal and returned once more to Scotland. My father had become ill, and needed my companionship. With my small savings I opened an institute in my father's house where individuals with interests similar to my own could meet, and converse on the very questions which now exercised my own mind.

Alas, how flimsy has been my resolve, and how great my reliance on the encouragement of others. How vulnerable one is, to that strange amnesia which vitiates all youthful faith and passion. As time passed, the clarity of my questions dulled, the need I had to answer them, undermined. My inspiration had departed. Worse than this, however, were the strange ideas that began to fester in my mind. I would find myself watching a sunset from the window of my *study, when the room would become unbearably hot – so much so, that I would begin to perspire heavily. Throwing open the window, I would find the temperature rising even more, as if the world had become a furnace. Behind the innocuous clouds floating on the horizon I could make out the flames of a ghastly universal conflagration, making its way towards me. I would dream of streets littered with dying birds, and empty fields where nothing lived ... Every time I heard of a death, the news would resonate in me like a knell for every human being. It was as if nothing was coming to life at all, that an inexorable mortality had the world in its grip.*

My cowardice was undoubtedly responsible. By temperament I should have been a revolutionary, a bomb-thrower, a sniper, a violent conspirator, a person capable of facing up to unpalatable solutions. My 'spiritual' inquiries concealed a feeble evasion of responsibility for action. Is faith not merely a device to make of life a hiatus in which no risks are taken, no mistakes made, no crimes committed – even though no advance in human welfare has ever been accomplished without risk, error, or crime?

Eventually I abandoned the confines of my Institute altogether and began to accost passers by: 'Look!' I would beseech them, indicating wildly the various cardinal points. 'Look!' as if it were all self-evident. 'This is no time to be squeamish or fearful! The time for common decency has long since passed! Man the barricades! Have we not exhausted the possibilities of patience? The oppressed are patient, but the oppressors, they too are patient – and not only are they patient, but they live longer, they are better fed, they are untroubled by human sympathy, they have unlimited resources at their disposal to sustain their patience.

I have searched the streets for others I could incite, but the oppressed are squeamish, hold no grudges, blame themselves for their predicaments. They merely suffer, are thankful for whatever relief is available and exist like myself in a state of thriving panic as their suffering increases and their compensations shrink. It is as if the very air of the world resonates with a prayer: 'Please do not drive me too far. Let me at least die as a human being and not a reactionary machine of mad revenge!'

Of course, I have retired now. My treatment has assuaged some of the more painful recollections. I am trying to reconstruct my barriers of irony. Behind them I may hide along with my compatriots, the routed army of the thin-skinned. There is much humour here; mordant laughter sweeps through the ranks; although, to be candid, it does not taste of joy. It does not nourish or fortify. It is not the laughter of the free.

I think of the Sirene on days such as this, and I wonder. Perhaps there are two species of human being. Once, long ago, when some apes were evolving and others were not, for generations they would have resembled each other. There would have been those who might have wondered, in their rudimentary fashion, why they were different, what it was that distinguished them from their fellows, when according to all appearances they were identical. They would have lived and died without ever seeing the process of which they were a part come to fruition. Why should this not be true today? Why should there not be two species of human? One, avaricious, violent, acquisitive, with a mind hermetically sealed in a glaze of impenetrable selfishness, and beside it, physically indistinguishable, at least for the present, another species, speaking the same languages, eating, procreating, participating in the same rituals and customs, proceeding resolutely, developing vision, awareness, kindness, free from the psychopathology of self-interest which has cauterised its redundant brothers and sisters?

Robertson put down his pen, turned and looked into the garden. Alberta was planting seedlings in a narrow bed by the pond. He could hear talking and assumed Martin was in the vicinity, although he could not see him. He turned back to the desk, pushed up the sleeve of his jacket and examined the stitched scar that almost encircled his lower arm. The story of the manatee was much better than the truth. The truth was unbearable, yet he had borne it. So many truths were, and so many people did. That denial must make us less than human in the end, surely. He shuddered, seeing himself again on the ship's deck, the cook's knife in his hand. It was only the slightest motion, a nothing, a gesture. Yet the result was shocking. Nothing in his imagination had prepared him for the speed at which blood could abandon a cut vein. In the moments before he lost consciousness the tidal power of its escape had confirmed that he had made a mistake in punishing his body for the torments in his mind. He felt nothing but pity for the thing that was dying all around him, the panic and bewilderment of his own betrayed flesh; and nothing but hatred for his cool and ruthless reason, which continued to the last to draw all strength and hope to itself, as its lifelong, blameless ally expired. He closed his journal and left the room.

Alberta looked up as he emerged from the kitchen door. 'Martin's going back to Canada,' she said, laying down the trowel.

'Ah.'

'There's no future for me here,' Martin said. He was sitting beneath the oak tree on the far side of the pond, stirring the water with a dead branch.

'The future,' Robertson echoed vaguely, as if puzzling over the concept.

'We bore him,' Alberta said.

'This country's dead,' Martin said. 'It's going to be the same for ever.' He dropped the branch and walked around the pond to join them.

Robertson and Alberta exchanged glances.

'I'm sorry,' Martin added. 'I don't mean to hurt your feelings.'

'Perhaps it's you that has no future, Martin,' Alberta muttered, as he turned back towards the house.

'What do you mean?'

'If you lose your family and your country, what will you become? You'll end up as some sort of ghost and you won't belong anywhere.'

Robertson rested his hand lightly on her arm. She shook it free.

'You think love is easy? You think you'll always find it?' She turned away and walked quickly back to the house.

Some hours later, towards sunset, Martin was awoken by laughter, and a jaunty, arrhythmical, accordion tune coming from the garden. He got up from the bed and went to the window.

Robertson and Alberta were dancing together on the lawn. Robertson, accordion strung over his neck and shoulder, advanced and retreated before his sister like a ridiculous, melodramatic bullfighter. His broken and missing fingers slipping over the keys produced a weird, staccato rhythm; Alberta teetered back and forth, stamping her feet down, or rising on to a toe, stopping suddenly as if suspended in time, waiting for a lost beat to catch up, then plunging gracefully into another step. They moved sinuously, laughing, synchronised, as if joined together at the nerves. As Martin watched the music and the silence turned inside out. The incidental sounds of the world became the melody, and the notes of the accordion percussive interruptions, as if someone were opening and closing a door on some great festivity taking place just out of his line of vision.

The following day he bought his ticket and a week later caught the plane to Toronto. Before leaving he phoned Carole but thought better of it at the last minute and replaced the receiver before she had time to answer. Neither Robertson nor his mother accompanied him to the airport, although, before Martin left, Robertson gave him his journal. As the 747 cruised over Greenland Martin read the journal and counted his money repeatedly. He imagined himself an urbane world traveller in a variety of amusing situations, playing poker with criminals, buying expensive cocktails for a beautiful woman, cruising the Trans Canada Highway in a sports car. He had to remind himself from time to time that he only had five thousand dollars.

On the day Robertson died, of a stroke on the Taigh nan Òran lawn, Martin was stretched out on a tall oak bed in a faded hotel in Spokane, Washington. He had been dreaming that he was drowning in the Taigh nan Òran pond. His feet were entangled in reeds and roots on the pond bed. A newt swam past his eyes, waving its speckled tail in a jolly greeting. Robertson's face, distorted by rippling water, hovered over him from a pale sky. He realised that, like all sailors, Robertson probably could not swim. After some moments of struggle he breathed in the water, but this did not affect his sense of well-being. Darkness came over his eyes and he awoke. A breeze blew through the curtains. The sun was rising. A cicada hummed in a sycamore by the window. He thought about what he would have for breakfast in the coffee shop downstairs.

He had been travelling for months, hitching across the continent from Baja to Vancouver, returning east, pausing here and there to work in a store or warehouse before moving on again. He had lost track of the notion of home, of there being any centre to the world. From time to time he would add another cartoon to the story of Saint Shabby, but one afternoon, in order to impress an anonymous waitress, he left the sketchpad on a table in a restaurant by Interstate 70, and didn't go back for it.

Sometimes he thought about Ray or Maggie, or Steve or the girl in the cornfield. Where were they at that moment? Were they drunk? Dead or alive? Despairing, or happy? Had they found love? He imagined Christine's skin beneath a stranger's fingertips. Was the light on? Was it raining? Was the room warm? Was music playing? He saw Alberta in the garden, looking back at him from the irretrievable past. He thought about his uncle, and at times he could feel Robertson's mind exploding inside his own, like a grenade filled with gifts and passions. Often it seemed to him there was nothing but a series of accidents to connect the people he had known. They had all just flashed up like meteorites, sparks in emptiness. Some of the dead too were as alive in his mind as the living. One day he might even walk into a bar somewhere and meet his father, sit with him for an hour, have a beer, and talk about the times they should have had.

Publishing May 2001

The Dark Ship
Anne MacLeod
This vast literary saga celebrates love, music and poetry in a finely woven story that reflects the complex past of a community on a Scottish island.
1-903238-27-7
£9.99

Dead Letter House
Drew Campbell
A bizarre trip into the surreal. On a twenty mile walk home a young man explores time and space and discovers his own heaven and hell.
1-903238-29-3
£7.99

The Gravy Star
Hamish MacDonald
One man's hike from post-industrial urban sprawl to lost love and a burnt-out rural idyll.
'A moving and often funny portrait ... of the profound relationship between Glasgow and the wild land to its north.' James Robertson, author of *The Fanatic.*
1-903238-26-9
£9.99

Strange Faith
Graeme Williamson
This haunting novel tells the story of a young man torn between past allegiances and the promise of a new life.
'Calmly compelling, strangely engaging.' Dilys Rose
1-903238-28-5
£9.99

About 11:9

Supported by the Scottish Arts Council National Lottery Fund and partnership funding, 11:9 publish the work of writers both unknown and established, living and working in Scotland or from a Scottish background.

11:9's brief is to publish contemporary literary novels, and is actively searching for new talent. If you wish to submit work send an introductory letter, a brief synopsis of your novel, a biographical note about yourself and two typed sample chapters to: Editorial Administrator, 11:9, Neil Wilson Publishing Ltd, Suite 303a, The Pentagon Centre, 36 Washington Street, Glasgow, G3 8AZ. Details are also available from our website at **www.11-9.co.uk.**

If you would like to be added to a mailing list about future publications, either register on our website or send your name and address to 11:9, Neil Wilson Publishing Ltd, Suite 303a, The Pentagon Centre, 36 Washington Street, Glasgow, G3 8AZ.

11:9 refers to 11 September 1997 when the Scottish people voted to re-establish their parliament in Edinburgh.

'They [the first six 11:9 titles] are my unreserved recommendation for this or any other year.'
Carl MacDougall, *The Herald*

Hi Bonnybrig 1-903238-16-1
Shug Hanlan
'Imagine Kurt Vonnegut after one too many vodka and Irn Brus and you're halfway there.'
Sunday Herald

Rousseau Moon 1-903238-15-3
David Cameron
'The most interesting and promising debut for many years. [The prose has] a quality of verbal alchemy by which it transmutes the base matter of common experience into something like gold.'
Robert Nye, *The Scotsman*

The Tin Man 1-903238-11-0
Martin Shannon
'Funny and heartfelt, Shannon's is an uncommonly authentic voice that suggests an engaging new talent.'
The Guardian and *Guardian Unlimited*

Life Drawing 1-903238-13-7
Linda Cracknell
'*Life Drawing* brilliantly illuminates the contradictions of its narrator's self image ... Linda Cracknell brings female experience hauntingly to life.'
The Scotsman

Occasional Demons 1-903238-12-9
Raymond Soltysek
'A bruising collection ... Potent, seductive, darkly amusing tales that leave you exhausted by their very intensity.'
Sunday Herald

The Wolfclaw Chronicles 1-903238-10-2
Tom Bryan
'Tom Bryan's pedigree as a poet and all round littérateur shines through in *The Wolfclaw Chronicles* – while reading this his first novel you constantly sense a steady hand on the tiller ... a playful and empassioned novel.'
The Scotsman

Already available from bookshops and the 11:9 website: www.11:9.co.uk